Craving All His Love

Tyrecka Liggons

Craving All His Love

Copyright © 2017 by Tyrecka Liggons

Published By: Shan Presents

All rights reserved.

This book is a work of fiction. Names, characters, places, and incidents either are the product of the author's imagination or are used fictitiously and are not to be construed as real. Any resemblance to actual persons, living or dead, business establishments, events, or locales, is entirely coincidental.

Text Shan to 22828 to stay up to date with new releases, sneak peeks, contest, and more...

Text **SPROMANCE** to 22828 to stay up to date on new releases, plus get information on contests, sneak peeks, and more!

Table of Contents

Chapter One

Ramsey Scott

I was thankful to be home from work, but seeing as how I was a mother of two… seven-year-old twins, a girl and a boy, to be exact. My job wasn't quite done, yet. I still had to make Luchi and Luna something to eat before it was time for us to call it a night. I had worked a twelve-hour shift at Thornton's. I was thankful when seven o'clock hit. Thanks to my sister and granny, I had a great support system for the twins. Their father hasn't been much of any help since I got pregnant at seventeen.

I wasn't pressuring my kids' father Lance to help too much with them, because anytime he came around, he was a huge pain in my ass. The only good thing that came out of me and Lance's relationship were Luchi and Luna. I was a single mother, struggling, but by the grace of God, I always found a way to get by. I lived in a three-bedroom house, thanks to being on section 8, I got a decent amount in food stamps, although I worked like a slave at Thornton's, and I've had the same Blue Toyota Camry since I was seventeen, but it was getting me and my babies where we needed to go, so I couldn't complain.

"Are you tired, mama?" Luna asked, climbing in my bed. My eyes were getting heavy, but I needed to make sure my babies were straight before I could close them.

"Yes, my Luna, my feet are killing me, but it's all worth it knowing, I can buy you everything you need." I tickled Luna's belly.

"Mama, while you're in here playing with Luna, I'm in the other room hungry." Luchi said, walking into my room. It was clear to me he had an attitude.

"Luchi, your hot dogs are on the stove now." I explained to my child, as if he was my parent and not the other way around.

"Hot dogs? You're not going to fry me some chicken?"

"No, Luchi, I've been standing on my feet all day. I'm tired. I'm off tomorrow. I promise to make you a nice meal. Tonight, it's chili dogs on the menu."

"Man, okay." Luchi climbed into my bed with an attitude.

"Mama, can we watch *Home*?" Luna asked, curling up under me, resting her head on my breasts.

"Naw, man, I'm tired of watching that movie. That's all you want to watch." Luchi yawned, curling under me as well.

"Sorry, Luna, I agree with your brother. Let's give *Home* a rest tonight."

"Okay." Luna pouted.

Kissing her forehead, I took in my kids' features, and my babies looked nothing like me. Everything about them screamed Lance. My skin was the color of a Hershey bar, but the twins inherited their daddy's light-skinned complexion. Luna had long curly hair that I often styled in a bun on the top of her head. My baby had the most beautiful smile that could melt even the coldest heart.

My Luchi was the most handsome little boy I had ever laid eyes on. I knew he would break many of hearts one day. Although I struggled day-to-day, I made sure my kids never went without, and I made sure their wardrobe was the latest. At six, Luchi already thought he was a trendsetter. I kept his curly fro tapered on the side. My handsome baby rocked a big diamond in his ear. Luchi's vision wasn't quite a hundred percent, so he wore glasses. At first, he hated the thought of wearing glasses until I bought him a pair of Ray Bans. I didn't have much in this world, but my twins were everything to me.

Watching the twins sleep peacefully under me, my eyes slowly closed. Sliding myself and the twins under my cover, I tried to get as comfortable as possible in my bed, the best way I could with my two little tiny monsters glued to me. The whole way home, I was praying the twins wouldn't give me a hard time when it came to getting ready for bed. Normally, it would take forever to get Luchi to fall asleep, but I guess God heard my prayers. Kissing both my babies goodnight, I joined them in dreamland.

**

Beep, Beep, Beep

I jumped from my sleep once I heard the sound of my smoke alarm going off.

"Oh, my goodness, the hot dogs!" I yelled, jumping from my bed.

I began to cough as smoke made its way into my room.

"Luchi, run to your sister's room and get her some pants!" I yelled, before rushing out of my room to see how bad things were. The moment I hit the corner, I saw my whole kitchen going up in flames and spreading. I started to panic once I realized we were trapped. Rushing into Luna's room, I found the twins curled up together in a corner beside her dresser.

"Mommy, I'm scared!" Luna cried out.

"I promise, baby. I'll get us out of here!"

I had to put on a brave face for my babies. I couldn't let them know I was just as scared as them. The fire was quickly spreading from room to room, and I needed to think fast before it got to us. Rushing over to the window, I quickly ripped down the curtain. Then, it dawned on me that the window in her room didn't open. We were trapped in Luna's room. It was something I've been complaining to my slumlord to fix since I moved into this house.

I began to panic and cry as I beat on the window, losing my cool. Hearing my kids cry broke me down inside. Before I could pull myself together, I heard loud banging on the window.

"Ay, Shorty, stand back." I heard the man on the other side of the window yell. Running over to my kids, I quickly grabbed them, pulling them into a bear hug, covering their body with mine.

"Ahhh!" The twins and I screamed once we saw a chair come crashing through the window.

We watched as two men knocked the rest of the glass out of the window.

"Come on, you need to get the fuck up out of here before you become burnt toast."

Picking up the twins, I quickly carried them over to the window. The stranger quickly hopped inside the window once he realized I was struggling trying to carry two kids.

"Thank you so much." I cried, as the stranger grabbed both Luchi and Luna out of my arms.

"Grab them, Za'Cari!"

"Ahhh," I cried out once I felt a piece of glass from the window go into the bottom of my foot.

"I got you, shorty." The stranger said, sweeping me off my feet and quickly moving out the window.

Once I was outside the house, I watched as it went up in flames. I watched on in horror with my neighbors and bystanders as all our belongings burned to ashes. I said a silent prayer thanking God for sparing me and my children's life.

"Ma'am, we need to check you and your kids out." The paramedics, said rushing over to us.

"Thank you!" I told the two strangers over and over again as the paramedics wheeled us away on stretchers.

Zouk (Zoo) Taylor

Today was another busy day at the Barbershop, and I couldn't wait to drop my brother Za'Cari off at home, so I could make my way home to relax. I was still salty I had to go out of my way to take this nigga places, because he didn't know how to keep his bitches in check. A crazy hoe named Sam fucked up his rides moments after she went through his phone while he was in the shower and found out he was fucking her sister as well. I told this nigga to get a rental car, yet he thought it was best that I drove him around.

I was a couple blocks away from his street when something told me to go a different way than I normally did, and I was thankful I did.

"Brah, do you see this shit?" Za'Cari asked, leaning closer to get a better view.

"Hell, yeah," I said, throwing my car in park before quickly hopping out.

"Does anyone know who lives here, and if anyone is inside?" I asked no one in particular.

"A young lady and her two kids live here. They're home, because I watched them go inside about an hour or two ago." An elderly woman told me as a lonely tear rolled down her cheek.

"Has anyone called the fire department?" Za'Cari question the elderly lady.

"Yes, I called, Father God, please let the poor child and her babies make it out alive. My heart can't take it." The elderly woman stood beside me praying.

Everyone watched in horror as the front of the tiny house and most of the right side went up in flames. Something in me told me to take off running to see if I could help. Hearing a mother and her two kids was stuck inside had me shook. Running around the side of the house, I watched shorty struggling to get the window open. The look of defeat quickly washed over her.

5

"Zoo, what the fuck are you doing?" my brother yelled running after me.

"Hand me that chair over there." I called out to him before running over to the window.

"Ay, Shorty, stand back." I yelled. Once I knew she was out of the way, I threw the metal lawn chair through the window with all my might.

Za'Cari carried the kids to safety while I carried their mother. She was so frightened and dead set on getting her kids safely out of the house, she cut her foot up stepping on the shattered glass from the broken window.

"Thank you so much."

The girl I rescued from the house thanked me as they willed her away. I had no choice but to follow her to the ambulance, because she had a death grip on my hand.

"Ma'am, can you give us your name?"

"Ramsey Scott." she spoke to the paramedic, never taking her eyes off her children.

"Okay, Miss Scott, we're going to get you and your kids checked out."

"Okay."

"Ay," I spoke, grabbing her attention.

"Yes?"

"I get that you're very appreciative, but can a nigga get his hand back?"

"Oh… oh, I'm so sorry." She said, stumbling over her words, as she quickly let my hand go. "I can't thank you enough for saving our lives! Before you go, can I ask you one favor?"

"What?" my tone came off rudely.

"Never mind, I'll just wait to call my sister when I get to the hospital." She looked nervous, and I could tell she was taken aback by my tone.

"We need to get going." The paramedic added, lifting her into the ambulance.

"I want my kids. You know what, I'm fine. I just want to make sure my kids are okay." She told one of the paramedics in a panic.

"Ma'am, you should really get checked out."

"I'm fine." she stressed, pushing the paramedic away.

"Ay, just calm down and go get yourself checked out. You need to make sure that you're straight. You won't be any good to your kids if you're fucked up somewhere. What's your sister's number? I'll tell her what's up and have her meet your young ones at the hospital." I offered.

"No, I'm fine. I just want to be with Luchi and Luna."

"Listen, Ramsey, just go to the fucking hospital. I didn't save your ass only for you to die from some internal bullshit." Her eyes bugged out, after hearing my harsh words.

"Yo, Zoo, ease up." Za'Cari spoke, not really shocked about the way I had just flipped on her.

"You're right; what the fuck do I care? Best of luck to you. Come on, bro, so I can drop you off at home."

I had to stop myself from getting in my feelings. Who was I to tell a complete stranger what to do? Hopping in my ride, I took one last look at the house as the firefighters tried to get control of the flames. Looking over my shoulder, I watched as Ramsey hugged her kids kissing them all over their face while crying. Starting up my car, I put my shit in drive and quickly pulled off.

"Are you good, bro?"

"Yeah, I'm straight."

"You sure?"

"I'm fucking positive, so drop the shit, Zay!" I yelled, frustrated about him trying to check me.

"I just asked a question; you need to check your fucking attitude. As your big brother, it's my job to check on you, my nigga."

"Well, when I say I'm good the first fucking time, you should've let the shit go." I yelled, pulling up in front of his house.

"You need to talk to somebody, Zoo; you're a ticking fucking time bomb."

"I repeat, my nigga. I'm good. Now, get the fuck out of my shit." I yelled, ready for my brother to get out of my ride.

"Alright." Za'Cari said, hopping out, shaking his head. "Be safe; I love you, bro."

"I love you, too."

"Hit me up to let me know you made it in safe."

"I got you." I said, speeding off before he could shut my door well.

Looking in my rearview window, I could see my brother walking up his pathway shaking his head. Za'Cari was only eleven months older than me, but this nigga swore up and down he was my daddy. I tried not to flip out on him too much, because I knew he was only worried about me. I'll be the first to admit that I haven't been myself the last few years, and my attitude was only getting worst. Everyone in my life knew not to talk about the situation that turned me into the dark motherfucker I am today. So, Zay pressing me quickly pissed me off.

I dealt with my problems by burying them deep, and I guess Za'Cari knew just like I did that old wounds from my past were reopened tonight. I thought I was tired and ready to go to bed, but somehow, I found myself pulling into the parking garage of Kosair Children's Hospital.

Taking the elevator down to the emergency room, I walked over to the information desk standing behind a lady as she talked to the security guard who sat behind the desk.

"I'm looking for my niece and nephew, Luchi and Luna Scott."

Hearing the name Luchi and Luna caused me to focus on what was going on in front of me. I remember Ramsey saying their names.

"Yes, your sister has been waiting for you. Follow me this way." A nurse appeared.

I followed behind Ramsey's sister and the nurse. Ramsey's sister was so wrapped up in getting to her family she never noticed me following behind them. The nurse on the other hand kept looking at me like she wanted to say something, so I played it cool like I actually belonged. I just wanted to make sure they were okay.

"Ramsey!" her sister called out pulling the sliding door open. I could tell in her voice she was relieved to see them okay.

"What are you doing here?" Ramsey asked.

"You called me." Her sister answered. I could hear it in her voice she was confused by her sister's line of questioning.

"Not you, him." Ramsey said, pointing at me.

"I asked myself the same question once I was getting off the elevator. I guess I wanted to make sure y'all were good."

I could tell her sister was taking back by my bluntness by the look on her face and the way she jerked her head back.

"Ramsey, how you know him?" her sister looked me up and down like I wasn't shit.

"I don't …I mean, he saved our life." I could tell she was taking me all in.

"What's your name?" Her little girl asks me with a smile that made me smile back at her.

"Zouk. What's your name, pretty?"

"Luna Lee, and this is my twin brother Luchi Lee, my mama, Ramsey, and my aunt, Jennifer. Thank you for saving us."

"Yeah, good looking." Her twin butted in.

"No problem, young one." I laughed at her little boy. I could tell little dude was as cool as a fan.

"How are y'all feeling?" I asked, making myself comfortable in one of the chairs next to their hospital bed.

"Good, just scared. I told my mama I was sad, because we lost all our stuff. I felt better when she told me the most important thing, which was us, got out of the house unharmed." Luna told me.

I glanced in the direction of Ramsey. Most women would've been pissed and bitching about the material shit they lost, but not her. Her main focus was her kids, I was feeling how she was teaching her kids not to value material shit, but to value family.

"Your mother is right. I'm glad you're feeling okay. What about you? How you feeling?" I asked the little boy Luchi.

"I'm good as long as my sister and my mama is good."

I nodded my head in understanding where the little nigga was coming from. "So, is his mama good?" I asked her, wondering if she let someone check her out.

"I'm good. The paramedics cleaned my cut I got from the glass in the ambulance. It wasn't as bad as I thought. I feel fine, and once I find out my kids are a hundred percent healthy, I'll get properly checked out."

"Fair enough." I said, getting comfortable in the chair, because I knew it would be a while.

The room grew quite as Luchi channel surfed looking for something to watch.

Ramsey

I knew now wasn't the time to be checking Zouk out, but I couldn't help noticing how fine he was, sitting across from me in the hospital chair. I didn't want to assume, but by his really light complexion, I could tell he had to be mixed. I was watching him so hard, I could tell his hair was freshly cut along with his facial hair. I love the fullness of his eyebrows and sexy, juicy lips. I could tell by the diamond in both his ears, and the two diamond necklaces he rocked around his neck, that his pockets were deep. I've always had a thing for thugged out dudes with tattoos, so looking at this growling tiger tattoo that covered Zouk's neck had me gone. Both his arms were covered in tattoos.

My thoughts had me ready to rip his clothes off and go exploring to see what other tattoos I could find throughout his body; I knew his tattoos didn't stop there.

"You need something?" Zouk asked in a tone letting me know he was trying to be a smartass. I guess he peeped the way I was drooling over him.

I quickly snapped out of the fixation I had on him, feeling embarrassed that he caught me staring.

"No, I'm sorry. My mind went off to la-la land thinking about everything that happened tonight." I lied, trying to save face.

Zouk gave me a look like *yeah right,* before turning his attention to the TV. Looking over at my sister, she had the same facial expression as Zouk.

"Shut up." I mouthed to her, causing her to giggle.

Zouk looked our way, I guess wondering what she was laughing about, but now it was my turn to focus on the TV. Zouk's presence and energy gave me mixed emotions. I could tell this is where he wanted to be. I don't know why, because he didn't know me nor my kids, but I appreciate him being here. Tonight had me feeling helpless and alone. On the other hand, his attitude wasn't very friendly, and everything that came out his mouth was rude.

"My babies are so tired." I spoke out loud to myself, as I watched them sleep with no care in the world. "I'm so thankful for God sparing our life, but we have nothing." I broke down crying.

"Surviving with your life should be more than enough. Material shit can be replaced. Fuck everything in your house. The only thing that matters is that you and the twins are safe." Zouk let me know.

"I know; I'm just tired of struggling. I'm tired of feeling like I'm doing well, only to be hit with another setback." I cried.

"Ramsey, wipe your face. God blessed you to live another day, so wipe your tears and worry about that shit tomorrow. Right now, I want you to be thankful for what you have right in front of you." His words made my heart flutter for some reason.

I knew he was talking about my kids, but the look in his eyes made me feel like it was something more. Doing as I was told, I walked over to the sink and splashed cold water on my face.

"Zouk, help us." Luna yelled crying in her sleep. My heart broke into a million pieces, as I rushed to Luna's side. My baby was traumatized, having nightmares of the fire.

"Luna, I'm right here. I got you." Zouk picked her up from the bed.

"I had a bad dream." Luna cried.

Luchi was now sitting up in the hospital bed looking frightened. Jen wrapped her arms around Lucci telling him everything will be okay, while Zouk and I tried to calm down Luna.

"Is everything okay in here?"

"Yes, but no. I want to know how much longer it will be? They've been through a lot tonight, and they need to be somewhere comfortable so they can try to get a decent night's rest." Zouk spoke to the nurse before I could open my mouth.

"Sir, I know your kids has had a rough night and may be tired, but we need to run all the proper tests to make sure your children haven't inhaled any harmful gasses.

"Don't you think you should be doing the same? Zouk asked. Chills ran down my spine at the sound of his voice so close to my ear. We were standing close because he had Luna in his arms and I was rubbing her back trying to soothe her. I was praying Zouk didn't see my true emotions through my eyes.

Zouk looked to be about 6'4, so at my 5'3 height, I had to look up to him.

"I'm fine, Zouk." Our eyes locked, causing the beating of my heart to pick up. Everything about him was so intense.

"The doctor should be in soon." the nurse spoke pulling Zouk's attention back on her.

"You wanna come to mommy, Luna?" I asked, trying to put some distance between me and Zouk, but I didn't want to leave Luna's side.

"No."

She tightened her grip around Zouk's neck. I found it weird how my kids were so open to Zouk being around. Both Luna and Luchi act like the two kids from *Are We There Yet*, when it came to men being around me. Most didn't make it through a full conversation with Luchi around. Jen must've realized it, too, because she wore the same puzzling look as me.

"You know you don't have to be here. I'm here, so they're fine." Jen told Zouk.

"Naw, you don't have to be here. I'm here, so they're fine." Zouk told Jen, sitting back in his chair still holding Luna in his arms.

"Ramsey, who is this nigga?" Jen asked pissed.

"Aunt Jen, he already said his name is Zouk." Luna answered.

"Exactly… enough said."

Zouk gave Jen a look that basically said shut the fuck up without saying it.

"Ramsey, do you think it's smart having a complete stranger, not only around your kids, but holding Luna?"

"What exactly are you trying to imply? I hope you're not on no funny shit?" Zouk questioned. I could tell he was ready to go off on my sister.

"No, I hope you're the one that's not on any funny shit. Tell me, what's your interest with my sister and her kids?" Jen yelled.

"Um, let's see. Well, for starters, I'm fucking human, and although I might be a rude motherfucker most of the time, watching a woman and her children being stuck in a burning house happened to move a nigga. I'm as real as they come. I don't sugar coat shit. I thought I made my intentions clear the moment I walked through the door?" Zouk spoke, in an even tone.

"Well, something about you rubs me the wrong way. I think you should go." Jen continued to yell. I didn't understand where all her anger was coming from.

"Is there a problem in here?" the nurse asked with a worried look on her face.

"Yes, could you get security to remove him?" Jen asked the nurse.

"Is something wrong, Miss. Scott?" the nurse asked me.

"I'm not sure. Did I miss something? Jen, why are you going so hard?" I asked confused.

"So, you're taking up for him?" Jen yelled.

"I'm not taking up for anyone; I'm truly lost at this point."

"Miss Scott, do you want me to get security?" the nurse asked looking around the room.

Looking at Luna, I knew she didn't want me to kick Zouk out. By the look on Zouk's face, it was like he knew for a fact that I wasn't going to kick him out as well. Luchi was looking at Jen like she was crazy.

"Bitch, is the decision hard?" Jen asked pissed.

"Jen?!"

"You know what, Ramsey, save it. This nigga has been rude to you since the moment he walked through the door, so kicking his ass out should be a no-brainer."

"Jen, I nor my kids need all this extra drama right now." I tried to explain, but she cut me off.

"You know what, say no more," Jen yelled, grabbing her purse, rushing past the nurse.

"Jen!" I called out.

"Ramsey, fuck her. Worry about your kids; she'll cool off." Zouk spoke, unbothered by Jen's outburst.

"What just happened?" I asked, frustrated and confused.

"Mama, you know Aunt Jen stay tripping." Luchi said, laying back with his hands resting behind his head. Looking over at Luchi, I could tell he was trying to copy Zouk's cool demeanor.

"Is everything fine now?"

"Yes, sorry about that." I apologized to the nurse, embarrassed by my sister's behavior, which was normal for Jen to make things about her. She often flipped out for no reason.

"Okay." The nurse walked away unsure.

"Did you have to be so rude to her?" I asked Zouk.

"I'm rude, period, but I didn't like the shit she was implying."

"Must you cuss so much in front of my kids?"

"Shorty, this is my mouth. Take it, or leave it?"

"We'll take it." Luna smiled.

"Will we?" I asked Luna, confused at when she started calling the shots.

"We will." Luna laughed

"Yeah, we'll see about that one." I smiled at my baby girl.

"I got you, Luna." Zouk said, basically disregarding what I was saying.

Chapter Two

Ramsey

I was so thankful my children were okay. After being in the hospital for hours, the twins were finally released with a clean bill of health. My car was still parked in front of what used to be my house, so Zouk offered to give the twins and me a ride to my Nanna Mae's house. I was so ready to shower and curl up with my loves to get some rest, but Zouk shot that down. He waited outside my nanna's house in the car while I got the twins ready for bed. My nanna agreed to watch the twins, while Zouk took me to University to get myself checked out. I was grateful for him staying by my side through it all. He didn't say much, yet his presence brought a sense of relief over my body. I was relieved knowing I had a clean bill of health as well. I was happy when I climbed in bed cuddling up with my loves. I was ready to put May tenth behind us. It had been a few days since the fire, and depression was starting to set in.

I fell apart when Jen took me to my house to pick up my car, and I saw the condition of the house, or should I say what was left of it. I was waiting for the fire department to finish investigating the cause. I knew it was my fault; that's why I was beating myself up about it. If something would have happened to my kids that night, I would have been the one to blame, and that thought alone was eating away at me.

I could tell my stress was starting to affect my kids, too. My nanna noticed as well, so she suggested we got out of the house to get some fresh air and do something fun. My mother was in the military; that's why my sisters and I were raised by my nanna. We didn't have much of a relationship, yet she always came through in a clutch.

I appreciated her wiring me a thousand dollars from Alabama where she was stationed, after she heard about the fire. I planned on taking my babies to the amusement park with some of that money. I knew I really couldn't afford it, but I really wanted to take Luchi and Luna's mind off the fire.

It was going on 11:30 A.M., and my plan was to be out of the house by noon, but Luchi was giving me hell, running around my nanna's house doing any and everything. Thanks to her keeping them over her house so often, the twins had everything they needed at her house. Putting Luna and Luchi's swimwear in Luna's *Monster High* backpack, I was ready to make my way out the door, when I heard my nanna's doorbell go off.

"I got it!" Luchi yelled out, running from the back of the house to the front door.

"Luchi Lee, you better not open that door!" I yelled from the living room.

"Girl, you better stop doing all that yelling at my Luchi. Baby, get the door. Nanna's right behind you." My nanna said doing what she always did when it came to Luchi. He did no wrong in her eyes. I was once my nanna's favorite until I had the twins.

"Hello, young man." I heard my nanna say, as I threw Luna's backpack over my shoulder making my way out of the living room to the front door.

"Hello." Zouk lightly smiled at my nanna.

"How may I help you today?"

"My name is Zouk. I'm a friend of Ramsey's." Zouk said pointing to me.

"Oh, you're Zouk?" My nanna spoke in a knowing tone, smiling at him.

Giving him the once over, she tilted her head to the side. Looking him up and down, she nodded her head in an approving manner, before turning around to look at me with a huge smile on her face. I almost died from embarrassment when she gave me thumbs up with a wink.

"I didn't mean to show up unannounced. I just wanted to come by and check on Ramsey and the kids."

"Well, honey, you're just in time, because you almost missed them. As you can see, she's on her way out."

Nanna and Zouk were having a conversation like I wasn't standing there.

"Where are you going?" Zouk asked, finally addressing me. He was questioning me like he had the right to.

"We're going to Kentucky Kingdom; do you want to come?" Luna asked, running out of her and Luchi's room.

"Yeah, come with us." Luchi added.

"No, I'm pretty sure he has things to do." I explained to the twins. "Love you, Nanna; we'll be back later." I said, kissing her cheek before rushing out the door.

"I'm actually free." Zouk announced, his response stopped me in my tracks, causing me to turn around to face him. "Come on. Y'all can ride with me." His voice held so much authority.

"Yayyy!" Luna yelled.

"That's what's up!" Luchi slapped hands with Zouk.

"Y'all have fun." My nanna smiled.

Just like my kids, my nanna didn't really care too much for guys being around me. After Lance, my nanna felt like no man was good enough for me. It was her shoulder I cried on when he broke my heart, so to see her push me out the door with Zouk was odd.

I wanted to put up a fight about Zouk going with us, but with three against one, I knew that was a losing battle. I made sure Luchi and Luna were buckled in before climbing into the front seat and doing the same. Looking out the window, I saw that my nanna was still on the porch watching us, smiling. Taking a deep breath, I prepared myself for a long day with Zouk's rude ass. His attitude was terrible and had no filter, so I knew the less I said to him, the smoother the day would go.

Starting his Dodge Charger, loud music blasted throughout the car, causing me to jump. Looking over at Zouk, I could tell he was amused by me being frightened, because of the faint smirk he wore on his face.

Turning the music down, he picked up his phone from the cup holder.

"Ay, Zay." Zouk spoke into the phone. "You and Ba'Cari trying to hit the Kingdom?"

I listened to Zouk's one-sided conversation, trying to figure out when this trip to the kingdom with the twins became a group thing.

"Yes, you can bring Angel." Zouk added before hanging up.

"I need to stop at Wal-Mart to get a bathing suit."

"Wal-Mart?" Zouk looked at me with a mean mug on his face like me asking to stop at Wal-Mart offended him.

"Yes, Wal-Mart."

"Naw," Zouk said, before pulling away from my nanna's house.

"What you mean no?"

"Exactly what I said." Zouk said, before turning the music up really loud.

Reaching over to turn down the music, Zouk smacked my hand, then shook his head no. I never met such a ruder person in my life. Zouk's attitude sucked. He was so nice to my kids and nanna but when it came to me, he acted like my presence bothered him.

I fiddled with my phone most of the ride until I realized the car had come to a complete stop. Looking up, I realized that we were sitting in front of a clothing boutique.

"Here, go inside and get you a swimsuit." Zouk said reaching into his pocket. Pulling out a wad of money, he handed me a hundred dollars.

"I have money." I shook my head declining the hundred-dollar bill.

"Here, man. Plus, hurry up." Zouk rudely shoved the money in my hands.

"Make it quick, Mama. I'm ready to ride some rides." Luchi called out from the backseat.

Hopping out the car, I quickly made my way into the boutique. Inside the store, I was in awe at all the sexy clothes. This store was most definitely for the grown and sexy.

"Welcome to *Louisville Trends*. How may I help you?" an older lady walked up to me smiling.

"I'm just looking for a swimsuit."

"Okay, right this way." She said, leading me to the back of the medium-sized store.

"Those two racks over there is where all our swimsuits are located.

"Okay, thank you."

"No problem. Let me know if you need any help."

Nodding my head, I looked through the rack of swimsuits for something that complemented my shape and figure. Most of the pieces were really cute, but too revealing to wear to the pool with my kids. Now, if I was going to Miami for a turn-up trip, these swimsuits would be perfect.

Finding a cute, two-piece, neon yellow, pink and orange bandage bikini, I looked at the price tag almost fainting. Did they seriously want eighty dollars for two tiny pieces of fabric? Looking at the price tag on several different swimsuits, I realized every last swimsuit on the rack was sixty dollars and up. Making my way to the register with the swimsuit I picked out in my hand, I decided to check out some of the clothes that I walked passed. I was curious to see the prices on the sexy dresses the mannequin wore, and they were all giving me a headache.

"Is this all for you today?"

"Girl, yes. Everything in here is cute, but y'all putting a hurting on people's pockets." I laughed.

"Yes, we're expensive, but I know for a fact you won't find what we have to offer here in any other store." She smiled, ringing me up for the swimsuit.

Just when I was about to reply, I heard a horn blowing nonstop. Looking out the window, I saw Zouk waving me to come on.

"Why is he so rude?" I rolled my eyes letting out a frustrated sigh, paying for my item. "Thank you." I said, before making my way toward the exit.

"Really?" I asked, climbing into Zouk's truck.

"Yeah. Luchi said you was taking too long."

"Whatever," I turned around to give Luchi a look. Smiling, Luchi focused his attention on looking at something out the window.

"Here's your change."

"Keep it." Zouk said, declining the change, smacking my hand away.

"Do you know how much this swimsuit cost?" I asked, removing it from the plastic bag, placing it in Luna's backpack. "You should've took me to Wal-Mart like I suggested. I could've found a cute, cheap swimsuit for fourteen dollars." I said, placing his change in a cup holder.

Yet again, Zouk rudely turned the music up on me while I was talking. I guess, that was his way of telling me to shut up. I wanted to cuss him out for being so damn rude to me, but I decided to hold my tongue, because I wanted this day to be drama-free for my kids. I sat mute the rest of the ride to our destination.

The kids screamed from the backseat once they saw the huge Ferris wheel at the amusement park as we rode down the highway nearing our exit. I had the same huge smile on my face, but my smile was for a different reason. I was happy to see my kids light up with so much joy.

The twins talked non-stop, as we made our way through the fairgrounds.

"I'm so excited!" Luna yelled bouncing up and down in her seat while Zouk looked for a parking spot.

"Are you ready to ride some rollercoasters, mama?" Luchi asked leaning in the front seat.

"Bro, ain't this car still moving?" Zouk asked Luchi.

"Yes."

"Okay, so why are you out of that seatbelt?" Zouk looked over his shoulder at Luchi. "Make that your last time standing up or getting out of your seatbelt while I'm driving." Zouk was doing a slow creep through the parking lot looking for a parking space but slowed completely down to look at Luchi.

"Okay." Luchi nodded his head before finding his place back in his seat. I didn't have a problem with Zouk telling Luchi right from wrong, because Luchi's hardheaded ass was always doing me the same way when I drove. I spent most of my car rides yelling for him to sit down.

After finding a parking spot, we exited the car ready for some fun. Popping his trunk, Zouk pulled some basketball shorts from a duffle bag.

"Here, Ramsey. Do you have room in your bag for my shorts?"

"Yes." I said, unzipping Luna's backpack, so I can put his basketball shorts inside.

"This is about to be so much fun." Luna grabbed Zouk's hand excited.

"I know." Luchi yelled, bouncing all around.

Walking the distance from the parking lot to the entrance, I enjoyed watching my kids' excitement.

"What's up y'all? Zouk addressed the group of people standing off to the side of the ticket booth. From the understanding I got from meddling in Zouk's phone conversation, I was expecting to see three people waiting for us, instead of a group of ten or so greeting him.

"Yo, y'all remember my big brother Za'Cari, right?" Zouk asked us. I nodded my head, while the twins answered with a yes.

"This is his son Ba'Cari and Zay's friend Angel."

Zouk introduced his nephew and the girl standing next to his brother. I could tell the girl looked at herself as more than just Za'Cari's friend by the way she looked at Zouk when he introduced her as such.

Smiling, I politely spoke hello as my kids followed suit.

"This is my baby brother Zoran, but he goes by Zoe." Zouk said, pointing his other brother out.

I tried to hide the shocked look on my face when I laid eyes on Zoran. He was so beautiful; if Zouk never introduced Zoran as his brother, I would've mistaken him for a girl.

"Hey, boo. Damn, your melanin is popping! You're a beautiful chocolate thing." Zoran said, smiling big at me.

"Thank you, you're beautiful yourself." I said, being completely honest.

Zoran, or should I say, Miss Zoe, was everything. He dressed his ass off to be spending his whole day at an amusement park. Zoe had the same light-skinned complexion as Zouk and Za'Cari. I didn't know if he identified as a man or a woman, but I was going to call her a she because little baby was HER.

Zoe's hair was styled in a short cut with a feathered bang with her sides shaved off and three lines designed each side. Her makeup was flawlessly done, but her eyebrows and pearly white teeth were what caught my attention. Zoe rocked a maroon, blue, and white romper with a pair of blue heels.

"Zoe, what do you have on? I better not hear you complain not once about your damn feet hurting."

"Now, you know I does this." Zoe said, striking several poses like someone was snapping pictures of him.

"Anyways, this is Amber. Zoe's home girl, and these niggas are Crash and Beans, and their young ones, Lil C and A'Shanti.

"Hey." I smiled, waving.

"This is Ramsey and her twins, Luna and Luchi." Zouk introduced us.

"And Jen." My sister said walking up.

Zouk gave me a look. I could tell he was instantly annoyed by Jen's presence.

"You didn't tell me your sister was coming."

"She didn't mention anything about your rude ass being here, either." Jen rolled her eyes.

"Umm, fall back miss thing." Zoe said, addressing my sister.

"Excuse me?" Jen questioned.

"You're excused." Zoe said rolling his eyes.

Not the one for confrontation, I closed my eyes saying a silent prayer that the drama wouldn't ruin my kids' first time at Kentucky Kingdom.

"Everyone, just relax. Let's have a good time." Za'Cari said, stepping in before things could get out of hand.

"Yes, lets." I said, walking over to the ticket line, which was long, but things seem to be moving fast. Luna and Lucci were getting to know Ba'Cari, Lil C, and A'Shanti, while Zouk talked to his brothers and friends.

"So, these are the type of people you have my niece and nephew around? A rude bastard you barely even know and a group of fags?"

"Jennifer, you really need to watch your mouth. If you're not going to be here and be positive, you can leave. You, nor anyone else, will ruin this day for my kids." I let my sister know I wasn't here for the BS.

"I'm just saying, you don't know him, yet you allow him and his weird friends around my niece and nephew. But, I'm done. I won't say anything else."

"Thank you, I would greatly appreciate it." I said turning around. I was determined to have a good day, but Jennifer and Zouk's attitude were making it hard.

After standing in line for fifteen minutes, it was finally our turn to purchase our tickets.

"Hello, welcome to Kentucky Kingdom." the girl behind the glass in the ticket booth spoke.

"Hello, may I have three tickets, please?"

"Why are you buying tickets that cost fifty dollars, when you can buy a season pass for damn near the same price. Think, Ramsey?" Zouk spoke rudely standing beside me.

"Stop talking to her like that." Jennifer's tone matched his.

"Stop talking to me period." Zouk said, dismissing Jennifer. "Can I get four season passes?"

I shook my head in embarrassment by the way they were behaving, and the way the young girl behind the glass was looking at us. She looked slightly nervous. I could tell it was because of both Jennifer and Zouk's rude attitude.

"Your total is two hundred-and-sixty-six dollars." The young girl said tapping on her computer.

Going into his pocket, Zouk pulled out a wad of money, counting out three, crispy hundreds, then handing them to the young girl. Counting out Zouk's change, she handed him his money before giving him further directions.

"Here you go, sir; here's your change. Take this to the building on your right, and they will print out your passes for you."

Looking to the right of us, I spotted the building with a huge sign that said "Season Pass".

"You didn't have to pay for us." I said, while we moved to the side, so Jennifer could pay for her ticket.

"I know I didn't. I do what I want."

"I would like to have a good day today." I let Zouk know.

"And we will. Especially, if your sister stay in her lane. I hate her vibe."

"Well, it's not like your attitude is warm and fuzzy."

"I'll be over here waiting for everyone." Zouk said, walking off.

I rolled my eyes at the fact that he refused to address his attitude, as he was making his way over by the entry of the season pass building. After watching Za'Cari pay for their passes, I started to make my way over to Zouk. The line for the season passes was starting to get crowded, and I wanted to get our place, since Zouk was letting people pass him up too busy fooling with his phone.

"That nigga paid for your ticket; you should've made him pay for mine." Jennifer said, catching up with me. I could tell she had an attitude.

"Jen, can't nobody make Zouk do anything he don't want to do." My attitude matched hers. I didn't see the problem. Before I even knew Zouk was coming, she agreed to pay her own way, so I didn't see the problem now.

"You're learning fast." Zouk said, walking past us over to his brothers.

"Whatever, I'll see you inside, since I only have a ticket, not a pass." Jennifer said being extra petty, walking over to the ticket line.

"Thank you, mama. I'm so excited." Luna said running up to me hugging my leg.

"You're welcome, love. Make sure you thank Zouk as well."

"I did." Luna said, running back over to talk to A'Shanti.

After standing in the season pass line for thirty minutes, we were finally inside ready to have a fun-filled day.

Zouk (Zoo) Taylor

I was really enjoying myself at the Kingdom with my family, Ramsey, and the kids. We spent the first hour of our day in King Louie's Playland, which was the kiddie area. Luna and A'Shanti ran around riding damn near everything. I even rode a couple kiddie rides with them, along with Beans, because A'Shanti and Luna asked us to. I found it hard telling her no.

Ba'Cari claimed him and the boys were too old to ride the rides in the kiddie area, although they all were the same age. Luchi co-signed excited to ride Fear Fall, a tower that took you a hundred and twenty-nine feet over the kingdom. Anxious to see their reaction, we let Luna and A'Shanti ride a couple more rides before getting in the long line for Fear Fall. The girls act like they were too scared to get on, so my niggas and I rode the ride with the boys. I challenged them that, if they rode this ride like a "G", I would buy them whatever they wanted.

Lil C didn't make it halfway up the ride before he started crying for his daddy.

"Look, Ba'Cari, you can see my car from up here." I joked, laughing at my nephew. He had his eyes squeezed shut.

"Unc..." Ba'Cari's words were cut off with screaming as the ride dropped. The way Ba'Cari and Lil'C screamed, you would've thought they were dropping to their death. Luchi, on the other hand, was laughing at them right, along with me and my niggas.

"You said anything I want, right?" Luchi laughed, running up to me after we got off the ride.

"Yes." I laughed.

"Same deal for the lightning run rollercoaster?" Luchi asked.

"Naw, it's clear that you're an adrenaline junkie, so get your mama on a rollercoaster, and we have a deal."

"Deal!" Laughing, Luchi walked over to Ramsey. "Mama, are you ready to ride this rollercoaster?"

"I been trying to prepare myself for this since I agreed. I promised you I would ride one roller coaster, so I got you." Ramsey smiled at Luchi pulling him in for a hug.

"You're not slick, Luchi." I laughed, feeling played.

"Let's get it! I'm ready to ride this rollercoaster. I'll let you know when I'm ready to cash out." Luchi laughed before grabbing Ramsey's and Luna's hand.

"Luna, I got us." I heard Luchi say, causing me to become curious about what he meant.

After Luchi dragged us around the kingdom riding anything he felt would give him a rush, we finally made our way to the waterpark.

"Dang, Unc, do you see all these fine honeys?" Ba'Cari licked his lips, as he watched half-naked teenage girls walked past.

"Sorry, little nigga, you're not quite there yet."

"I'm a Taylor. I was born with the sauce."

"Well, what the hell happened to it when you were riding the Fear Fall or them rollercoasters? Nigga, you're out here embarrassing me." Za'Cari joked, laughing.

"Yo' chill, OG." Ba'Cari laughed his daddy off.

"Do y'all want to get lockers and change over here, or do y'all want to walk over there?" Zoe asked, pointing in two different areas of the waterpark where you could change and buy lockers for your belongings.

"You know what, let's just go over here. My feet are killing me." He said, answering his own question.

"What I tell your ass, Zoe?" I asked my brother pulling him into a headlock.

"Zay, get him off of me." Zoe called out to Za'Cari.

"Zoo, do I need to put my hands on you? Or are you going to let my peoples go?

"I told his ass not to complain about wearing these damn heels. What? He thought I was playing?" I asked, smacking Zoe a couple times before letting him go.

"Y'all need to stop doing all this fucking playing; y'all got people looking at us crazy and shit." Jennifer spoke with so much hate in her voice causing my head to snap in her direction. The sound of her voice irritated me. Anytime she spoke, it was something negative flying out of her mouth. Ramsey was catching on, well. That's why I wasn't surprised when I looked her way, and she wasted no time checking her sister.

"Chill out, Jen."

"Whatever, Ramsey." Jennifer spoke, smartly, walking away in the direction of the changing room.

"Don't invite me to anything else if you know her hating ass is attending." I walked over to Ramsey to let her know.

"Yes, I think you're a sweet girl, but your sister keeps trying me." Zoe spoke looking like he was ready to fight. Sometimes, I think he forgets he is truly a man and can't fight a girl.

I could tell Ramsey wasn't about to say anything bad about her sister, so she brushed us off by smiling faintly.

"Let's go change."

Ramsey grabbed Ashanti and Luna's hand walking off. Everyone else followed suit. Ramsey knew her sister was a hating ass bitch. I could tell she got on her nerves as well. I respected Ramsey for always sticking by her side, because I did the same for my brothers. I hung out with Zo just as much as I hung out with Zay, and I wish a nigga would come out of pocket about Zo being gay or had any foul shit to say about Zay. Although I didn't support a lot of Zo and Zay's life decisions, they were my brothers, so riding for them wasn't a question.

"Here, Luchi, go with Zouk to change. Luna and I will be over here changing. If you finish before Zouk, wait until he's done before leaving out of the changing room. Don't be trying to roam around like you're grown." Ramsey said, handing us our swimwear out of Luna's backpack.

"Man, go change. I got him." I said, dismissing her.

"Luchi, you heard me."

"And you heard me; I got him."

Waving me off, Ramsey grabbed A'Shanti's swimsuit from Beans before walking into the girls' dressing room while the guys did the same.

Zay and I allowed Zoe to change first before changing. People often put a target on Zoran back because he dressed like a girl, but what they didn't know was that he had two crazy niggas who were willing to murder a nigga's whole family all the way down to the dog on the strength of him.

After changing into our swimwear, I went ahead and bought a locker for our belonging since the girls were taking forever. Lil C, Luchi, and Ba'Cari were enjoying the scenery. I couldn't believe my ears when I heard Ba'Cari and Luchi yell Bingo at the same time as a chocolate chick in a two-piece bathing suit walked past them. These little niggas were actually playing Bingo picking out girls like they were nice cars.

"You can have shorty that just walked past. I call Bingo on that right there." I heard Ba'Cari say while pointing.

Looking in the direction of where he was pointing to, my eyes landed on Ramsey. I couldn't deny how beautiful she was, and the way her swimsuit was hugging her shape had a nigga feeling some type of way about her standing there in that revealing ass bathing suit thang.

"My little man got taste." Zay laughed.

"Ay, little nigga, watch out." Luchi said, heated, when he realize Ba'Cari was checking out his mother.

"Damn, Ramsey is bad as fuck! Her sister is cute, too, but shorty's attitude is a huge turn-off. Damn, Zoo, you lucked up on this one." Beans said, licking his lips lusting over Ramsey.

"That ain't me; y'all know how I get down."

I thought Ramsey was a beautiful girl, but I wasn't looking at her like that.

"So, you don't mind if I tried to fuck with shorty. She's already vibing with my daughter, so that's a plus. And got damn look at that ass. She better stop bending over like that, before something slides up inside her." Beans lustfully watched Ramsey's every move as she bent over to put Luna's backpack in our locker.

I could feel myself getting pissed off while I listened to Beans talk. I wasn't feeling Ramsey like that, so I wasn't understanding why I was getting mad. I brushed it off blaming it on my anger issues. It was normal for me to get pissed off over nothing.

"Do you." I said playing it cool.

"Y'all ready!" Ramsey asked, walking up to us smiling.

"Yeah, we was waiting for y'all; where to first? Lead the way." Beans flirted with her letting his eyes roam her body.

Faintly smiling, Ramsey looked over at me.

"What? You got it; lead the way." I spoke being my normal rude self. I could see Jen shaking her head out of my peripheral vision.

"Let's go right here first." Angel announced pointing to the River.

"Yes, I can't wait until my feet touch this water. They are burning on this hot ass concrete." Amber said, bouncing from one foot to the other making her titties jiggle as she looked at me. I told Zoe about bringing her thirsty ass around me. No matter how many times I told her I wasn't interested, it seemed like, she tried harder.

"Zoo, don't be trying to look at my booty." Amber flirted.

"No worries, I won't." I said, causing my brothers to laugh.

"Zoo, be nice." Zoe hit my shoulder.

"I would like to see that."

Ramsey gave me a side-eye as we walked over to whatever this river ride was.

"Everyone grab a tube and move to your right." The lifeguard yelled.

"I'm going to get on first, then can you help her on?" I heard Ramsey ask Beans for help as she hopped onto her yellow floating tube.

"I'll help her so you can handle A'Shanti." I butted in.

"Blocking," Zoe fake sneezed.

"Grow up, Zoe; you're childish as fuck."

Laughing, he blew me a kiss before hopping on his floating tube. After Ramsey had laid back comfortable in her tube, I sat Luna in her lap.

"Can you hold onto our tube, Zoo?" Luna asked me, as I grabbed a tube from the lifeguard.

"Okay, pretty."

"Help me, too, Zoo." Luchi walked over to me. He was tall enough to stand in the water, because it was only two-and-half feet.

"Luchi, are you sure you want to float around this river by yourself? I'm pretty sure Zouk will let you on with him. Right?"

"Mama, I'm good."

I could tell by the look on Luchi's face he was embarrassed by his mama treating him like a baby.

"Just stay close, please."

"Okay."

Letting go of his tube, Luchi began to float away, followed by Ramsey and Luna, then myself. It was refreshing being in the water seeing that the heat was blasting at damn near a hundred.

"This is so relaxing." Ramsey said, leaning back with her eyes close.

"Man, did you try that shit on before you bought it?"

"What?" Ramsey asked looking over at me. I was trying not to say anything about her swimsuit, but I didn't like the way niggas was looking at her as they floated on by.

"What? You got water in your ears? That swimsuit is showing damn near everything; that high ass motherfucker didn't come with a wrap?"

"I don't get how you still uptight when this is so relaxing."

"Ramsey, your ass is out."

"What's it to you, Zoo?" Ramsey asked, slightly raising her sunglasses up to get a good look at me.

"Man."

"Thought so." she said, relaxing.

"Lulu, are you having fun?" I asked, changing the subject.

"Aw, I like that name,. Yeah, today has been fun. All I need is a funnel cake, and everything will be complete." Luna showed off her beautiful smile.

"I love funnel cakes, too." I told her.

"Thank you, Zoo, for everything. You're really nice."

"Aw, that's sweet baby. I bet that was the first time he heard those words." Ramsey spoke smartly with her eyes still closed.

"Shut up." I said, splashing water all in Ramsey's face.

"Zouk!" she yelled.

"Aw, shut up. Water won't make your chocolate melt." I said, rubbing some off her face.

"Ay, Zoo, what you up there doing to my future baby mama?" Beans yelled out from behind us.

"His future?" Ramsey asked, confusedly.

"Let me leave you for your future." I said, letting her floating tube go. Don't ask me why I was so damn rude to Ramsey, because I didn't know myself. I thought she should find herself lucky; I barely gave anyone conversation outside my family and friends. Most of the shit I was saying may be rude, but at least I was talking.

I guess Ramsey felt some type of way about me letting her floating tube go, because she asked Zay to help her off the float, and she ignored me the remainder of the time we spent at the Kingdom. She also asked her sister for a ride home, which Jen gladly agreed to do knowing it would piss me off.

I found it funny that Ramsey didn't want to say goodbye to me, because she called herself being mad, yet she was sending messages through Luchi and Luna. She didn't have it in her not to thank me for the day. I was rude to her, but I couldn't deny that I liked who she was as a person and a mother. Pissed or not, she let me know she was appreciative of the day. I was ready to go home and call it a day; a nigga was beat.

Chapter Three

Ramsey

It had been a few weeks since I moved in with my nanna because of the house fire. Come to find out, I wasn't the cause of it. The stove caught fire because of some faulty wires, which I wasn't surprised about, because my landlord had a lot of outdated appliances in my home, my stove being one. That damn stove was ancient, and my landlord was as worse as they come.

I was thankful that my nanna talked me into getting renter's insurance when I first moved, because now, I was getting back everything me and my kids lost.

It had also been a few weeks as well since the last time I heard from Zouk, or Zoo, as his family and friends called him. That man was too confusing for my liking, and with all the things I had going on in my life, I didn't have time to sit down and try to figure him out. I didn't like how he thought he could give me to his homeboy as well. I noticed the way Beans looked at me, and I thought he was a handsome guy, but I wasn't looking at him like that. I didn't know what kind of girl Zoo took me for, but I wasn't her. I was very much attracted to Zoo when his mouth wasn't moving, but when he talked to me like I was a child, it instantly turned me off.

I knew my sister hated him and thought I was weak for not standing up to him, but I wasn't a confrontational person. Plus, he was good to my kids, and they loved him. I was also the type of person who accepted people for who they were. I realized his attitude was who he was. It wasn't like he talked to me any different than he talked to anyone else.

But enough about Zoo. Today was week two of me trying to find my loves and me a new place to stay. It was also my birthday, but I wasn't in the mood to celebrate. I would do so when I found my babies and me a decent place to live. The first week was a huge bust. Every house that I went to view was a hot mess, and I wasn't having that again. My section 8 voucher was enough to find us a nice place, so I was going to take my time doing so.

My nanna was keeping the twins, which I was thankful for. Luchi was already on ten, and it wasn't even eight o'clock yet. I made my kids and Nanna breakfast before getting myself dressed. The heat was already pushing ninety, and it was only eight-thirty. I wore my hair pulled up in a high ponytail and a tank and shorts. I was thankful for my outfit of choice, as I made my way to my car.

I was shocked to see Zoo's car blocking mine, as I made my way down the driveway. Walking over to his car, I knocked on the window. Watching it roll down, I came face to face with Zoo, as he looked over at me for a split second then continued breaking down his weed in his lap.

"Get in." He looked up at me again.

"I have somewhere to be. Can you let me out?"

"Get in!" His voice held so much authority.

I let out a frustrated sigh, as I opened the door to get inside.

"Zoo, what are you doing here?"

"Where are you going?" he asked, ignoring my question.

"What are you doing here?" I asked again.

He finished rolling his blunt before lighting it up.

"Hello?" I said, fanning the smoke away from my face.

"Man, where are you going?"

"House hunting. Now, tell me what are you doing sitting in my nanna's driveway at eight o'clock in the morning, rolling a blunt at that. Don't you think that's a little disrespectful?"

36

"Chill out; you acting like I asked nanna to hit this motherfucker."

"You'll do anything to avoid my question. Why are you here, Zoo? I haven't heard from you in a while, and now you're just popping up."

"So, what's first on your list?" Zoo asked.

Shaking my head, laughing, I opened the door stepping one foot out as Zoo grabbed my arm.

"Ay!"

"What Zouk?"

"Where you going at?"

"How many times I gotta keep saying I have somewhere to be?"

"I know; you're riding with me. Shut the door."

"No, thank you. I don't have time for you today."

"Fuck you mean you don't have time for me?" Zoo raised his voice.

"That's what I mean right there. I don't have time for your attitude. It's too early."

"Man, get in, and shut my damn door. I been looking around, and I found a couple places for you to look at."

"You sure you don't want Beans to take me?" I asked, sarcastically.

"Keep it up, Ramsey." Zoo said turning the music up.

Rolling my eyes, I buckled my seatbelt. Pulling out my phone, I decided to do my morning scroll down my Facebook timeline. I didn't have any friends, so I got most of my entertainment from the internet.

"Are you going to give me an address, or do you want me to drive around the city of Louisville until I see a *For Rent* sign in a front yard?" Zoo rudely asked.

"If I'm not mistaken, you said get in, you have a couple houses to show me."

"The first appointment is at ten-thirty. We have time to view at least one or two of your houses on your list before we go."

"Okay, there's a house for rent on Cecil and Greenwood."

"Hell, naw. Next." He quickly shut that down.

"We can go look, Zoo. You never know; the place could be nice." I tried to plead.

"Fuck what the house is looking like. I'm pretty sure you know down that way is wild as fuck. You're not moving down there."

"Zoo, it won't hurt to go look."

"I said no; there's no need for you to go look, because I said you're not moving over that way. Now, what's next?"

Shaking my head, I wasn't about to argue with him. I made a mental note to go look at the house by myself.

"There's another on thirty-second and Hale."

"Fuck no! Next!"

"What's the point if you're just going to turn down everything I say?"

"So, you're telling me there's not one house on that listing that's in a decent neighborhood?"

"Yes, I just gave you a few." I spoke slightly annoyed.

"Let me see the listing."

Going into my purse, I pulled out the section 8 listing that I received from the section 8 office.

Pulling into the gas station, Zoo pulled over to the side, so he could look over the papers. His mood was very hard to read, because at this moment, his face was emotionless, as he flipped through the papers that were stapled together.

"So, you didn't see these houses out on St. Matthews?"

"Yes, I saw them, but they are too far away from my nanna."

"What does that mean? It ain't like you're catching the bus around. Stop being scared to put some mileage on that bucket."

"I don't want to be that far away from her, just in case of emergency."

"Okay, man, let's take a ride to look at some of these houses in the east." Zoo said, putting his car back in drive.

Just like Zoo suspected, the houses I wanted to look at were a bust. I thought some we looked at wasn't that bad, but Zoo felt like they weren't good enough.

Pulling up at the house Zoo found, I fell in love, and I was only looking at the outside.

"Oh my goodness, I love it already." I said, excitedly undoing my seatbelt.

"Yeah, the inside is nice as well."

"You've seen the place already?"

"Yeah, I looked at it the other day when I was riding through." Zoo said exiting the car.

"Hello, Mr. Taylor; it's nice to see you again." A lady dressed in a two-piece pant suit greeted him.

"Good morning, Mrs. Peters; this is Ramsey, the young lady I was telling you about." Zouk said, extending his hand for her to shake.

"Hello," I smiled, shaking her hand as well.

"Follow me, and I'll show you around."

"Okay." I was so excited to see the inside.

"Okay, so this house is a three bedroom with two baths. To the right, is the living room, and to the left, as you can see, is the stairs that lead to the bedroom, but first, before we make our way upstairs, let me show you the kitchen and backyard. As you can see, the kitchen has stainless steel appliances."

Seeing the kitchen made my eyes light up. Everything looked brand-new.

"I love it," I said, running my hands over the counter.

"Let me show you the backyard." Mrs. Peters said, leading the way over to the back door. "This backyard is perfect for a family." she smiled, stepping to the side, so I could take it all in. I fell more in love with the house after seeing it. I knew, after I got my money right, I could do so much with it for my kids. This backyard was so big, having a pool, a playground, or a trampoline was an option.

"Stop daydreaming so she can show you the bedrooms." Zoo pulled me back inside.

The bedrooms were big and spacious, and I was for certain this was our new home.

"Zoo, thank you for finding this house. I love it."

"Yeah, it's nice. Plus, it's only a couple blocks away from me."

"Well, in that case, I pass. "I joked.

"She'll take it." Zoo said, pulling me down the stairs back into the living room.

After talking to Mrs. Peters, I was excited to get home and tell my babies I found us a new home

Chapter Four

Ramsey

The kids and I were finally back in our own place. Moving day was exhausting yet exciting. Zoo was by my side to make sure the move went over smoothly. He was truly a lifesaver with his rude self. Most of the times, his attitude could be a bit much, but he was always here with a helping hand. He insisted on buying Luna and Luchi furniture for their room, but I declined. I used my renter's insurance check to furnish my whole house. Of course, Zoo felt like he had to go with me to give his input.

The twins loved our new place. Luchi loved the backyard, and Luna loved her room and all the toys Zoo bought for her. I didn't have to work today, so I was lounging around my living room while the twins were upstairs doing their own thing. Reading a good book on my new tablet, was how I was going to spend my day. Just when I was about to log into my Kindle app, a Skype call came through from my big sister Rory.

"Hey ladies!" Rory yelled into the camera once I answered. I smiled at the sight of both of my sisters' faces on my tablet screen.

"Ro, I miss you!" I yelled, happy to see her beautiful face for the first time in months. She had been so busy lately that this was the first time in months she had time to call home.

"Hey," Jen spoke dryly rolling her eyes. I took a deep breath preparing myself for Jen's attitude.

"Don't start, Jennifer. What's with your attitude?" Rory questioned, her attitude quickly changing. Jen was receiving the same attitude she was giving out, and Rory had no problem going toe-to-toe with her.

"Jen's attitude has been real unpredictable lately." I added.

"Not lately, honey, because this is me all day every day. I never switch up. I just don't like how you been a weak bitch again over another rude ass nigga." Jen rolled her neck, as she yelled into the camera. It never failed. She always found a way to bring up Zoo.

"Jennifer, tell me what does Zoo have to do with this conversation? What? You want him or something? Every time we talk, it's Zoo this, Zoo that. We haven't talked to our sister in a couple months, and the first few seconds of the conversation you want to start stuff. I swear, I don't get you."

"I'm confused. Who is Zoo, and why are you beefing over a nigga? Come on, we don't do that."

"Trust me, I'm not beefing over him." I said, letting it be known. Jen was really starting to get on my nerves.

"Rory, Ramsey don' found her another nigga that treat her like shit. Only this time it's this new nigga Zoo, and he's worse than Lance's sorry ass, but Ramsey is too weak and stupid to see that. You know what, I can't take looking at her face. Rory, call me when you're done talking to her. I'm in the middle of something, anyways." Jen bitched before hanging up.

"I swear, her ass is really starting to work my nerves with her attitude. I can't wait until you come home. I proceed with caution when it comes to her ass. I don't know what mood I'll get when it comes to Jen. Her snapping on me like that is becoming the norm."

"What was that about? I hate being so far away from everyone."

"I hate it, too. So much has happened in the last month or so. My house caught on fire, so the twins and I had to move back in with Nanna for a while. We're back in our own place now. "

"Oh my goodness, your house caught fire? When did this happen?" Rory asked in a panic. "I can't take being here. I'm ready to come home."

"Don't stress about it, Ro, but it happened about a month o"

"So, why is Jen tripping so hard off him?"

"Because his attitude is rude, but he looks out; Luchi ad Luna loves him."

"What about you? Do you like him?"

nr so ago. The kids and I are okay, thanks to Zoo. He saved our lives."Yeah, he's cool. He treats the kids well, plus he risked his life to save us. He never left my side after the fire when we had to get checked out. He's always doing something with the kids, which they love. He goes out of his way to show them a good time."

"Yeah, all that is nice or whatever, but do you like him?" Rory stressed.

I could tell she was getting excited about the thought of me having feelings for someone. She hated that I gave up on dating or finding love after Lance broke my heart.

"Do you mean is he fine? Yeah, he's very handsome ,but do I like him like having feelings for him? Um, that's hard to say. Like Jen said, he's rude. His mouth has no filter. He's very stubborn, or maybe the better word for it is demanding. He's very closed off, and most of the time, hard to handle. Jen hates him, because he doesn't take her slick mouth and rude attitude, and the fact that he's unapologetic about his rude attitude. I handle him the same way I handle Jen. I accept him for who he is." I shrugged.

"You said all that, but you didn't answer my question." Rory laughed.

"I don't know if I like him." I laughed.

"Whatever, you know if you like the man or not." Rory continued to laugh with me.

"Speak of the devil." I laughed, getting up from the couch as I heard my doorbell ring. Jen and Zoo were the only people who knew where I lived, and by the way Jen had just act, I knew it wasn't her on the other side of my front door.

"Hurry up and open the door. I'm ready to see the nigga that's driving my sisters crazy."

Looking out the peephole, I made sure it was Zoo before opening the door.

"Hey, Zouk." I greeted him, opening the door wide enough for him to enter.

"What's up? Where's the twins?"

"Upstairs." I said feeling nervous. His voice always did something to me, and the way he was looking right now wasn't helping none. He looked so good standing before me.

"What are you in here doing?" Zoo questioned, walking over to me, looking over my shoulder down at my tablet that I held in my hand.

"You in here on a pen pal call with some Army nigga?" Zoo asked with an attitude. "Tell homie you have to go."

"See?" I asked Rory, laughing.

Zoo had mistaken Rory for a boy, because the lighting in Rory's apartment was dimmed and her hat was pulled down low over her head hiding her face.

"Does this nigga see what? What you in here talking to this nigga about?" Zoo stood closely behind me lurking over my shoulder, looking back and forth at me and my tablet.

"Did you stop by for a reason?" I asked, slightly turning around to look at him.

"Who is this nigga?" Zoo asked, ignoring me.

"Zoo, focus."

"I am focused; I want to know who this nigga is you're talking to."

"You came over here for a reason, so what was it?"

"My reason just changed. Now, I want to know who this nigga is." Zoo looked down at me intensely.

Rory's giggle made Zoo's scowling expression soften. He no longer looked angry; he looked confused.

"Zouk, this is my sister, Rory." I shook my head, staring at him while he looked down at my tablet at her.

"Damn y'all look just alike. Are y'all twins?" Zoo asked.

Looking at my tablet, the lights in Rory's apartment were no longer dimmed and her hat was off revealing her face.

"No, not twins. Just really strong genes." Rory smiled.

"Well, I'll let y'all finish talking. I'm about to go out back and play football with Luchi. Nice meeting you, Rory."

"You, too." Rory smiled waving bye.

"Luchi." Zoo yelled up the stairs.

It sounded like elephants tramping above my head once the twins heard the sound of Zoo's voice.

"Zoo!" They yelled from the top of the stairs.

"You still trying to throw the football around?" Zoo asked Luchi.

"Yeah!" Luchi's face lit up.

"Get your football. I'll be waiting out back."

"Wait for me, Zoo." Luna yelled, running down the stairs, while Luchi ran to his room to get the football that Zoo had bought him.

"Lulu, be careful on the steps. I don't want you to hurt yourself." Zoo explained, once she reached the bottom of the stair, grabbing his hand.

"Yes, sir." Luna smiled brightly, as they made their way through the kitchen and out the back door. Luchi wasn't too far behind.

"Sooo, I'll ask you again," Rory laughed. "Do you like him?"

"Shut up." I laughed, brushing her off. I tried to hide my face, because I was blushing.

"Babyyyy, I get it." she playfully fanned herself. "That man is fine, plus he don't play about you. He said tell homie you have to go." Rory made her voice deep, doing her best impression of Zoo. I laughed at her silliness.

"Girl, he's not looking at me. He just don't want no other nigga looking at me, either." I rolled my eyes. Zoo stayed blocking, yet he never really showed interest in him wanting me for himself.

"It doesn't look like that to me," Rory gave me a knowing look. "He is rude, tho, I'll give Jen that. It's clear dude be trying to handle you. It's also clear that the twins love him as well. It sounded like the ceiling was about to cave in when they heard his voice."

"I know, right, and get this. Nanna loves him."

"What? That's a shocker. Aw, yeah, you most definitely need to sit on that." Rory winked, causing me to giggle. "Nanna like him, the twins like him, fuck Jen. She barely likes herself." Rory playfully rolled her eyes, causing me to laugh harder.

"I miss you, sissy." I pouted. I loved Jen, but Rory was my ace. We were only a year apart, and were inseparable until she went off to the military.

"I miss you, too. I can't wait until this is over and I'm back home."

"Do you know when that will be?"

"No, but when I do, you'll be the first to know. I'm about to get my day started. I love you!"

"I love you, too. Be safe, sissy."

"Kiss the twins for me. I'll Skype you again soon."

"Okay." I said, blowing her a kiss before hanging up.

Hanging up with my sister always made me sad. I hated the fact that she was so far away in South Korea. I couldn't wait until she was released and back home.

Placing my tablet on the table, I made my way outside to see what the twins and Zoo were doing in the backyard. Luna was in the way, while Zoo taught Luchi how to properly hold the football.

"Come on, Ramsey. We were waiting for you."

46

"For?" I asked, confused.

"We're about to play two-on-two touch football. You and Luchi against Me and Luna." Zoo announced.

"No, I don't know how to play football."

"Come on, mama. Just play. It will be fun." Luchi added. I could tell he was excited being that this was something new for him. I was happy Zoo was around to do things like this with Luchi.

"Okay." I relentlessly agreed.

Playing football wasn't really my thing, but Luchi had a way of making me do things I didn't want to do, like riding roller coasters and rolling around in grass playing football.

"Y'all about to go down." Luna screamed, putting her arm in the air for Zoo to high-five.

I didn't know the first thing about football. Luchi was trying to coach me with the little knowledge he soaked up from Zoo. Luna didn't care about the rules, as she did her own thing running all around the backyard until Lucci touched her. I'm convinced she thought we were playing a game of freeze tag, but it didn't matter, because we were having a good time. After playing in the backyard for two hours, showering, and changing, Zoo treated us to dinner.

Chapter Five

Ramsey

Time seemed to be flying by since Zoo entered our lives, and I must say, things were interesting. He wasn't my biggest fan, but the twins I could say felt otherwise. He had quickly become the man in their life. If he wasn't taking them to Toy-R-Us buying them anything that made their eyes light up, he was taking them somewhere showing them a good time. Kentucky Kingdom was damn near their second home. Last month, Zoo took them to Holiday World Amusement Park. Jen was still in my ear with her negative opinions of Zoo. Yeah, his attitude sucked 90% of the time, but it was clear he had a good heart. He didn't have to do half the stuff he did for my kids but he did.

Today was the Fourth of July, and Zoo had invited us to Za'Cari's annual Fourth of July Bar-B-Que. I had to work a few hours, so Zoo offered to keep the twins. Although I agreed, I was somewhat against it. Jen's voice telling me I didn't know him kept ringing in my head. Although it was some truth to her words, I felt like I'd spent enough time with him in the past two months to know he wouldn't do anything to cause my kids any harm. Strangely, in that short period of time, Zoo grew an attachment to my kids.

My work hours flew by quickly. My day at Thornton's went like most, some rude customers and countless guys coming in wasting their time trying to get my attention. I wasn't interested in getting to know any of them, because I wasn't up for my time to be wasted. For the last six-and-a-half years, my life revolved around Luna and Luchi, and I planned to keep it that way.

I had thirty minutes left in my shift, and my co-worker Lesley worked the counter, while I moved around the store making sure everything was in its rightful place. Thornton's was in the heart of the hood on 18th and Dixie Highway. People stayed coming into our store making a mess at the fountain drink station. After throwing a few used cups away, I wiped down the counter.

"Hey, Mommy!" Luna ran up to me. I was shocked to see her, Zoo, and Luchi standing behind me.

"Hey, Love." I cheesed "What are you doing here?" I asked, wrapping my arms around her. Luchi bypassed me going down the aisle that held the chips and candy. "Hey, Luchi!" I called out to my rude boy.

"What's good, Ma? Are you ready to clock out?" Luchi asked. I smiled at my little man trying to sound grown.

"Yes, just about." I watched him walk up to me with a bag of chips, a Slim Jim, and a bag of skittles.

"You got me on this?" Luchi asked Zoo.

"Don't you think you should've ask that before you started picking up shit?" Zoo asked Luchi, while going in his pocket. "Luna, you want something?" Luchi ignored Zoo, as he placed his things on the counter.

I shook my head, because Zoo was creating monsters. He never told them no. That's why Luchi thought it was okay to pick up whatever he wanted without asking first whenever they walked into a store.

While Lesley rang them up, I went to gather my things and clock out. Lesley was giving Zoo the eyes, but he was so into his phone he paid her no mind. If Luna and Luchi wasn't my kids, I would've thought they were perfect angels the way they stood next to Zoo well-mannered. With me, on the other hand, they were all over the place.

"I'm ready." I smiled, walking over to them. My babies looked so cute in their Fourth of July outfits.

"Bye, Ramsey, Happy Fourth of July, Love!" Lesley called out. Now, Lesley and I weren't enemies, but we weren't cool like that, either. I had to chuckle at her breaking her neck to say goodbye to me. I knew it was really about Zoo, and by the look on his face, he did, too.

"Bye, Lesley."

"Come on, man. Her loud ass is doing too much." Zoo said, guiding me out of the store.

"I need to go home and change. Come on, Luna. Do you want to ride with mama?"

"Umm…" she looked at me nervously. I could tell she wanted to say no.

"We'll meet you there." Zoo said, coming to her rescue.

"I guess. "I fake pouted hoping Luna would change her mind. She used to be my little shadow, but when it came to choosing between Zoo and me, I was losing every time.

"Alright, see you there." Luna smiled, unbothered by my fake pout. She grabbed Zoo's hand pulling him in the direction of his car.

**

After showering and changing, Zoo drove us over to Za'Cari's house. I was expecting just a little family get-together barbecue, but boy was I wrong. Za'Cari's annual Bar-B-Que was a huge block party, and it was a kid's dream. Za'Cari's street looked like a mini carnival. There was a different type of bouncy houses in each yard on both sides of the block. The different food station that aligned the street was what made my eyes light up. Bar-b-que wasn't the only thing on the menu; it was a variety of everything. I loved all the different activities they had for the kids. Face painting, henna tattoos, games, rides. You name it, Za'Cari went all out.

"Welcome, welcome." Zay smiled brightly greeting us. It was written all over his face; he was proud of himself.

"Happy Fourth, nigga. You did your thing, yet again." Zoo dapped his brother up.

"Shit turned out better than last year. No, lie, I'm glad it's over. Shit was stressful."

"How you doing today, beautiful?" Zay smiled, pulling me in for a hug.

"Hey, Zay. Nice seeing you again. Thanks for the invite."

"No problem; enjoy yourself. Help yourself to anything."

"Okay, I'm going to go over to speak to Zoe, then have a look around." I was with Zoo, but I wasn't with Zoo, if that makes sense, so I walked off without saying so much as a word to him.

"Hey, Zoe!"

"Hey, beautiful; you look cute as always."

"As do you."

"Well, hello to you too, Ramsey." Amber smirked.

"Hey!" I spoke, dryly.

Amber rubbed me the wrong way. Not only did she beg for Zoo's attention, she begged for mine as well. She stayed trying to get my attention with a smart comment or a look. She stayed throwing me shade over a guy I wasn't even looking at like that.

"So, you came with Zoo?" she asked, looking over at him biting on her bottom lip. I guess she called herself trying to be sexy. Don't get me wrong, Amber wasn't an ugly girl. It was just that the way she carried herself that made her ugly. She was a pretty, brown-skinned girl, but she overdid her makeup and dressed very slutty. There were kids running around everywhere, yet she was sitting in Zay's front yard dressed like a lady of the streets.

"Yeah."

"So, are y'all together?"

"Naw," I kept it short. Zoo and I wasn't together. I'm pretty sure he had no romantic feelings or attraction to me. I didn't even know if he even considered me as a friend.

"So, I still have a chance is what you're saying?" Amber licked her lips at Zoo like he was a mouth-watering steak. "I been trying to wait until…"

"Amber!" Zoe yelled, cutting his best friend off. "Amber, you know better."

"I'm just saying, but I'll chill. I'm about to go speak to Zoo." Amber smiled at me, standing up, pulling her skirt she got from Hooker-r-Us down.

"Girl, no worries. She been trying to get with Zoo for years, but he's not looking at her." Zoe gave me a reassuring smile.

"I'm not worried. Zouk and I are not like that. The only thing we have in common is Luna and Luchi. He enjoys being in my kids' life, and they enjoy having him around, so who am I to stop that?"

"Thank you, Ramsey." Zoe smiled hugging me.

"For?" I asked, confusedly.

You'll soon find out. Now, let's go find some food." Zoe smiled, looping his arm through mine. Amber had herself wedged between Zay and Zoo. "Come on, Amber."

"Thank you; take her thirsty ass on." Zoo was clearly irritated by her presence, which made me smile. She was threatened by me about a man who didn't want her.

"Zoe, you stay blocking." Amber playfully rolled her eyes, but I could tell she meant some truth in her statement.

"It comes with the job, now come on." Zoe pulled a relentless Amber away from Zoo.

"Come on, Luna and Luchi. Do y'all want to walk around with Mommy?"

"Yeah, I'm down, because I'm looking for Cari."

"You coming, Zoo-Zoo?" Luna asked. I rolled my eyes as I watched Amber get excited behind Luna's question.

"Go ahead with your mama. I promise I'm right behind y'all."

"Okay." Luna said, running over to me grabbing my hand.

I tried to grab Luchi's hand, but he gave me a look like he was embarrassed.

"What would y'all like to do first?" I asked the twins once we got in the mix of things.

"Mama, I'm not trying to hang out with y'all. I'm looking for my boys. Once I find them, I'm ghost."

"Luchi, you're not about to run around by yourself."

"Man," Luchi said, giving me attitude sounding like Zoo.

Zoe and Amber walked ahead of us mingling, while I stopped to get Luna's face painted. Luchi stood off to the side pouting as he watched kids of all ages run carefree.

"Luchi, what's wrong with you?" Zoo asked, coming up behind us startling me.

"He wants to run around without me, and I said no."

"Cari!" Luchi yelled, once he spotted Lil C and Ba'Cari running around.

"My nigga is finally here!" Cari ran up to Luchi. They were hyped to see each other.

"Come on; we were just about to go play basketball." Lil C announced.

"I can't. I have to follow my mama and sister around like some little kid." Luchi talked about me to his friends like I wasn't standing here.

"Luchi Scott, you are a little kid." I spoke slightly angry. I didn't like how he was talking about me like I wasn't there.

"Cari and Lil' C are six and seven, and they're running around by themselves." Luchi argued.

"Well, I'm not their parents."

Luchi looked at Zoo with pleading eyes. "You little niggas stay together. When I call your phone, Cari, you better answer on the first damn ring. If I have to come looking for y'all, it's going to be a huge problem. Cari, don't go pass Ms. Robertson's house." Zoo did what he always did pissing me off.

"I know, Unc. My daddy already gave me the rundown." They ran off before I could tell Luchi no.

"Zoo, he's six. He doesn't need to be running around by himself. Someone could snatch him."

"Trust me, Ramsey, if someone takes him they'll bring him back." Zoo joked. Well, I at least I think he was joking. Zoo never really laughed or smiled. "What's next Lulu?" Zoo asked her, dismissing me. I wasn't done bitching about it, but I guess it would be a waste of breath, since Luchi was long gone.

"Play a couple games, get something to eat, and some cotton candy and popcorn." Luna hopped up from getting a butterfly painted on her face. "Can you win me a teddy bear?" Luna asked, excitedly, jumping up and down.

"You know, I forever got you." Zoo took her hand walking her over to the first game we saw.

Hearing him say that kind of bothered me. I guess it was the thought of my kids getting attached to someone who could walk away at any moment. That's why I didn't date. I wouldn't play my kids by bringing a man into their life and things didn't work out between him and me. Not only did Zoo win Luna a stuffed animal, but she also made him win me one as well. It was crazy how many evil stares I got from so many different women for being by Zoo's side. Of course, I thought he was sexy, but I wasn't coming onto him or anything. Nothing about us gave off we were a couple or sexually attracted to each other, so I didn't understand their problem.

After getting us some food and junk food, we made our way back over to Zay's front yard, where he had tables and chairs set up. Zoo sat next to Luna, and they talked to each other like I wasn't here. It made me sad; I wished Luna would have this type of relationship with Lance the way she had with Zoo. He listened to her talk, even when she told the same story twice just to have something to talk about, and Zoo would listen intently like it's his first time hearing it.

After eating, Zoo got up to throw our trash away. I noticed one of the girls who eyed me on the road while Zoo and Luna were playing games was making her way up to him. Minding my own business, I focused on my phone. Going through Facebook, I liked all the pictures of everyone in their cute Fourth of July outfits.

"Ashanti!" Luna cheered, causing me to look up from my phone. Beans and Ashanti were making their way over to us with food in their hands.

"Hey, pretty mamas." I smiled at Ashanti; she was such a cutie.

"Hey, Miss Ramsey. I like your dress."

"I like it, too." Beans said in a flirty tone. He looked handsome today, but I wouldn't tell him that.

"Thank you, both." I politely smiled.

Looking over at Zoo, he was already looking my way. I couldn't really read his facial expression, so I didn't know what he was thinking. The girl he was talking to realized he wasn't paying attention, so she wrapped her arms around his neck turning him to face her.

"What's up with that?" Beans asked, looking over at Zoo as well.

"What do you mean?" I asked, looking away from Zoo and his lady friend.

"Ain't that your man over there hugged up with the next?"

"No, Zoo and I are just…." I paused, because I didn't know what we were. "It's nothing like everyone thinks. Zoo's been there for us during some hard times. I appreciate him for always willing to show my kids a good time like now. So, what he does in his free time isn't really my business."

"Is that so?" Beans smiled sipping his drink. "So, does that work both ways?"

"What?" I asked, confused by his question.

"Is your free time any of his business?"

"I would hope not."

"So why is he watching you right now with a look like he's ready to snap. I know that look when a nigga think the next is trying to make a move on his girl."

I didn't want to look over at Zoo. I pretty much knew what look Beans was talking about. "You and I both know that's just Zoo's natural look; the man is just evil." I joked, causing both of us to laugh.

"I guess you're right, but something is telling me it's more behind it." Beans said, taking a bite out of his hamburger. Shrugging my shoulder, I brushed it off.

"Daddy, when we're done eating, can you and Ms. Ramsey take me and Luna over to play some games?"

"You rocking with me?" Beans asked me. I didn't like his tone, like what he was saying had a double meaning.

"I don't mind."

"Cool."

After agreeing, it seemed like they both were swallowing their food whole, not interesting in chewing. Ashanti and Beans were both excited for different reasons.

Zoo and his little friend had walked away, which was none of my business. My main focus was Luna and Luchi. I was worried about Luchi, at first, but I had no problem spotting him in the crowd.

"Y'all want me to win y'all some stuffed animals?" Beans asked Luna and Ashanti.

"Thanks, but no. Zoo already won me and my mommy one." I could tell by Luna's tone that she didn't like Beans. She wasn't rude like Luchi, who would've spoken what was truly on his mind.

"I'll take one, Daddy." Ashanti hugged him. I could tell she was a daddy's girl.

Beans chose basketball, which wasn't a good choice. He ended up playing three games losing them all. I tried not to roll my eyes when he started throwing his pockets around. After buying Ashanti two stuffed animals, we walked over to the face painting station. Ashanti wanted to have a matching butterfly like Luna's.

"So, how old are you, Ms. Ramsey?" he asked, while we stood in line.

"Twenty-four, and you." I asked, not really caring but didn't want to seem rude and stuck up like I was too good to talk.

"Twenty- Seven. You know I think you're beautiful, and I would really like to get to know you."

"Thank you, but I'm not trying to travel down that road right now. I'm still trying to regroup after the fire."

"Can I just be your friend, and somewhere down the line, we can see where this could go?"

"I don't mind having friends, but that's really all I can offer."

"Okay!" Beans cheesed like I agreed to be his wife or something.

After Ashanti got her face painted, we let the girls bounce in the bouncy house before making our way back over to Zay's. It was getting dark outside, and pretty soon, the fireworks show was about to start. I was happy to see Luchi and his boys were finally sitting still. Luna and Ashanti joined them at the table while I made my way over to Zoe and Amber. I wasn't a big fan of Amber, but I didn't want to hang by myself. Zoo gave me a look while I walked past him as he chilled back with his brother and a couple of their friends. The same girl was glued to his hip.

"Why is shorty on our nigga?" Amber asked, trying to be funny once I sat down.

"He could be your nigga, but he's not mine."

"You need to go break that shit up."

It was clear that Amber was a special one. I wasn't about to entertain this conversation with her. I was thankful my attention was pulled away by a text coming through on my phone.

Zoo: *It's getting dark, so stay where I can see you.*

Looking over at Zoo, he was having a conversation with his friends, not paying me any attention, so I did the same with him ignoring his text. I didn't care if it was dark or not. If I wanted to walk off, I didn't need Zoo's permission to do so. I did want to get up and walk off, because I felt out of place. Everyone seemed like they belonged, while I sat next to Zoe trying to think of something interesting to say to spark up a conversation.

Zoo's little lady friend kept giving me a smirk look as if she was saying she stole my man. Amber must have realized it as well, because she had no problem speaking up on it. Ignoring them both, I got up from my seat. The kids were running around the yard, so I was going to use this as my moment to sneak away. I knew taking Luna with me meant stopping at several different booths. I was hoping I could go get a funnel cake without stopping a thousand times.

I walked across the yard, not wanting to walk past Zoo and his friends. I didn't have time for him to act like my daddy or taking the chance of Beans trying to follow after me. It was annoying me that Beans was keeping an eye on me like I was his girl. All I did was agree to be his friend. I loved how I looked around, and there was no drama. It was known to be drama whenever the city did something to link up. Families were out having a good time.

"What I say?" Zoo's voice was so close to my ear, he caused me to jump.

"Why do you keep sneaking up on me?" I asked.

"This is why; your ass is too scary to be moving by yourself."

"Zoo, it's hundreds of people out. Ain't nobody thinking about little old me. Plus, I'm more than capable of protecting myself. Been doing it for twenty-four years."

"You know all that stopped months ago. You now have a new protector, so what I say goes."

"Zoo, I think the overprotective daddy role is cute with Luna, but when you try it on me, I find it very annoying."

"Ramsey, I don't care what you find annoying; your ass is still going to do what I say."

"Zoo, while you're watching my every move, I know two women who's watching yours and would be more than happy to have the attention you're giving me."

"You sound jealous," Zoo said, slightly raising his eyebrow.

"Jealous?" I laughed. "Trust me, I'm not."

"Good, because I'm not really looking at you or them like that."

Rolling my eyes, I turned back around. I silently waited my turn to get my funnel cake. Zoo and his wishy-washy attitude was about to work my nerves. We really didn't have many conversations, but when we did, they always went left. We stood in awkward silence, as I waited for my funnel cake. Once it was done, I thanked the middle-aged lady and walked away. Zoo quickly moved in front of me acting like a bodyguard. It was no point in speaking up on my frustration with Zoo. I was quickly learning he did what he wanted when he wanted.

Zoo's little lady friend was still sitting in the same spot looking silly. It was clear she was pissed about him chasing after me. Amber was shaking her head like she had a problem. Not in the mood to be around negative energy, I walked over to Zay's white F-150 that was parked in his driveway. Letting the latch down, I climbed inside. Soon after I sat down, my twins, Ba'Cari, and Lil' C came over bumming for my funnel

59

cake. I took this time to talk to them to see how they were enjoying their day, since they were somewhat calm and not bouncing all over the place.

Luchi and his boys were telling me a story, which they found hilarious. I guess me and Luna missed the joke. but I laughed. Anyways. because their laughs were so genuine and contagious.

Of course, Luna was having a good time. I wouldn't be surprised if she had several cavities, too. She ate so much junk food. I was such a mom; moments like this was what I lived for. Out of all the adults out here, I found hanging out with my kids and their friends more enjoyable. The love wasn't fake or forced.

Zoo

Cleo sat beside me talking about a whole lot of other shit I wasn't paying attention to. My focus was on Ramsey and the kids sitting in the bed of Zay's truck having a good time. I had been watching Ramsey over the last few months. I looked out for her so much, because it was rare to find women who were all about their kids nowadays. Their needs always came before hers, and that's why I tried to lighten her load.

Although she thought I wasn't watching, my eyes were on her most of the day. I watched how niggas looked at her, yet it seemed like she never noticed, because her main focus was making sure her kids were having a good time. This was Zay's sixth year doing his Fourth of July Bar-B-Que, and with every year, it got bigger and bigger. He started it when most of our crew started having kids. This was only the second year of him doing the huge block party. We were well-known in our city since Zay and I owned a franchise of barbershops, so the city came out to show us love. It was crazy how a lot of these sorry ass bitches came out only to go fishing for a nigga instead of showing their kids a good time. Ramsey wasn't thinking about that, but I did peep how Beans was all in her personal space. She wasn't my girl or anything, so I wasn't going to stand in the way of the nigga trying to shoot his shot. I wasn't feeling Ramsey like that, but I was drawn to her for some reason.

Cleo was still rambling on about why I followed after Ramsey when she walked off. I had to look at her crazy, because she was tripping right now. Her jealousy was allowing her to think she was more than just a fuck to me, and I couldn't have that. Cleo was a bitch I called up on a late night when I didn't have shit else to do. I wasn't trying to wife no bitch, and she knew that. I didn't understand why she was questioning me.

"Cleo, you know better. Don't question me like you're more to me than just a fuck. I'll holla at you later. I'm about to chill with my peoples." I said, before getting up, using my key to let myself inside Zay's house.

Walking upstairs to the hall closet, I grabbed a couple blankets before going back outside and over to Zay's truck. "Everyone out!" my voice held a lot of authority. I didn't mean to come off so aggressive, but fuck it; that was me.

All the kids hopped down; Ramsey stayed put. "Ramsey, you too!"

"I found my own little bubble, but he couldn't help himself; he had to bust It." she complained under her breath, yet did was I asked.

I wasn't trying to "bust her bubble" as she said. I might be a huge ass, but it was funny to me how she didn't see I was just trying to make their life more comfortable. Yeah, I was an evil nigga, but I did care a little. Luchi felt the need to help while I laid the blankets down. The firework show would be starting soon, and I wanted us to be comfortable.

"Zoo how romantic are you making this spot just for us?" Amber asked, walking up to Zay's truck.

Amber didn't understand that, her face alone got on my fucking nerves. No, she wasn't ugly; she was just annoying as fuck, and I didn't find shit sexy about a bitch throwing herself at me constantly. Shit, since I could remember, she's been Zo's best friend, and since the moment she came into his life, she's been a huge pain in mine. Every time I turned around, her ass was in my face, literally. Amber didn't give a fuck if it was Winter, Spring, Summer, or Fall, her ass and titties were out.

"Do you ever fucking go away? I mean, damn." No matter how mean I was to her ass, she never stopped trying to get with me.

"I know you're only putting on, because Ramsey is right here. She already told me she didn't want you, so you don't have to play like you don't want me here.

"Why is it hard for you to understand that I really don't? And leave me out of whatever y'all have going on." Ramsey added.

"I don't have shit going on with her."

"Boy, you know you want me." Amber walked away putting an extra switch in her steps.

The rumbling from the fireworks began to grab our attention. The kids hopped in the bed of Zay's truck getting excited. I sat next to Ramsey pissed that she had a conversation with Amber about me. The kids jumped around as the fireworks filled the sky.

"You told Amber you didn't want me?" I pulled her close to me, so she could hear me over the loud booming.

"Yes,"

"What? You told her you're feeling Beans?"

"You sound jealous?"

"Naw."

"Good, because I'm not really looking at you or him like that." she smirked, mocking me.

"Zoo-Zoo, look!" Luna yelled, squeezing in between Ramsey and me. She didn't know she was coming to her mother's rescue.

Ramsey smiled at me like she knew Luna was saving her. I was going to let the conversation go for now. I didn't know why I was so pissed off at Ramsey saying she didn't want me. She acted like she didn't see niggas, including me. I think that's something I wanted to change.

Chapter Six

Zoo

Ramsey had to work today, so I had the twins spending time with them. We had been running errands most of the morning, and I needed to stop by the shop to go over a few things with Zay. After that, we'd spend most of our day at the Waterfront water park. After letting them get wet, I took them to Fourth Street to have lunch at TGI Friday.

I couldn't help spoiling them, so after leaving TGI Friday, we made our way to the toy store. They had no limit so they ran around the toy store going in. That bet I made with Luchi at the Kingdom was pointless, because I balled out on them on a regular.

Luna wanted Barbie's and a Barbie dream house. Luchi wanted new art supplies and a DS. After running around the toys store for two hours, it was time for me to drop the twins off to Ramsey.

"Luchi, put your seatbelt on." I looked back at him.

"Hold on; can you turn the light on?" He asked.

"Come on, Luchi; I'm ready to pull off."

"Hold on." He said before going in his bag handing me his headphones. "Open this."

"Man, you couldn't wait until you got home?" I asked, snatching the headphones from him.

"I could, but I don't want to." He said, pulling his DS out of the bag as well.

Ripping the shit open, I turned back around to face him. "Here, now put your damn seatbelt on." I said, handing him his headphones back pushing him back into the seat.

"Luchi!" I yelled. Dude was really trying my patience. He knew I wasn't moving until he had his seatbelt on. I guess he wasn't doing so until he turned his game on.

"I'll wait, since I'm on your time." I spoke, sarcastically.

"Good looking." Luchi smiled. I knew the little nigga was trying to be smart as well.

"Come on, Luchi, so we can go." Luna whined.

"Shut up. I'm ready." Luchi said, after putting his headphones on before sitting back and buckling his seatbelt. "We can go now." he smiled up at me.

"Do you have your seatbelt on Lulu?"

"Yes, sir."

"Okay, well, let's roll." I smiled at her through the rearview mirror before starting up my car.

The car ride to Ramsey's was silent, which I enjoyed. At the waterpark, all you heard were kids running around yelling and having a good time. At TGI Friday, it was nothing but moving around, the toy store had bad kids running around, either crying because they didn't get their way, or excited because they did. The silence was welcoming.

Hearing vibrations, I looked down at my phone that was sitting in the cup holder trying to figure out how my shit got on vibrate. Oddly, the vibration wasn't coming from my phone. Looking around, I tried to pinpoint where the sound was coming from. Luchi was moving his DS around, I guess he was playing the driving game I bought him.

Looking over at Luna, she was humming staring out the window. Smiling, I refocused on the road but quickly did a double take looking back at Luna. I just knew my eyes were playing tricks on me. I knew I had to be tripping.

"Lulu, hand it here now." I spoke pissed. "Where did you get this from?"

"I had it in my purse," She answered with a look of confusion.

"How did it get in your purse?" I asked, looking from the road into the rearview mirror.

"I put it there. I found it in Mommy's room."

I was so pissed right now. Not at Luna, but at Ramsey. I couldn't get to her fast enough.

Ramsey

By the look on Zouk's face, I could tell it was about to be some bullshit. The way he marched up the steps in my direction, Zouk looked like a raging bull.

"Hi, Mama," the twins yelled, running past me to their room with what I assumed was a bag full of toys.

"Hey, my loves," I called after them. "Thanks for spending time with them." I said, trying to rush Zouk off, before he could start in on his bullshit.

"Right, but check this." Zouk spoke with an attitude. "So, I'm riding down the street with Luchi and Lulu, and I heard some shit vibrating. My first thought was maybe my phone got on vibrate somehow, but no. That wasn't the case, so I looked to the backseat to see what Luchi and Luna were doing, and guess what the fuck Luna had in her hand having a great fucking time?" Zouk spoke, beyond pissed, as he held up my purple bear-style tiny vibrator. The feeling of embarrassment washed over my face as I tried to snatch my vibrator from his hand, but I was unsuccessful, because he quickly moved away every time I reached for it.

"Fuck you need this for, Ramsey?"

"Why do you think, Zoo? May I have it back, please?"

"Naw, you don't need it." he opened my front door hurling my vibrator as far as it could.

"Why must you live to make my life a living hell? Zouk, I needed that?" I whined. "You of all people know I barely have money. Now, I have to find extra ends to replace it."

"What I tell you? Whatever you need, I got you." he let me know with a small smirk. If I would've blinked, I would've missed it.

"I appreciate your help, but I wouldn't need it if you didn't throw my shit across the street."

"Who are you cussing at? You better watch that shit." Zoo pointed in my face. "Yo, Luchi and Lulu, come holla at me. I'm out." he yelled up the stairs after them.

"Bye, thanks again for the toys." Lulu hugged Zouk. Seeing them interact, calls my heart to melt.

"No need to thank me; you know you're my favorite girl." Zouk gently pinched her cheek, causing her to blush.

"Are you still taking me to try out for football tomorrow?"

"Oh, yeah. Have him ready tomorrow around five-thirty."

"Wait, what's going on?" I asked lost.

"Zoo is taking me to try out for the Jets football team tomorrow." Luchi spoke, excitedly.

"Luchi, who did you ask?"

"He ask me; the fuck?" Zoo's face balled up like he was insulted by my question.

"And you are?" I asked, confused with what parental authority he had.

"About to fuck you up, if you don't miss me with the bullshit."

"Zoo-Zoo, you cuss a lot." Luna frowned.

"I know. I'm sorry, Lulu."

"It's okay. I forgive you," she smiled hugging him.

"And that's why you're my favorite girl."

"Have him ready by five-thirty; I'll see y'all tomorrow, but call me if you need me." Zouk hugged Luna one last time before dapping Luchi up. "Call me if you need me; I'm out." he repeated before walking out the front door closing it behind him.

"Damn, for once, can I get some love?" I whined to myself.

"I love you, Ramsey." Luchi gave me a reassuring smile.

"I love you, too, little man, but don't call me Ramsey. Put some respect on my name."

"Zoo calls you Ramsey." Luchi spoke to me in a tone, I didn't like.

"I'm not Zoo's mama; I'm yours, so that's what you will call me."

"Okay." Luchi said running off.

"Luchi, don't turn on that game. Run your bath water and get ready for bed."

"But, Mama, Zoo just bought me some new games!" Luchi yelled from his room.

"Zoo this, Zoo that." I mocked, walking into Luchi's room. "Are y'all hungry?"

"No, we ate."

"Okay. Lulu, get you and your brother some pajamas out. Bye, Luchi. Go get in the shower."

"But, Mama."

"But mama nothing, Luchi. I won't keep doing this every night with you. Stop telling me what you're going to do. I'm telling you to get your shit, walk in the bathroom, shower, and get your ass in bed." I hated cussing at my kids, but sometimes, Luchi took me there.

"I swear, I wish Zoo would've let me stay with him." Luchi mumbled under his breath, as he snatched his pajamas from Luna's hand making his way to the bathroom.

Counting to ten in my head, I tried not to put my hands on my kids, but with every passing day, Luchi would try my patience. "Once your brother is done showering, you get in, Love."

"Okay, Mommy."

**

The constant ringing of my phone pulled me from my sleep. Looking at the clock on my nightstand, it read 4:30.

"Ugh…" I let out a frustrated moan, as I reached for my ringing phone. I was beyond tired, thanks to Luchi giving me a hard time like always.

"Hello?"

"Come open the door."

"Zouk, it's four in the morning."

"What's your point, Ramsey?"

"My point is it's four in the morning."

"I'm still lost to why you're telling me this. Just open the door, man." Zouk said before hanging up the phone.

Rolling out of bed, I made my way to the front door to let him in.

"Why the fuck are you answering the door like that?" Zouk spoke with a clear attitude.

Looking down, I totally forgot I was practically naked. My tank top was so tight, my breasts were coming out of the sides. All I had on was a thong. I felt so embarrassed standing before him dressed like that.

"I…," I tried to speak, stumbling over my words.

"Go put some fucking clothes on." he said, walking into the living room.

Rushing to my room, I quickly threw on a bra and a different shirt. Zouk knocked on my bedroom door, as I was sliding into my shorts.

"Is your ass decent, so I can come in?" he asked, pushing the door open.

"Yes, don't think I was on some slick shit by answering the door like that. I was sleep when you called. I just rolled right out of bed to open the door."

Zouk gave me the once over before kicking off his shoes. "Zoo, what are you doing here so late?"

"Sometimes a nigga can't sleep."

"So, you decided to wake me up from mine?"

He looked me up and down before pulling a Swisher and a bag of weed from his pocket.

"You need to work on that." I spoke, angrily, climbing in my bed getting back under the cover.

"Work on what?" Zouk asked rolling up.

"The way you treat me. You're rude as fuck, and I'm tired of kissing your ass and being nice to you when you're nothing but an ass to me. I only put up with your shit, because my kids love you, and I truly appreciate what you've done for me, but don't get it twisted. Watch how you talk to me."

"Are you done?" Zouk asked lighting his blunt.

"Get out!" I yelled.

"Ramsey, you better lower your fucking voice; take your ass to bed or something."

"Why are you here if you're just going to be rude?"

Zouk continued to ignore me as he smoked his blunt. Fed up, I snatch the blunt from him taking a couple pulls. I stopped smoking once I found out I was pregnant with the twins, but at this moment, I had the urge to smoke. Zoo did that to my nerves.

Passing his blunt back to him, I turned over and got comfortable in bed. "What are you doing?" he asked me.

"I'm taking my ass to bed or something." I mocked.

"You're just going to go to sleep on me? I came over here, because I didn't want to be alone."

"If you keep it up with your terrible attitude, you'll spend many of nights alone."

"I'm not even trying to hear all that, man. Just hit the lights."

"Asshole." I mumbled, before doing what he asked. I didn't understand Zouk. It was crazy how I didn't really know this man, but I trusted him with my most prized possessions, my kids. I trusted him to lay next to me in my bed. I knew he would never cause harm to me and my kids. He risked his life to save ours. Why he was here in my bed at this moment was still unclear to me. What *was* becoming clearer was that he didn't want me to understand him. He didn't want me to be a part of his life.

Zouk

I laid next to Ramsey, asking myself how I ended up there. Just like many other nights, sleep didn't come so easily. Most nights, I would drive around until I got tired, and tonight was no different, besides the fact I found myself parked on the street in front of Ramsey's house.

I didn't know why I was so rude to baby girl. For some reason, I was drawn to her and her kids. No matter how rude I was to her, I couldn't stay away from them. Luchi was my little nigga, and Luna was my favorite girl. Ramsey, on the other hand, something about her made me want to be around her, but at the same time, I hated the way shorty let me say anything to her. Most of the time, she just stood there looking silly. I wanted to smile when her sweet ass called herself going off on me, but I continued to sport my poker face.

"Why are you here? You're lying next to me in my bed. I allow you to spend time with my kids, and it just dawned on me that I don't know you. Jen is right. I been acting stupid." I could hear the panic in her voice as she spoke.

"Don't you think it's a little too late to go into a panic? If I was going to hurt you, trust me, I had several different opportunities to do so."

"Jen has been warning me of how dumb I been acting. It just dawned on me that I know nothing about you, but your name and where you live.

"That's not enough?" I asked being sarcastic. Her having a panic attack was blowing my high.

I didn't give a fuck about her realizing she didn't know my life story. Her ass needed to snap out of what she was going through and ask the questions she wanted to know.

"No, that's not enough. I allowed a complete stranger in my home, around my kids." She said, turning the light back on.

"Man, if it wasn't for this complete stranger busting into your home, you would still be stuck inside. Man, you're blowing my high being dramatic as fuck." I run my hands over my face.

"I'm not being dramatic; it's true. I know your name is Zouk, nickname Zoo, you're rude as hell, and where you live."

"That's enough to give the police, since you act like a nigga is going to do something to you."

"I'm not saying you would do something to me. I'm saying Jen is right, and it just hit me that she has every reason to be concerned.

"Ramsey, ask your damn questions, so this annoying ass conversation can end. You know what, I'm just going to tell you what you feel like you need to know to ease your mind."

"What?" Do you hear yourself? Don't just tell me anything just to shut me up."

"Man, I'm not. My name is Zouk Taylor as you already know. I'm twenty-five, I was born April third. I'm the middle child of three boys; you already met my brothers. My folks are still together married twenty-eight years. Blessings. You're tripping off not knowing little details about my life but you know who I am as a person, so stop tripping. I showed you who I was the moment I met you. I never sugar coated how I was or switched up, so fuck what Jen talking about." I said, getting up from her bed. "Come lock up; I'm leaving."

"Why? Because I'm asking questions?"

"Naw, I'm leaving, because it sounds like you don't trust a nigga. You went into panic mode and shit like I would do something to hurt y'all. All because you don't like a nigga's tone or delivery. I'm up; you blew a nigga's high and every fucking thing." I said, before walking out of the room. I wanted to check on the twins, but I was more than ready to get away from Ramsey.

I loved being around her and the twins, because that brought out something that I haven't felt in a while... peace. I liked Ramsey, because she wasn't expecting anything but appreciated everything. She was always grateful for the small things. It could be as simple as opening a door for her.

Tonight, she flipped the script on me. I thought lying next to her would bring me the peace I longed for on so many nights. It pissed me off to hear her say she didn't know me, because a nigga wasn't on no bitch shit breaking down my life story. My action toward her and the twins the last three or four months should've been enough. I knew that was my cue to back off.

Chapter Seven

Ramsey

The summer was over, and it was now time for my babies to go back to school tomorrow. I was thankful Za'Cari told me I could bring Luchi up to his barbershop to get his hair cut. After buying everything the twins needed for school, my pockets were hit. Luna was with Jen getting her hair braided, so that gave me time to sit in the barbershop with Luchi. I'd never been there before, but I knew it would be mad packed since school started tomorrow.

Walking into the barber shop, I felt out of place seeing that it was filled with mostly men. I looked around for Za'Cari when Luchi took off running.

"Zoo!" he yelled, pushing his way through the crowded barbershop.

"Luchi, get back here." I called out following after him. By the time I made it over to them, Luchi was dapping Zouk up as if he was a big dog.

I haven't seen or heard from Zoo since he stormed out of my house a few weeks ago. The day after our little blow-up, he had Zay come pick Luchi up for football try-outs. I'm glad he still found a way to keep his promise to Luchi, although he called himself being mad at me.

"What the fuck are you doing up in here?" Zoo asked, being his normal angry self. He had a little boy in his barber chair cutting his hair.

I rolled my eyes before answering "Za'Cari told me to come up here, so he could cut Luchi's hair."

"Za'Cari hasn't come in yet; why didn't you hit my line? I would've picked him up."

"Because it's not your responsibility. Come on, Luchi, let's wait over here for Zay." I said, grabbing his hand so we could find an empty seat to wait our turn.

I pulled Luchi's DS out of my purse to past time. I didn't want him to get bored; he was known to be very mischievous when he felt like it was nothing for him to do. Pulling my headphones from my purse, I plugged them into my phone turning on Pandora. Chris Brown's radio station was always on point, delivering the hits. Picking up a magazine off the table beside me, I begin to flip through the pages while I bopped to my music.

"You see right thru me; how do you do that shit? How do you do that shit? How do you? How do you?" I snapped my fingers, singing along with Nicki Minaj.

"Mama." Luchi pulled my earphones from my ears to get my attention.

"Yes, baby?"

"Don't call me baby in here, mama, and stop singing. People can hear you." Luchi looked at me like he was embarrassed.

"Excuse me. What, am I embarrassing you?"

"Yeah, and people keep looking at you."

"Lil homie, we're not watching baby because of her singing." A guy sitting across from us said looking at me, licking his lips.

"Lil homie, you need to stay in your lane. My mama ain't looking at you." Luchi addressed the dude before I could.

"Okay, Luchi, just play your game."

I knew how my son was; his attitude was terrible, and being around Zoo only made it worst.

"I'm saying, Mama. These niggas need to keep their eyes and comments to themselves."

"Luchi, what I tell you about your mouth?"

75

"I see his problem; he needs a daddy in his life. Don't worry, baby. I got you covered." Another dude smirked while winking at me.

"You don't have shit covered! The only nigga that's going to be playing daddy to him is me." Zoo's voice boomed with authority, anger dripped from his voice.

"My bad, Zoo. I didn't know that was you."

"I'm not! Nor do I need a nigga trying to play daddy to my son. Nine times out of ten, you're probably not being a father to your own. With that being said, I'll appreciate it if you don't address me or my son again, please and thank you."

"Shorty, your little speech was cute and all, but I don't need your damn help." Zoo called himself checking me.

"You can save it as well, Zouk. I'm not here for your shit today, either."

"I don't give a fuck what you're up for."

"Come on, Luchi, grab your stuff." I stood from my seat, grabbing Luchi's DS and throwing it in my purse. "Tell Za'Cari I said thank you, but no thank you. I would rather my son go to school with a nappy head before I deal with your fucked-up attitude today." I stood toe-to-toe with Zoo. I was truly fed up with his shit.

"Good! You had no business in here in the first place! Got niggas in here whispering about your body and shit. Niggas coming for you, thinking they got a chance at my spot."

"Bye, Zoo, you're causing a scene for no reason. You're the reason Luchi's attitude's so screwed up." I said, shaking my head before practically dragging my son out of the barbershop.

Getting in my car, I wanted to, not only scream, but break down crying. All I wanted to do was get my son a haircut for the first day of school, but Zouk was always doing something to piss me off. Resting my head on the steering wheel, I tried to calm my nerves; I refused to cry about it.

"Come on, Luchi." Zoo spoke the moment he opened the backdoor "He's not going to school without a haircut, so fuck what you're talking about. After I cut his hair, I'll bring him home."

"I'll wait for him." I said, opening my door to get out.

"Take your ass home; I'm not feeling how niggas are looking at you." I stared at Zoo confused. I didn't understand the jealousy that was held in his tone.

"I'm not worried about no niggas." I proceeded to get out of the car.

"Mama, I agree with Zoo. The barbershop is no place for you."

"Okay, just have him home before eight. I'll pay you when I get my next check."

"Ramsey, get out of my face with that stupid shit; this is me." Zoo said, pointing at Luchi.

The huge smile on my son's face is why I put up with Zoo's smart mouth. My kids adored his rude ass.

"Give me a hug Luchi. Make sure you behave and watch your mouth."

"He's good; he's with me."

"That's what I'm afraid of." I mumbled, hugging Luchi.

I watched until Luchi and Zoo walked back inside the barbershop. Taking a deep breath, I shook my head. That whole little scene inside the barbershop quickly escalate, which was becoming the norm for Zoo and me.

Pushing what happened to the back of my head, I drove home to get the twins' things ready for school in the morning while I was kid-free.

Ramsey

By the constant ringing of the doorbell, I knew it was Luchi at the door. After placing the spaghetti in the oven to bake a little, I rushed to answer the door.

"Don't just answer the door without asking who it is." Zoo started in on me the moment he walked through the door.

"Zouk, I didn't need to ask who it is because I know my son. He's the only pain in my ass who ring my doorbell like that."

I locked the door before following behind them to the living room.

"What's all this?" I asked, as Luchi and Zoo carried in several bags from Wal-Mart."

"Luchi, go get ready for bed." Zoo told him ignoring me.

"You don't need help with the rest?" Luchi asked him.

"Naw, I got it. Go take your shower." Zoo said, as he made his way back out the front door.

"Luchi, your pajamas are already on your bed."

"Okay, good looking, mama."

Making my way into the kitchen, I checked on the food I was cooking.

"Rah!" I heard Zoo yell, as he shut the front door. "Rah!" he yelled, again, as I was taking the last of the chicken out of the frying pan.

"Ramsey!"

"Yes?" I smiled once I realized he was calling for me the first two times. Maybe, he was warming up to me since he gave me a nickname.

Walking into the living room, I realized my floor was filled with Wal-Mart bags, along with a lot of other bags from multiple stores.

"You didn't hear me fucking calling you?"

"Is cussing at me fucking necessary?" I looked over my shoulder to make sure my kids wasn't around to hear me cuss. "I was cooking, Zoo."

"What does that have to do with you answering me?"

"What's all this?" I asked, changing the subject.

"Go finish getting the twins ready for bed." Zoo spoke in a tone that was basically dismissing me.

I was really getting to the point where I was so fed up with Zoo's attitude. Walking into Luna's room, I saw her sitting on her bed, watching the movie *Home*. "Hey, Mama's baby; what are you doing?"

"Watching the Boovs crazy selfs." Lulu laughed at the TV. "Mama, one day, can you do my hair like Tip's?" Lulu's eyes lit up at the thought of rocking a curly fro like the main character from the movie.

"Of course, anything for my favorite girl in the world."

"Mama, I'm not your favorite girl. I'm Zoo's."

"Speaking of Zoo, did you know he was in the living..." Before I could finish my sentence, Luna took off running. She hadn't seen Zoo in weeks as well.

"Luna, watch where your big-headed ass is going!" Luchi hopped out of the way just in time before Luna could run into him as he was making his way into his room.

My eyes nearly popped out of my head when I heard the cuss word leave my son's lips. "Luchi!" I yelled shocked.

"Luchi, don't get popped in your shit. Watch your damn mouth." Zoo threatened, walking down the hall carrying Luna in his arms.

"Ay, where did y'all even come from?" Luchi smiled, unbothered by Zoo's threat.

"Luchi, do you want to sit in timeout before bed?" I asked, still shocked he cussed.

"Timeout?" Luchi and Zoo asked at the same time with their faces turned up like they were confused.

"Yes, timeout. You'll stand in the corner."

"Rah, just go make their plates, so they can eat and get ready for bed."

"Yeah, I'm hungry as hell." Luchi said, walking past Zoo.

"Ahhh!" Luchi yelled once Zoo's hand connected to the back of his head.

"Nigga, what you thought I was playing? Watch your mouth."

"Good one, Zoo-Zoo." Luna laughed.

"I wonder where he get his bad mouth from." I sarcastically questioned walking past Zoo making my way to the kitchen.

"Make their plates and meet me in the living room."

"Yes, sir." I said, after placing spaghetti on the twins' plate while watching Zoo leave out the kitchen.

"Mama, are you just going to let Zoo smack me?" Luchi asked salty.

"Boy, that lick didn't hurt." I laughed along with Luna, who thought Luchi getting smack was hilarious.

"Ma, it kinda did. Plus, it's the principle."

"The principle? So, Luchi, he can buy you anything your heart desires, and do everything else for you, but he can't discipline you when you get out of hand?" I asked.

"I guess you got a point."

"I guess I do," I smiled, placing their food in front of them. "Eat up, so y'all can get ready for bed. School's in the morning. Yay!"

"Yay!" Luna yelled excited.

"Yay my…"

"Zoo!" I yelled before Luchi could say ass.

"Okay, mama, dang." Luchi looked scared.

"Now, eat your food." I laughed, walking out the kitchen.

"Zouk, did you buy all this?" My eyes widened when I looked around my living room.

"Naw, I stole it." Zoo gave me a look like stop asking stupid questions. "Check this," Zoo said, walking over to me taking my hand into his, which shocked me. I tried to control the butterfly feelings I got in the pit of my stomach the moment our skin touched.

"I already picked out the outfit they're wearing to school tomorrow."

"Zoo, this is too much." I said, shocked, looking at all the clothes and shoes Zoo bought for the twins.

"Rah, how is this too much when they go to school a hundred-and-eighty days out of the year?"

"So, you went out and bought an outfit for each day?" I asked laughing.

"No, but I got damn near close to every day." Zoo laughed. He was full of surprises tonight.

"I like it." I smiled.

"What, the clothes?"

"No, your laugh." I smiled.

"Anyway…" He got serious, again, causing the smile to quickly wipe from my face. "As you can see, Luchi and Luna has six storage bins apiece. I already labeled them Monday through Friday. The last bin is for their shoes."

"Okay, thank you! I really appreciate everything besides your smart mouth."

"No problem." Zoo smirked.

"Mama, can I have some juice?" Luna called from the kitchen.

"Naw, all you're going to do is piss in the bed." I heard Luchi say.

"Bye, Luchi. You're done eating; go get ready for bed." Zoo walked into the kitchen.

"Alright, just let me get some juice." Luchi smirked.

"Naw, nigga, but your ass can get some water." Zoo said, making Lulu a glass of juice and Luchi a glass of water.

"But, mama." Luchi whined.

"What the fuck you crying to her for? She heard me just like you did. You want to keep cussing like you're grown, nigga, why are you crying over some juice?"

"You right; why the fuck am I crying for?" Luchi said, laughing.

"Luchi, keep cussing, and I swear I'm going to beat your ass." I yelled, trying to grab him up, but he ran out of the kitchen laughing before I could.

"He's so bad." Luna laughed between taking sips of her juice.

"Good night, Luna, I love you."

"Good night, Mommy. I love you, too. Good night, Zoo." Luna said running off to her room.

"Night, favorite girl."

"Good night, Luchi." I called out.

"Goodnight, mama. I love you! You know I F's with you the long way!" Lucci yelled.

"Luchi!" Luna cracked up, laughing at her brother.

"Go to bed, Luchi!" I yelled, trying to hold in my laugh.

"I know you love me, too." Luchi yelled, laughing.

"Dude is bad as fuck." Zouk shook his head.

"I wonder who he's trying to be like."

"Hell if I know." Zoo smiled.

"Right." I laughed, letting down the ironing board and plugging up the iron.

"Right." Zoo winked at me before walking away. I pray he didn't see the way he had me blushing.

"You leaving?" I called out.

"Naw, I'm staying the night. I want to be here for their first day of school."

This was the stuff that pulled at my feelings when it came to Zoo. The way he was always there for my kids let me know it was more to him than this angry person that he showed everyone.

"Are you asking me can you stay or telling me?"

"Come on, Ramsey. Stop asking stupid questions. When have I ever asked your permission to do any fucking thing?"

"Do you always have to be so evil?" I asked, walking into the living room to get the twins' school clothes they were wearing for tomorrow.

Chapter Eight

Ramsey

I was off for the next two days, and my plan was to relax around the house. Nanna said she'd been feeling lonely lately, so she's been getting the twins almost every weekend. I wish Rory was home, because I didn't want to spend my Saturday night in the house. I wasn't that bored to ask Jen to go out, though, so I guess it looked like I was spending my Saturday night by my lonesome.

It was like Zoo could read my thoughts, because the moment after I got the idea to step out for some drinks, he texted telling me to get ready, because he was taking me to a party. This was a first. Zoo and I didn't do too much hanging out together without the twins. I was somewhat skeptical, because I didn't want to deal with his rude mouth if I didn't have to. I also didn't want to stay in the house, either, so I made my way to my room to look for something to wear.

The weather in the middle of October didn't get above sixty degrees, so I dressed accordingly. I wasn't the type that dressed half-naked all year around no matter the weather just to look cute for the club. I wasn't willing to get a cold for the cause.

Going into my closet, I found the dress and boots I ordered off an online boutique. Lying them on my bed, I stripped out of my clothes so I could shower. I had no time to waste, because I knew doing my hair and makeup would take a while.

After showering, I sat at my vanity, with my towel still wrapped around my body. I was going to apply my makeup first, because I planned to go big tonight with a full beat. The looks I got whenever I stepped out with Zoo didn't go unnoticed. If I was going to be the topic of so many people's conversation, I wanted to give them something to talk about. The dress I was wearing was a somewhat sexy little, long-sleeve, deep neckline, red number. I loved that dress, because of the geometric hemline. My thigh-high, red, crush velvet four-inch heel boots were going to set my whole look off. After doing my makeup, I styled my hair in big, wild curls.

Zoo called my phone telling me he was outside the moment I slid my foot into my thigh-high boot and zipped it up.

Moving around my house, I made sure everything was turned off before grabbing my keys off the living room table. Locking up, I made my way over to Zoo's car. Surprisingly, he was standing on the passenger's side with the door open waiting for me.

"What's up, Rah?" Zoo greeted me with a quick hug.

"Hey!" His cologne filled my nose, and not only did he smell good, but he looked good as well.

"Let me see." He stopped me from getting in the car. Opening my Peacoat, he took in my outfit.

I stood nervously waiting to hear something smart fly out of his mouth, but shockingly, that didn't happen.

"You look really cute and classy. I'm not feeling the fact that your titties are on display, but I guess I'll let you breathe." Zoo said, while fixing my coat back.

"Thank you, Zouk." I smiled. Hearing a compliment from him was rare.

"So where are we going?" I asked after leaning over to open the door for him.

"Zay's having something at a pool hall."

"Sounds fun." I said, buckling my seatbelt.

"It's going to be chilled and laid back, nothing major."

So far, things were going well between Zoo and me, and I planned to keep it that way. Sadly, that meant little to no conversation. Taking out my phone, I snapped a couple selfies. No lie, I was truly feeling myself. I was always on my mommy mode, so it was always nice to put some clothes on and just be Ramsey.

"Is that what you do when you go out with your girls?"

"What?"

"Do you just take pictures by yourself like they're not around? Come on; capture our moment. Let me in on that shit." Zoo looked at me smiling.

I blushed, because Zoo was truly surprising me tonight. Seeing him with a full smile was also rare. I waited until he stopped at a red light before leaning over, making sure I had a good angle to get us both. I took advantage of this moment and took several pictures before the light turned green.

"These are cute." I wore a cheesy smile, as I looked through the pictures of us.

"I'm a fine ass nigga, and you're straight, so what do you expect?" He looked at me smiling for a split second.

"Just straight?" I asked, laughing. "All this fine chocolate is what makes the picture."

"You might be right about that." Zoo cut his eyes at me, while wearing a smirk.

I decided not to touch that comment with a response, so I turned my attention to my phone uploading the pictures to my social media sites.

"I went to check on the twins and nanna not too long ago, just to make sure they were straight. They were more than good. Nanna was over there cutting up in the kitchen, and I walked in just in time. I had dinner with them before going home to get dressed. I fucks with Nanna. She had an early Thanksgiving dinner cracking, and everything was on point." Zoo beamed, looking back and forth between me and the road. He was being really talkative and attentive.

"So, y'all just going to have a family dinner without me?" I pouted. I could only imagine what the layout looked like. Nanna stayed showing out in the kitchen. I couldn't lie, I was jealous right now.

"Babes, it ain't even shit I could say to make you feel better about missing it. I could've called you, but I didn't. Truth be told, I didn't want to share."

I couldn't take it. Now, I was babe? I couldn't wait until we made it to the pool hall. I needed a drink. I complained so much about Zoo and his rude attitude. Now, I was getting what I've been asking for, and I didn't know how to act or take it. I guess my silence didn't go unnoticed, because I felt Zoo staring at me, although I was staring straight ahead. The rest of the ride to the pool hall was chill, as music softly played throughout the ride.

Pulling into the pool hall, by the look of the many cars in the parking lot, you could tell the place had a nice crowd.

"Get your I.D and put your little purse thing under the seat. Leave your jacket as well." Zoo said, before hopping out.

I would've protested about leaving my jacket, because it was cold out, but since we were close to the door, I let it ride.

"I said leave your purse." Zoo said, after opening the door for me. Grabbing my purse out of my hand, Zoo stopped me for stepping out of the car.

"I need it. I want to buy some drinks."

"Rah, I'm trying not to be an asshole today, but keep saying dumb shit, and this cool vibe we got going on won't last too much longer between us. You don't need your purse whenever you're with me, and you know that. Whatever you need, you know I got you? Now, grab your I.D, and let's go."

He was right, and I didn't want to ruin the night with a petty argument. Hitting the locks, Zoo placed his hand on my lower back guiding me to the door. Looking over at him, I smiled. I liked this Zoo.

He actually smiled back. He was so handsome. Everything about him was on point. His hair was freshly cut, jewelry brightly shining, and he only had on a pair of jeans and a solid V-neck shirt that showed off some of his chest tattoos, yet he was still sexy as hell and made his simple outfit look as good as some designer clothes, but that was a line I wasn't about to cross.

Walking into the pool hall, we were met with the normal crew. Zay, Beans, and Crash hung out at the bar with a couple of other dudes I saw with them a lot. I didn't know most of their names, because Zoo didn't care to introduce me, so I didn't care to learn them. Zoe and Amber were on the little dance floor, and although I didn't care too much for Amber, she and Zoe always seemed to have a good time together. They were dancing all over each other.

I was shocked to see Jen in the cut with two dudes. I wanted to be offended that she didn't call to invite me out.

"What's up, niggas?" Zoo greeted his brother and friends.

"Yo, the gangs all here!" Zay yelled.

"What's, up Ramsey; you look good as fuck." Bean licked his lips, flirting with me.

"Thanks Beans." I politely smiled. I didn't want to say too much. Anything could set Zoo off.

"I'm going to go speak to my sister." I told Zoo. I was ready to get away from Beans. I wasn't about to let his flirting ruin Zoo and my peaceful night.

"You want a drink first?" he asked, grabbing my hand to stop me from walking away.

"Yes, I'll have a Vodka Spritzer, please."

I tried not to blush. I was feeling this calm, relaxed Zoo.

"Yo, let me get a Heineken and a Vodka Spritzer." He called out to the bartender.

"Okay, baby, coming right up" The bartender flirted with Zoo.

I rolled my eyes, although I was used to it. Women flirting with Zoo was normal.

"What was that about? Is something in your eyes?" Zoo watched me with a smirk.

"I'm rolling my eyes because women can be so rude. I know she sees me standing here." I rolled my eyes again. "She's flirting with you. How does she know I'm not your lady? She doesn't care; just so disrespectful." I rolled my eyes at the bartender as she moved around making drinks at the other end of the bar.

"You're not my lady, so her flirting should be the least of your worries."

Rude Zoo had reappeared. His tone came across offensive and harsh, which I found rude, yet sadly, I was used to his attitude. I always expected the unexpected when it came to his mood.

"Okay." I smiled, before grabbing my drink once the bartender sat it on the counter in front of Zoo. I was smiling, because he never practiced what he preached. Who flirted with him wasn't my concern, but somehow, who flirted with me was his.

Walking over to Jen, she acted as if she didn't see me standing in front of her.

"Hey, sister." I greeted.

"Oh, you see me now?" Jen asked with an attitude.

"I saw you when I first walked in,.I just wanted to get a drink first before coming over here. Why didn't you invite me out tonight?" I questioned.

I didn't really have an attitude about it, because I probably would've declined anyways if she did. I just wanted to hear her reasoning.

"I knew you would be here with your peoples. Y'all are basically one." Jen's eyes wondered over in Zoo's direction as she spoke. I hated that my sister sounded so jealous when speaking on me.

"So, who are your friends?" I questioned, changing the subject. One of the guys was watching me intensively.

"I'm Dell." He answered before Jen could, extending his hand out for me to shake.

"Ramsey." I smiled.

"Ramsey, this is my new baby, Light, and his homie Dell. This was supposed to be a date. I'm still trying to figure out why Dell's here, blocking, being the third wheel." Jen slightly turned to look at her friend Light. He wasn't paying any of us any attention as he enjoyed his beer, while bobbing his head to the music.

"I'm not the third wheel, now, since Miss Ramsey showed up." he smiled, licking his sexy lips.

Dell was a cutie. I didn't have a type when it came to physical appearance. His skin tone was maybe a shade lighter than mine, his milk chocolate skin looked smooth. His bushy eyebrows and sexy, full juicy lips had my attention. I wanted to take back what I said about not having a type when it came to physical appearance. Height was a factor when it came to me being attracted to a man. I couldn't do anything under 5'7, and Dell barely made the cut.

"Trust me, she won't be staying long." Jen's snotty attitude pulled me away from taking all of Dell in. I swear, I didn't get where all her anger came from, but she was my baby sister, so I just dealt with it.

"Jen, I'm here to have a good time just like everyone else." I said, taking a sip from my drink.

"I'm always up for showing a beautiful lady a good time. Ramsey, can I get to know you?" Dell asked.

"Right now, I'm just here to hang out." I wasn't there to sit down and talk. I wasn't trying to make a love connection in the middle of the club.

"Well, can I give you my number, so I can get to know you on a later date?"

"Sure, why not." I said, shocking myself. I'm just going to blame this Vodka spritzer that I was now downing like it was a glass of water.

"What?" Jen asked, shockingly. "The bartender must've put something in your drink."

Ignoring Jen, he read his number off to me while I typed it into my phone, before excusing myself to get another drink. I thought it was time to walk away.

"Hey, sexy chocolate." Zoe was now at the bar.

"Hey, baby." I hugged him.

"Hey, Ramsey."

Amber waved her hands around in a rude manner. Like, speaking was doing me a favor, her hand gesture was as if she was brushing me off or dismissing me. If she thought I was going to speak to her after that dry ass greeting, she was playing herself. Looking around, I spotted Zoo and his boys in the corner booth chilling.

"Can I buy you another drink?" Beans stood next to me.

"Sure." I smiled.

"Ay, Shay-Shay, let me get another Vodka Spritzer." Beans called out.

"What have you been up to, Miss Lady?" He asked, invading my personal space.

"Same ole, same ole. Being Luchi and Luna's mama twenty-four seven. How's Little Miss A'Shanti been doing?"

"Good, all she talks about is Luna and Ms. Ramsey. Since I can't seem to get you out on a regular date, maybe we can set up a playdate for the girls."

"Smooth Beans. Real smooth." I laughed hitting his arm.

"Was it? So, does that mean we can set up a playdate?" He looked me up and down. His eyes lingered on my breasts a little longer than they should've before making eye contact with me again.

"Let me run it by Luna." I laughed, shaking my head. I couldn't believe Beans was trying to use our kids to get some play.

I sat at the bar with Beans, Zoe, and Amber laughing and working on my third drinks. It had been a minute since I been out enjoying myself. I saw Zoo watching me from across the room, so I excused myself making my way over to him.

"I'm having so much fun." I smiled, sitting next to him.

"Ay, you're cut off on drinks." Zoo whispered in my ear, as he pulled me close to him.

"Why?" I asked, confusedly.

"Because you're drunk, and you're being too fucking friendly."

By his tone, I knew cool, calm, and relaxed Zoo was gone, and controlling, possessive, and aggressive Zoo was back.

"Zoo I'm not drunk. I'm just having a good time.

"I been knowing Beans for years, and he's not that motherfucking funny. The way you were smacking his arm, laughing at his jokes. And who is this clown ass nigga who standing over there by Jen, and why does he keep looking this way? Do you know dude or something?"

"He's one of Jen's peoples. He just gave me his number. He said he would like to get to know me. I told him yes, because I didn't see the harm in it."

"Any nigga that Jen hangs around has to be a fucking lame."

"Zoo, don't start with my sister. Please, not tonight. We've been having a good time."

"We have, but you need to let her know you don't need her playing matchmaker."

Zoo was blowing me trying to act like my daddy. I thought we were out to have a good time, and he was ruining it.

"I'm going to get a drink." I quickly stood up causing me to get a little lightheaded.

"I said you don't need anything else to drink. You got to be drunk giving niggas your number and shit." I didn't like the way Zoo was raising his voice, and the way people was looking at us.

"You're tripping." I mumbled under my breath sitting back down beside him. "Zoo, I'm not drunk, but even if I was, don't you think I deserve to be a little carefree?"

"No."

"Well, come on. Are you ready to go then, since you want to be a Debbie Downer?"

"Y'all not going anywhere. Come on, nigga. Let this girl have some fun. You stay riding her like you're her damn daddy." Zay said, coming to my rescue.

"Y'all know how Zoo is." Beans added.

"Mind your business, nigga." Zoo mean mugged Beans.

"I'm trying to make Ramsey that, if she stop playing and use my number. She know she's feeling a nigga." Bean winked at me.

"Nigga, if it ain't happen after seven or eight months, it ain't going to happen. Just fall the fuck back." Zoo said, shutting Beans down.

"For a nigga who claims he not feeling shorty, you stay blocking." Beans spoke with a slight attitude, which shocked me, because he was always so laid back and flirtatious.

"Nigga, don't worry about how I'm fucking feeling." Zoo said, before getting up bumping Beans before walking off.

"What did you do to my brother?" Zay smiled. I didn't find anything cute or funny.

"Zay, I don't know why Zoo stay tripping on me. It's crazy how he switch up." I spoke disappointed. "We were doing so well today."

"Give it time; it will all make sense." Zay smiled, confusing me more. Zoo was a complicated man. I guess, if no one on this earth understood him, his brothers did.

Zoo's family always reminded me to be patient with Zoo. Sometimes, he was just too much. We were out to have a good time, and right now, he was acting like an overbearing dad or more like a controlling boyfriend. After ordering a beer at the bar, I went on a search to find Zoo. He was standing by the pool table with a pool stick in his hand.

"Here, I bought you a beer." I said, placing the beer on the table in front of him.

"Good looking," Zoo said, being really short with me. He barely made eye contact.

"Would you like for me to roll you one up to ease your mind?" I asked, moving closer to him.

Looking down at me, I couldn't quite read his facial expression. Shaking his head, he reached into his pocket, then pulled out his weed and a wrap.

"We've been having such a good time together, let's not mess that up. Zouk, try to relax and enjoy yourself." I smiled rubbing up and down his arm. I was starting to realize that he was like a little kid. He liked to act out when he felt that someone else had my attention.

"You can roll my blunt in the car. I'm ready to go." Zoo said, laying the pool stick on the table.

"Ay, Zay, we're out." Zoo said, grabbing my hand.

I didn't get to say bye to anyone. I knew I would hear Jen's mouth about that.

Zoo

While Ramsey was in the shower, I picked up her phone off the nightstand. She didn't have a lock code on it, so it took me no time to find what I was looking for. First, I wanted to look through her text messages. I know y'all probably think I'm crazy, but I didn't give a fuck. I wanted to see who Ramsey was texting.

93

She had a few niggas hitting her up on the regular, but she would never reply back. Most of her other texts were between us and the others were from her sisters. Going through her contacts, I wanted to delete the number she got tonight, but I didn't know the name of the lame nigga, so I just went through her contacts deleting any nigga's number. Don't ask why. I just felt the need to.

Hearing the bathroom door open, I looked up at Ramsey for a split second before looking back down at her phone.

"Zoo, what are you doing with my phone?"

"Going through it; what it look like?"

"We was going so good. Now, why you tripping out?" she asked, climbing into bed.

"I'm not." Clicking delete, I erased all the niggas numbers she had on her phone.

"You sure, because it looks like it by telling me who I can and cannot talk to and going through my phone."

Standing up, I made my way to the bathroom. I wasn't about to explain myself. I felt like I didn't have to. My night with Rah started off with good intentions. I wanted to show her I could be cool, and we could be friends. I thought shit was going smooth on the car ride over. Once we got to the pool hall, I felt like she was doing too much conversing with Beans. That's what pissed me off. Not only did the nigga want Ramsey badly, but he looked at me as a threat, so he stayed throwing shots. That was Zay's boy, so I tried to keep my cool off the strength of my brother. Plus, he was a barber in our shop, and he brought in a nice amount of money. But the tension between he and I was getting worse.

I thought Ramsey would be sleep by the time I got out of the shower, but she wasn't. She was sitting up in bed waiting for me.

"Zouk, why would you delete all my male contacts?"

"Ramsey, I'm tired." I said, climbing over her, too lazy to walk around the bed to the other side. "Turn off the lights."

"You not gon' answer my question?" she asked as the room went dark.

"No," I said, pulling Ramsey down, then pulling her close to me. "Good night, Rah."

"Ahhh, you're such a pain in my ass." I could tell she was frustrated with me, but I didn't give a fuck. She would get over it.

"The feeling is mutual." I said, holding her tightly. My body quickly relaxed as I drifted off to sleep.

Chapter Nine

Zoo

After the night at the pool hall, a decent friendship between Ramsey and I was formed. Going out on the weekend while the twins were at Nanna's had become our normal thing. Zay always had some shit planned, so we always had some shit to get into. I knew the twins were spending time with Nanna, but I still wanted to stop by to see what Ramsey was up to.

Ramsey lived in a decent neighborhood, but I was still pissed to find her front door unlocked once I reached her porch.

My first thought was to go in raising hell. Feeling like this was the perfect time to teach her a lesson, I crept inside, locking the front door behind me. I searched throughout the lower level of her house. Not seeing her around, I made my way upstairs. I could hear the shower running from the hallway. Ramsey had the door open. I guess she thought she was home alone. I needed to take a leak, anyways, so I made my way into the bathroom. Pulling my shit out, I proceeded to handle my business not caring that Ramsey was in the shower.

I watched her quickly move the shower curtain back revealing only her face.

"Zouk, what the hell?"

I could tell by the deer caught in headlight look on her face she was frightened by my presence. "How did you get in my house, and do you believe in privacy and boundaries?"

"Privacy and boundaries, huh?" I looked over at her. "Says the same chick that's openly staring at my dick." I could tell she was embarrassed by me calling her out; it was all in the look on her face. Rolling her eyes,

Ramsey disappeared behind the shower curtain. "Why the fuck did you leave your front door unlocked?" I asked, finishing up my business, then washing my hands. "Ramsey!" I called out. I knew she could hear me, because I was now standing next to the bathtub. "You don't hear me talking to you?" I asked, pulling the shower curtain back, exposing her body.

I felt my dick jump as my eyes roamed her body. Ramsey was bad as hell. Just one sight of her naked body had a nigga stiff. The way she was shaped had me thinking irrational thoughts. It was so many things I wanted to do at this very moment. Her titties were the perfect size, not too big, not too small. She didn't have rock hard abs, yet you could tell she worked out. Ramsey's body was shaped like an hour glass. Her wide hips and fat ass had me stuck as I watched drops of water run down her body. I couldn't stop myself from reaching out and pinching her nipple. I really wanted to suck them; her shit looked like Hershey's kisses.

I listened to her let out several moans, making my dick jump some more.

"Keep leaving that door unlocked, and it might be another nigga up in here looking at your body and rubbing on your nipples, and I'm pretty sure you won't be up in here moaning and enjoying it. Get your ass out, so you can lock the door behind me."

I let my hand run down her side until I was caressing her ass, before walking out the bathroom. I could tell she was pissed by the way she was stomping throughout the house.

"What was that?" she asked, stopping in front of me, while I stood by the front door.

"Stop leaving the door unlocked." I said, before making my exit.

Hopping in my car, I quickly started that bitch up. I needed to get far away from Ramsey and fast. Y'all wanted to know why I wasn't fucking with Ramsey on that level? Well, I let y'all in on how a nigga was feeling. I won't lie. Ramsey was everything I wanted out of my lady, but

I knew she was something I wasn't ready for. I probably sounded soft as fuck, but I knew I was emotionally unavailable for Ramsey. I also didn't want to bring the twins into something I wasn't a hundred percent sure of with their mother. I know things could end terribly, and the last thing I wanted to do was hurt Luna and Luchi. I was fucked up, mentally. I had been rocking with Ramsey and the twins for months now, and she knew little to nothing about my personal life except what I was willing to share.

Thanksgiving was quickly approaching, and I had invited Ramsey, Nanna, and the twins to spend the holiday with my family and me. At first, Ramsey was hesitant about agreeing, because she didn't want to leave Jen out. I *was* going to say fuck Jen, but I decided to chill and let her join, because I wanted to spend my holiday with them.

I was on my way to the outlet mall in Simpsonville, Kentucky; I needed to find something for us to wear for Thanksgiving. This was some of the shit I loved about having Luchi and Luna in my life. I loved being a family, I loved them like they were my own, and they loved me the same. Luchi was my main man, my mini-me. Whatever I bought myself, he got the same. The same went for Luna. Shit, sometimes she even got the same exact outfit as me and Luchi. I just had Ramsey style her out with bows and shit to add a girly flair. If I was telling the truth, she got more. Luna was my heart. She was the reason my cold heart was melting.

The ride to the outlet was a quick one, because the traffic wasn't that bad. Plus, I didn't give a fuck about the speed limit. I planned on copping our shit from off Saks Fifth, but I loved to shop for my young ones, so stopping at Oshkosh B'gosh, Justice, Gymboree, Polo, and the Nike Factory was a must. I stopped by Charlotte Russe, Lucky Brand, H&M, and Gucci to grab Ramsey a couple things, as well.

With a hand full of bags, I made my way to Saks Fifth. Grabbing a shopping basket, I placed my bag inside, so I didn't have to carry them heavy motherfuckers around the store. I guess shit was working out in my favor, because it didn't take me long to find the perfect outfits for us. I found me and Luchi the same white, long sleeve, London Burberry Sweater. I was matching everyone's outfit off the white Burberry, long-sleeve shirt and beige plaid skirt I found for Luna. I found Ramsey a similar sweater as mine and Luchi's, but for women.

After dropping several stacks at the outlet, I was ready to go. Walking out of Saks Fifth, I realized I was hungry and tired as fuck. I was ready to get back to Louisville.

"Hey Zoo." Amber sang my name, as she walked over to me with her two friends. All these bitches had goofy looks on their faces lusting over me.

"What's happening?" I asked, not really caring.

"Shit, trying to ball like you. You got something for me in one of them bags?" Amber playfully flirted.

"Not unless your name is Luna, Ramsey, or Luchi, I ain't got shit for you."

"You're so silly, Zoo." Amber laughed me off as if I was joking. She knew I was dead serious. I guess she was trying to save face in front of her girls. "So, what are you about to get into?" she asked me.

"Shit. About to get on up out of here."

"Can I leave with you?" Amber smiled, biting down on her bottom lip. I don't know if she was trying to be sexy or she was nervous, because she was afraid I was going to turn her ass down.

Amber's ass was persistent. Over the years, I've turned her ass down so many times, yet she never gave up, but today was her lucky day. Ramsey had me so damn sexually frustrated I found myself shrugging my shoulder basically giving this thirsty bitch the okay. I guess I could see what her head game was like on the way back to Louisville.

"Bye, Ladies." she damn near yelled, as excitedly waved bye to her friends. I could tell her fake friends were envious, but they had no reason to be. I wasn't about to wife her. I was just going to let her suck my dick.

Amber's mouthpiece was proper. We actually hit traffic on the way back to Louisville, so her sucking me off quickly passed the time. I appreciated the head; it wasn't in my top five, but it probably ranked number six. Shorty thought she did a good enough job to get some dick, but the only thing I had to offer her was a callback. I took her number, because I didn't trust that her thirsty ass wouldn't blow up my shit if I gave her mine. After dropping her off at home, I grabbed some Taco Bell and took my ass home to get some sleep.

Chapter Ten

Ramsey

Rolling over, I was expecting to see Zoo lying next to me. Looking over my shoulder, the bathroom door was open with the light off. I knew he said he had to do a few things to help his mother with for Thanksgiving dinner, but the least he could've done was say he was leaving.

I wasn't ready to get out of bed. Looking over at the clock on my nightstand, the clock read ten o'clock. Dinner at Zoo's parents' house started at three. Although that may have seemed like a long time to most, it felt like thirty minutes when you had to get three different people ready.

I wanted to make breakfast beforehand, because we all know that, considering CP time, three really meant six-thirty, seven. I didn't want to hear my kids complaining every ten minutes about being hungry. Getting out of bed, I made my way to the bathroom to handle my morning hygiene. After washing my face and brushing my teeth, I made my way down the hall to Luchi's room to see if Luna wanted to help me in the kitchen.

Luchi was on the top bunk of his bunk beds with his headphones on, drawing. I loved how passionate he was about his Art. At six, he wasn't the greatest artist, but he was well on his way.

"Good morning, Luchi." I said, although I knew he couldn't hear me, while waving my hands around in the air to get his attention.

"Huh?" he questioned, pulling his headphones off.

"I said good morning, handsome; where is your sister?"

"In the kitchen." Luchi said, keeping it short, before placing his earphones back on.

I wonder what she was up to in the kitchen by herself. She knew not to play with the stove. I hope she wasn't getting like Luchi thinking she was grown and didn't have to listen to anyone.

"Good morning, Happy Thanksgiving, Mama." Luna smiled, brightly, as I entered the kitchen.

"Good morning, my love. What are you two in here doing?" I asked, looking at Luna and Zoo's prep area on my kitchen counter.

"You see eggs, bacon, pancake mix, and peeled potatoes, so what do you think we're doing?" Zoo questioned.

I was just making small talk with Luna, and he couldn't help himself from being sarcastic "I see you woke up on the wrong side of the bed. It's Thanksgiving, Zouk. Lose the attitude."

"Don't ask dumb ass questions." Zoo said, helping Luna mix the pancake batter as she sat on top of the kitchen counter.

"Anyways, Lulu, I was looking for you, because I wanted you to do the same thing with mommy. I guess Mr. Grump beat me to it."

"You can help us,. Why don't you cut up some fruit?" Luna suggested.

"I can do that." I walked over to kiss her cheek causing her to giggle. "I love you, Luna."

"I know, Mama. I love you, too."

I cut up the fruit over in my little area, allowing Zoo and Luna to have their moment. Watching them together was the cutest thing. Luna was the only person that Zoo didn't do all that cussing and aggressive talking to. When he talked to her, his voice was always relaxed. He treated her like a princess. I loved that she had him to set an example of how a man should treat her.

Luna wanted to have a dance party while they cooked, so I quickly ran to the living room to turn on the stereo before Zoo could protest. I wanted to see how far she could take Zoo. I died laughing watching Luna and Zoo have a dance battle. I guess Zoo didn't care that he was battling a seven-year-old girl. He wasn't down for taking an "L". He was Harlem shaking and C-walking around the kitchen.

"What the hell is this goof doing?" Luchi asked, entering the kitchen, laughing.

"Luchi, language!" I scowled.

"How did making breakfast turn into a dance-off?"

"Luna's idea. I guess you and I are the judges." I laughed.

Zoo was running out of dance moves, so he started copying everything Luna was doing. These kids nowadays created a new dance craze every week, so it was no surprise that Luna was winning.

"Zoo, keep to running business and cutting hair. Cutting up on the dance floor, ain't you." I laughed turning the music down.

"You don't want me." Zoo said, seriously, doing the Harlem shake dusting his shoulders off.

I laughed so hard; I couldn't believe Zoo was really in my kitchen acting a fool.

"I hope this breakfast is better than your dancing." Luchi said to Zoo before leaving out of the kitchen.

"I agree." I laughed, following behind him. "Call us when the food is ready."

Going into the living room, I sat right next to Luchi on the couch grabbing the remote. I cherished this moment as I cuddled on the couch with my prince. It didn't take long before Luna was curling up under Luchi on the couch as well. I did my normal morning scroll through Facebook, while the twins watched Nickelodeon.

"Dang, Lulu, you just forget about me, huh?" Zoo pretended to be hurt about Luna leaving him in the kitchen to cook alone.

"Join us." she smiled.

Sitting down next to me, Zoo was a little too close for my liking.

"Why so close?"

"Ramsey, shut up. I'm just sitting next to you on a couch. You sleep with your ass in my lap damn near every night, but me sitting next to you is a problem?"

"About that; are y'all together?" Luchi asked.

"NO!" I quickly answered.

Zoo had no chill to say that around the twins. His sleeping here almost every night was innocent. For him to imply it was more made me want to hurt him.

"That's odd." Luchi cut his eyes at me like I was lying.

"It's not for you to understand. Cartoons, toys, and drawing is your thing, so stick to it." Zoo said.

"Ramsey and Luna comes before all that."

"Oh, word? Well, say what's on your mind, young one; it's clear you're in your feelings."

Shaking my head, I just listened to these two. I wasn't clueless to why Luchi was so grown. Zoo treated him like he was already a man. Luchi was already headstrong, so Zoo only made him worse.

"Any nigga laying in Ramsey's bed needs to have a title. That's why I asked are y'all together. If not, the sleepovers need to chill."

Zoo laughed at Luchi. "I love your heart, little nigga. Always keep that."

"I already know." Luchi smiled, slapping hands with Zoo. I didn't understand these two fools. Luchi was acting like he was ready to fight Zoo, and Zoo's attitude seemed like he had no problem putting hands on my seven-year-old if needed.

Hearing Zoo praise him about stepping to him with heart had Luchi hyped. Luchi did his own thing, no matter who didn't like it, yet he lived for Zouk and Zay's approval; he looked up to them. They were the first male figures in his life.

"Come on; let's eat, so we can get our day started." Zoo announced, pulling me off the couch. Luchi and Luna raced to the kitchen.

"No, bra." Zoo smirked, pinching my nipple through my shirt.

"Boundaries, Zouk."

I smacked his hand away. My feelings for him were growing stronger. I wanted to control them, but sleeping next to him almost every night and little stuff like this wasn't helping.

"Shut up." Zoo smacked my ass before grabbing my hand pulling me into the kitchen.

We enjoyed a nice breakfast together before getting dressed. Zoo had to go help his mom, and I needed to pick up Nanna, so we agreed to meet at his parents.

**

"Where y'all at?" Zoo answered on the third ring.

"I believe we're outside." I said, slowly creeping down Zoo's parents' street. I knew I was at the right address. I was just nervous about being there. I knew his family would have a lot of questions. Like most people didn't understand our relationship. Hell, most of the time, I didn't understand our relationship, either. This would be our first time meeting Zoo's parents, and if they were anything like him, I was in some trouble.

"Pull over right here," Zoo stood in front of my car still talking to me on the phone.

Hanging up, he moved onto the sidewalk, so I could park. I could tell a lot of guests had already arrived, because there were cars everywhere. People stood outside on the porch and on the sidewalk in front of his parents' house. Zoo opened the door to help Nanna out of the car.

"Thank you, sweetie; that's why you're my baby." Nanna kissed Zoo's cheek while hugging him.

"What is she V.I.P? Is she the reason why I couldn't park there? Who is she? We're family, Zoo. Picking some random over me is fucked up." A girl standing close by my car called out, doing a lot of finger pointing and neck rolling.

"Yo, Jo'Tanya, respect your elders. You couldn't park right here, because I said so."

I could tell he wanted to say more, but bit his tongue because Nanna was right here. Zoo looked her up and down before guiding Nanna up the walkway. Jo'Tanya rolled her eyes at me like I was the problem. Brushing her off, I followed behind Nanna and Zoo holding the twins' hands.

I politely smiled as we walked pass Zoo's family members, who were chilling on the front porch. It was like they stopped what they were doing as we walked past. I was in love the moment I entered Zoo's parents' house. It was so big and beautiful. I dreamed of one day owning a house like this for my babies and me.

Zoo was being a gentleman helping Nanna out of her coat. She used this opportunity to kiss his cheek again.

"What's up, family?" Zay greeted us, hugging me and Nanna.

"Happy Holidays, baby." Nanna hugged Zay longer than she should've, causing him to laugh. "I'll take their coats and put them away. You can introduce them to everyone." Zay offered.

"Thank you, baby." Nanna smiled. Seeing another opening to be fresh, she kissed Zay's cheek. She loved her some Zoo and Zay.

Moving further into the house, we were stopped by Zoe. "Yesss, y'all better come through." He squealed. "Oh, where's my little family, so we can be cute as a unit. Look at y'all."

"Okay, nephew. Damn, I see you're doing It." a loud mouth lady approached us. "Introduce me to wifey."

"Chill, Aunt True." Zoo laughed. "This is Nanna Mae, Ramsey, Luchi, and Luna."

106

"Somebody finally got that girlfriend title again. I like it." She smiled doing a full circle around me checking me out.

"It's not like that, Aunty." Zoo laughed her off. I wanted to show my emotions, but I kept my cool. It was starting to bother me that I had no clue what my title was in Zoo's life.

"Whatever, it's like I'm feeling it, Nep. Cute family."

"Thanks for the approval, Aunt True."

"Come on; my dukes is in the kitchen cooking." Zoo was holding my hand and Lulu's, while Luchi held Nanna's.

The strange looks didn't go unnoticed, as we walked through. "Hey, Mama," Zoo called out to get his mother's attention. She had her back to us, dancing to the music as she stirred whatever was in the pot.

"Yes, Zouk Taylor? Don't start getting on my nerves. I already know what you're about to ask and the answer is no! The food is not done yet." She said, never turning around still dancing.

"Mama, I want you to meet Ramsey, the twins, and their grandmother Nanna Mae."

"Oh, hello, I'm sorry." She turned around, wiping her hand on the dish towel. She turned down the music before walking over to us. "Hello, I'm Renee; it's so nice to finally meet y'all." She smiled, hugging each of us.

"Nice… Nice to meet you as well." I stumbled over my words. I was so nervous, and I could tell Zoo noticed.

"Can I help you with anything?" Nanna offered Ms. Renee.

"Yes, I would love that. You know, with all these people moving through here, not one person offered to help." Ms. Renee fussed.

"Aww, yeah!" Zoo got excited, clapping his hands together "This food is about to be fire."

"Zoo, get out with all that noise." Ms. Renee pushed him.

"Would you like my help as well?" I offered.

"No, beautiful. I think we have it covered. Go continue to keep my boy here sane," She winked at me. I liked her vibe. She reminded me a lot of Zoe.

"Zoo, is Cari here?" Luchi asked.

"All the kid are in the basement. Come on."

I followed Zoo to the basement. I wanted to see what was going on. After seeing the basement, I wanted to ask could I move in. It looked like its own little apartment. Toys were everywhere, along with board games.

"The basement is for the kids, so they won't be running around everywhere. My little cousin Sid and Traci down here too. Watch them." Zoo explained.

"Okay, Lulu and Luchi, make sure y'all behave." I said, before turning around to go back up the stairs.

"Okay!" They called out at the same time.

Zoo patted my ass, as I walked up each step. Quickly turning around, I gave him a look. "Boundaries, Zouk."

"Shut up."

Amber popped up the moment we walked out of the basement. "So, I guess the cute little family matching outfits is y'all coming-out party?" she asked. I could tell she was in her feelings like always.

"Why do you care so much?" I asked, annoyed by her always being in my damn face. She was forever in my business.

"Why do I care? Well, let's see…." Amber started up, but Zoo quickly cut her off.

"Ay, real shit, Amber, don't disrespect my parents' house with no bullshit."

Walking away, I found an empty seat on the couch. So much was going on in the living room. Zay shot me a reassuring smile like he knew I was about to get in my feelings. I hated that my feelings for Zoo were starting to grow, and this bitch was always in my face with hers. I wasn't the type to fight over a guy. Wait, I used to be that girl, because I did a lot of fighting when I was with my baby daddy Lance, but I didn't want to go back to them days.

"I've been looking for you. Where have you been?" Jen asked, sitting next to me.

"We haven't been here that long." I tried not to let my attitude show. Jen fed off negative energy.

"This house is nice as fuck. What does Zoo's people do for a living?" Jen asked, looking around.

"I don't know."

"Figured. Well, what do you know about Zoo?" She asked, smartly.

"What's going on with you and your little, boo?" I asked, changing the subject. I wasn't about to go there with Jennifer.

"We're good. Dell keeps asking about you. He wants to know why you haven't hit him up yet?"

I wasn't about to tell Jen about Zoo deleting all my male contacts out of my phone, because that would only set her off. She already felt like Zoo was controlling.

"I haven't had much time for dating." I kept it short with her.

"You would if you stopped kidding yourself."

"I'm not kidding myself." I rolled my eyes. She was a piece of work.

"It's clear that you're waiting to see what can happen between you and Zoo. Give it up, and give Dell a chance. He's a cool dude for you. I think you should give him a call. Every time I see him, which is often, he always asks about you."

"When I find the time, I'll see if I want to spend it with Dell."

"Girl, you're not like that." Jen turned her face up, waving me off. She was not my sister. In my eyes, she was just like the rest. Jen was a huge hater.

"Jen, apparently, I am, if you say that nigga ask about me every time you see him, which is often." I smirked.

"Hey Pud, have you seen Amber?" Zoe asked, walking up to me and Jen, interrupting what I knew was about to turn into a heated argument. The look on Jen's face let me know she was about to go there.

"Oh yeah. I just saw her and Zoo sneak off that way." Jen pointed in the direction of the stairs. By the smirk on her face, and the way she was watching me, I could tell she was waiting for my reaction. Although my heart was broken, and I wanted to break down, I played it cool.

"Well, that answers your question." I put on a fake smile.

Zoe shook her head at Jen. I could tell he had something smart to say, but he bit his tongue.

"I'm going to mingle." Jen smirked, walking away. I could tell she was satisfied that she got under my skin.

"Are you okay, Pud?" Zoe asked, rubbing my back. He didn't seem too surprised about hearing the news of Amber and Zoo messing around. That let me know this wasn't something new.

"Yeah, why wouldn't I be?" I forced a weak smile. No, I wasn't okay. I was dying on the inside and felt disrespected. I looked like a fool. Grabbing a beer, I checked on the twins before grabbing my keys and making my way outside. I needed a moment to myself to breathe. Going into the glove compartment, I pulled a Black and Mild out to smoke. I really needed a blunt. I normally got my weed from Zoo, but I guess I had to settle for a Black.

Starting up my car, I plugged my phone into my aux cord leaning back all the way, I needed to clear my head. I didn't want to be in my feelings over Zoo, yet. I was so pissed knowing he was upstairs doing God knows what with Amber. I was so hurt, but did I have the right to be?

I'm pretty sure I looked stupid in the eyes of others. From the moment we walked through the door of Zoo's parents' house, all we heard was how beautiful "our family" was. If Jen saw them sneak upstairs, there was no telling who else did. Everything in me wanted to

110

put my car in drive and go home, but I didn't want to ruin my nanna and the twins' time.

Closing my eyes, I softly sang along with the music while puffing my Black.

After sitting in my car for twenty-minute a text came through my phone from Zoo.

Zoo: *Ay! Where you at?*

Rolling my eyes, I ignored Zoo. Starting up my car, I drove to the corner store. I didn't know why I was going. I just needed to get away. Going inside the store, I purchased another Black. To pass more time, I sat at the gas station freaking my Black.

Zoo: *Where the fuck are you. Dinner is ready, brah, and we're waiting on you.*

Taking a deep breath, I started up my car, making my way back to Zoo's parents' house. Pulling back up to my spot, I tried to get my attitude together before I joined Zoo's family again. I wasn't about to mess up everyone's holiday being salty over a man that wasn't mine.

Zoo was standing on the front porch waiting for me as I made my way up the driveway.

"Where the fuck have you been?" Zoo barked, stepping into my personal space. Stepping around him, I made my way inside.

"Rah!" Zoo grabbed my arm, pulling me back in his direction.

"Zouk, you better get your hands off that girl now." Zouk's father looked on with a disapproving look on his face.

"Thank you, Mr. Taylor." I smiled, before walking away to stand next to my nanna.

"Okay, so before I bless the food, let's go around the room and all share what we're thankful for." Mrs. Taylor announced.

I listened while everyone said their thanks, and it made my heart smile listening to my kids speak so highly of me. Zoo had the nerves to add me in his thanks, causing me to let out a sarcastic giggle. I straightened up when I felt my nanna pinch my arm, taking me back to the time when I was a little girl acting up in church. Zoo shot me darts with his eyes.

It was now my turn to say what I was thankful for, and Lord knows I wanted to use this opportunity to be shady, but I would never disrespect my nanna or Zoo's parents. Putting on my fake smile, I told the room what I was thankful for, purposely leaving Zoo out. I knew I was being petty, and by the look on Zoo's face, I could tell I succeeded in pissing him off.

Throughout the dinner, I sat next to my nanna mute. Every so often, I would laugh at Zoo's aunty. She was truly a character. I enjoyed watching my nanna enjoy herself. Jen was sitting next to Zoo's messy cousin, who had the attitude about the parking spot. I'm pretty sure by the constant eye rolling and childish giggles they were throwing major shade everyone's way.

Amber and Zoo took turns throwing me dirty looks. I couldn't help but giggle. I was trying to figure out what this dumb hoe Amber was mad at me about. She finally had him, so why was she tripping. Zoo was in his feelings like I was the one who disrespected him. I was more than ready for this dinner to be over, so we could go home, but Zoo's mother had other plans. After dinner, they had a tradition of decorating the Christmas tree. Everyone had to create an ornament to put on the gigantic tree that sat in the corner of Zoo's parents' living room. I chose a high heel to decorate and my Luna chose a snow boot. Luchi picked an "L" because Zoo chose a "Z"

I guess Zoo didn't know I knew about him and Amber. He kept trying to start up a conversation with me, and I had no problem shutting him down. After a while, he got the hint. Well, that's what I thought until he followed me to the bathroom.

"Man, what the fuck is your problem." Zoo asked, pushing me into the bathroom.

"Get the hell out. I need to use the restroom."

"Yo, who do you think you are talking to?" Zoo pushed me against the wall. "I don't know what's up with you, but you better kill the fucking attitude. "

"I don't need to kill shit. You lucky I don't kill your ass. I have every right to be mad. You got me looking dumb and shit. You have me and my kids walking around looking like your damn doppelgangers, and you're upstairs fucking the next bitch. Now, you're down here in my face with your filthy hands on me."

I couldn't hold my anger in any longer. I could tell Zoo was taking back by me going off on him by the shocked look on his face. He quickly pulled it together.

"You're really mad because I let that bitch suck my dick every now and then?" Zoo asked, confirming some of what I already knew, crushing me. "You act like I fucked the bitch on the regular, and if I was, Rah, that's none of your business, because I'm single. Right or wrong?"

"You're saying all of that, so why are you here? I haven't said shit to you. You should've let me be in my feelings in peace."

"Man, I see you're upset, so I'm always going to look out. I can't believe you really tripping on me about fucking with someone else like we're together."

"I'm so done with this." I said, more so speaking to myself.

"Done with what?"

"Don't worry. I'll play my hand soon enough."

Zoo let out a pissed off chuckle. "Yeah, okay!" Zoo nodded his head up and down.

"Are you going to get out?" I asked, shifting all my weight to one side as I undid my pants.

"You're pissed off for no fucking reason, and I'm not about to kiss your ass."

"I didn't ask you to. I asked you to get out so I can use the restroom. No one asked you to follow me. You did that on your own."

"Your mouth is real fucking slick right now."

"Leave, and you won't have to hear my mouth." I yelled. I really needed to go, and he wanted to stand here arguing.

"Rah, on everything, stop playing with me."

It was clear that he wasn't getting out. He had already seen my body, anyway, and I really needed to go, so I pulled my pants down sitting on the toilet. I felt so relieved as I emptied my bladder. I looked up to see Zoo looking at me crazy.

"What? If you had a problem with me using the bathroom in front of you, you should've removed yourself."

"Man, I'm not tripping off that. I'm tripping off you and your attitude."

"Don't be; it won't happen again." I said, wiping myself, pulling my pants up, and flushing the toilet.

"I thought we understood each other?"

"We do." I laughed, washing my hands. Zoo was a joke right now. How could I understand him when he kept me at arm's reach when it came to really getting to know him? I was done talking to Zoo; it was truly like talking to a brick wall with him. He was so closed-minded. Done with the conversation, I reached around him, opening the door, hoping he got the hint to move out of the way.

"I know my attitude is fucked up most of the time, and it seem like I don't give a fuck about nobody but myself, but you're my best friend Ramsey, and I don't like when you're walking around with an attitude."

"I'm here with you, right?" I questioned. I still wanted to be pissed at him, but I found it hard. It was different seeing him show a different emotion besides anger.

"Yes."

"Okay, so show me the same respect, because the same shit you're doing to me wouldn't fly if I did it to you, together or not. Show me the same respect you want me to show you."

"I got you, man." Zoo said, moving out the way so we could exit the bathroom.

"Well, well, well. It looks like Zoo's getting a lot of backroom action today. Now, that's something to be thankful for." Jen laughed, standing outside the bathroom door.

"Why did I invite this hoe again?"

"I'm the hoe, but you keep easing out of back rooms."

"Y'all chill, and Zoo, watch your mouth. Don't call my sister out of her name."

"Man," Zoo brushed me off brushing past me. He gave Jen a look before walking away.

"Remind me again what the fuck you see in this nigga? All he do is play you." Jen said, shaking her head. "Move, I need to use the bathroom." Jen rolled her eyes before pushing me out the way.

It was sad to say, but I was really starting not to like my own sister. I didn't know why she was so bitter and judgmental of the decisions I made in my life. It was like, every chance she got, she told me how stupid I was or looked at me as if I disgusted her. I didn't understand why she was there, if she couldn't stand Zoo and me so much. I was so glad this day was coming to an end.

**

"Sissy, Happy Turkey Day!" Rory yelled, excitedly the moment her face appeared on the screen.

"Hey, baby, same to you." I smiled, happy to see my sister's face like always.

"I wish I was home to have Nanna's cooking. So, how was your Thanksgiving?"

Girl, let's not," I said, picking my wine glass up off the table, then taking a sip. "Nanna kind of took this year off; we went to Zoo's parents' house for Thanksgiving." I rolled my eyes thinking about my day.

"Look at you, a part of the family and shit." Rory teased.

"Girl, today was low-key a mess, and your little sister is messy as hell. I'm seriously tired of her ass."

"Oh, shit, what happened now?" Rory moved closer to the camera.

"I found out Zoo was messing with his brother Zoe's best friend Amber. Guess who was reporting live on the scene with the breaking news? Your evil ass little sister. Jen couldn't wait to see my face crack. She was so proud to see me hurt."

"I keep calling that bitch, and she act like she can't answer." Rory spoke pissed.

"Something is up with her. I just don't know what. I met a dude while I was out with him at the pool hall with everyone. He's cool with Jen, and her little friend. I think I'll give him a chance. It's clear that Zoo isn't thinking about me." I was sad, because a part of me wanted the title of being Zoo's girl.

"Yes, do your thing. Don't wait around for him. If he can't see what he has, sister, that's his lost. Ramsey, you have a beautiful heart, you're a great mother, and woman, anyone would be lucky to have you. If Zoo can't see that, fuck him."

"Yeah, I agree. Can you come home already." I pouted. I was ready to have my best friend back.

"I swear, I'm more than ready to come home. Today, shit hit me hard. I just want to be around my family. My niece and nephew barely know me, Nanna getting old, I'm not there to referee you and Jen. I want a love life, and I just miss the states period. I called to talk to mama; she's always a big help when I'm feeling like this, because she knows what I'm going through. She talks me down from saying fuck everything and hopping on the first thing smoking out of South Korea.

"Sister, I was trying to find some encouraging words to help you through your tough time, but I've come up with a blank." I said, laughing. "Good thing you didn't call me when you were feeling down, because I would've been the little devil on your shoulder encouraging you to go AWOL and run your ass home. Of course, Melissa knew the words to say to make you feel better about not leaving." I said, rolling my eyes. Of course, our mother Melissa knew the right words to say to Rory. After all, the military was the most important thing in her life.

I stayed on the phone with Rory, until it was three in the morning. Like clockwork, Zoo was calling my phone. Nine times out of ten, he was out front trying to get in, but not tonight. There was no way I was allowing him to sleep next to me knowing he was with Amber only hours before. After I let the first phone call rollover to voicemail, Zoo called several more times before giving up.

Chapter Eleven

Ramsey

Since finding out about Zoo and Amber, I decided to give the guy Dell a chance. He was a good friend with Jen's boo, so I had no problem with getting in touch with him. We had talked on the phone a few times, and I thought he was a nice guy, more of my speed. I was kind of mad at myself for being too stuck on Zoo to give him a chance sooner. Dell was handsome, but a little corny, a different speed from what I normally went for. I had no such luck with my type, so I was trying something different. I didn't plan on bringing the twins around Dell until I got to know him a little better.

Today, he was taking me out on a date to a dinner and a movie. I often did things with the twins and Zoo, and it had been a while since I went to see a movie without it being animated. I won't lie, I was actually excited to be going on a real date.

I had a few hours to get ready, and I still had to drop the twins off at Nanna's. I knew they wouldn't like the idea of me going on a date, so I decided not to mention it to them.

"Hey, Nanna," I greeted her, as I walked into the kitchen after letting us in with my keys.

"Hey, babies!" Nanna greeted us with kisses and hugs.

"What are you cooking my big baby?" Luchi asked her hugging her tightly around the waist.

"You know, I'm frying your favorite, baby. Some fried chicken. Go put your things away while I talk to your mother."

"Alright, come on, big head." Luchi said, pulling Luna away with him by her arm.

"So, what do you have planned for the night, little girl?" Nanna asked, flouring some more chicken.

"I have a date." I smiled.

"With who?" She stopped what she was doing, and the look on her face was everything but nice.

"A guy I met one night while we were all out. I met him through, Jen."

"Strike one, I love your sister, but her track record and the company she keeps is a hell no."

"He seems like a nice guy, Nanna. Plus, it's only one date. If I don't like it, I won't waste my time."

"Honey, I'm letting you know now you're wasting your time. You have a thing for Zouk. Going out with someone else won't change that."

"Nanna, me and Zoo are just friends. He's out here living; it's time for me to do the same."

"You young people today get on my last nerves," Nanna shook her head. "Willing to waste your time with someone you know you don't want to be with just to fill a void."

"Nanna, Zoo is dating a girl named Amber." I tried to explain to my nanna before she started in on a rant that could have me sitting at her kitchen table for hours.

"That hussy that was at Thanksgiving dinner?" She asked. Her facial expression made me giggle.

"Yes, Ma'am."

"Girl, that thot-thot ain't got nothing on you." Nanna rolled her eyes.

"Oh, no, Maelean Devereaux; who taught you that?" I asked in between laughter.

"Sadly, your disrespectful ass son called Jen that. I love that boy; he keeps me Young." Nanna laughed adding more chicken to her frying skillet.

"On that note, bye Nanna. I have to get going." I said, getting up from my seat still laughing.

"I would say good luck and have a nice time, but I'm team Zoo. Zoo gang!" Nanna yelled.

"Nanna, who are you right now?" I laughed so hard holding my stomach.

"Gang, Gang!" Luchi yelled running up to Nanna.

"Boy, don't be teaching my Granny that type of stuff; it's bad enough that you know it." I laughed.

"Mama, Nanna know ain't shit popping but a whole lot of gang shit."

"Right, Nephew!" Nanna laughed.

"Nephew?" I asked, shocked. I couldn't believe my seven-year-old was corrupting my grandmother. "This can't be happening right now. I got to go. Nanna, don't be letting him cuss."

"Ramsey, I been raising kids before you were thought of. Don't tell me how to raise my great grandson. You need to be on your way before you're late for your date."

"Date? Who did you ask?" Luchi questioned. By his tone, you would've thought he was my daddy.

"Bye, Luchi." I rushed toward the door.

"Nah, for real, Rah. Stop for a moment, and tell me what's up. So, you wasn't going to tell me you was out here seeing niggas?" Now, Luchi sounded just like Zoo, and I hated it.

"Luchi, stay in a child's place, and mind your business."

"Rah, last I checked, your last name is Scott, and so is mine, so what do you know.... that makes your business, mine." Luchi was pissing me off with his attitude like Zoo's.

"Bye, Luchi. I love you. See you tomorrow."

"Mama!" Luchi yelled after me as I walked to my car.

"Bye, Luchi! I love you. Be good for Nanna."

He gave me a look before running back into the house. I kind of had a feeling of what he was up to.

Luchi

My mama thought she was slick. I should've known something was up when she dropped us off over Nanna's house. She was a little too excited to drop us off. I didn't wait for Rah to pull off before running back inside locking the door behind me.

"Nanna, where is your phone at?"

"Luchi, leave your mother alone."

"I'm not thinking about her. I'm trying to call my lil peoples real quick." I said, grabbing the phone off the counter going into my room I shared with my sister. I dialed Zoo's number.

"Hey, Nanna, is everything good?" Zoo answered on the fourth ring.

"Nanna's good, but Rah is out here doing shit she has no business doing."

"What you mean?" Zoo asked. I knew what I said about my mama had his full attention, because he didn't get on me for cussing.

"Rah just dropped us off at Nanna's, so she could go on a date with some lame ass nigga. I tried to stop her, but she tried to play me like a lil nigga talking about I need to stay in a child's place."

"I'll swing by to see what's up."

"Alright, hit me back on Nanna's line."

"I got you, young one." Zoo laughed.

I knew Zoo wouldn't let this date go down; that's why I wasted no time calling him. I liked my mama with Zoo. I didn't want to see her with someone else.

**

Zoo

I was at the shop cutting hair when I got the call for Luchi, telling me Ramsey called herself going on a date. I wasn't shocked by the way she was moving. Ever since the dinner on Thanksgiving at my parents', her attitude had switched up. Whenever I came around to see the twins, she would hide away, locking herself in her room. When I took Amber home that day from the outlet mall, I never thought it would bother Ramsey so much. I kind of missed her ass, but I wouldn't let her know it. What I was going to do, though, when I finished up the client in my chair, was go over to her house to see what was up. I still had two others waiting to get their hair cut, but I was going to pass them off to Zay.

I didn't bother to clean my station before leaving out the shop. I was already there longer than expected, so I needed to quickly rush over to Ramsey's before whoever this buster was showed up to take her out. An hour-and-a-half later, I was pulling up to Ramsey's house. Stepping out my ride, I made my way up to her front door. Knocking twice, I waited for her to answer.

"Coming!" She yelled out, sweetly. I guess she thought it was her date at the door. Hearing the lock click, I turned the knob before she could open the door all the way.

"I was expecting you way sooner than now." Ramsey rolled her eyes at me blocking my way.

"Where do you think you going?" I asked, gently pushing her back, shutting the door behind me.

"Zoo, stop acting like Luchi didn't call you. You know I'm going on a date. Now, would you leave. He should be showing up soon."

"Man, so you really dropped the twins off at Nanna's, so you could go out with some square ass nigga? That nigga couldn't take you out while the twins were at school? Lunch dates are more suitable for friends."

"Friends?" she questioned, laughing. "I don't want to go out on a lunch date. I want to enjoy a date night out on the town with a handsome guy." Ramsey laughed like I was a joke, pissing me off.

"Man, let's go pick up the twins, and I'll take y'all out. We can do something together."

"No! I'm going out with my friend, and I wish you would go before he shows up, Zouk." Ramsey whined.

"Rah, this ain't really what you want."

"But it is. I'm dressed up, looking cute, my makeup is flawless, my hair is laid. Oh, this is what I want, and I also want you to go." Ramsey stated as the doorbell rang.

She tried to rush to the door, but I quickly pulled her back moving her out my way.

"Move, Zouk!" She whined, as I blocked the door.

"You move, man. I got this." I mean mugged her opening the door. The smile on this nigga's face once I opened the door only pissed me off even more.

"Is Ramsey home?" This dumb motherfucker asked looking at me then looking over my shoulder at Ramsey. It was clear that this corny nigga was nervous.

"Nigga, I know you see her standing here."

"Bye, Zoo, stop being rude." Ramsey looked embarrassed, but I didn't give a fuck.

"I'll leave, but in a moment. First, I want to know where this nigga plan on taking you."

"Zoo, leave."

"Real shit, Rah, chill." I gave her a look letting her know to fall back. "So, where are you taking her?"

"Who are you?" Dude asked like he had the right, looking from me to Rah.

Letting out a light chuckle, I looked over at Ramsey, who looked like she was going to be sick.

"Don't worry about who I am. Now, where are you taking her on this little date?"

Dude gave Rah a look. "Please, just answer his aggy ass, so we can be on our way." Ramsey rolled her eyes.

"To dinner and a movie."

"What movie and what restaurant?" I asked. I wanted to know full details, and dude was trying to feed me bullshit.

"Um, I was going to let Ramsey pick the movie, and we'll probably go to Applebee's for dinner."

"So you're going out with a two for twenty ass nigga." I shook my head, laughing. "Call me if you need me. Don't stay out too late." I said before pecking her lips. It was quick and innocent, something I never did before, so I knew it was inappropriate, which was the reason I did it. Sadly, I wanted to fuck with Ramsey's head, and by the look on her face, it worked.

"What's going on? Who is he?" I heard him ask as I walked past him.

"He's my best friend, something like my brother." Ramsey explained. Hearing her say that, I wanted to turn around and do some wild shit, but I kept it moving.

Hopping in my ride, I didn't pull off until they did. In my eyes, this nigga was a cornball. I knew this shit wouldn't last, so I was going to let Ramsey go on her little date.

Ramsey

I think it was Zoo's goal to make my date awkward. Since leaving my house, Dell had been pretty quiet as we rode down the street. No music was playing… just silence. I couldn't stop thinking about Zoo's kiss; that's why I didn't have much to say. I knew he stopped by on a mission, and boy, was it completed. He wanted to make sure my mind wasn't on the date, and he had succeeded. I was going to give Luchi an earful. I know he was the one who told Zoo I was going on a date.

Feeling my phone vibrate in my purse, I searched around until I found it. I rolled my eyes realizing it was a text from Zouk. Looking over at Dell, I made sure he wasn't looking before opening the message. I didn't want to be rude.

Text from Zoo:

I forgot to ask you, what's that corny ass nigga's name?

Text to Zoo:

Can you leave me alone? What would Amber think about you being all up in mine?

Text from Zoo:

Fuck Amber, she's not my girl.

Text to Zoo:

Neither am I, so let me be great.

Text from Zoo:

What the fuck is that nigga's name before I pull up and ask that nigga myself.

Trying not to let my frustration show, I told Zoo what he wanted to know so he could stop texting my phone being a pain in my ass. Every so often, Dell would look my way. I wanted to know what he was thinking.

Text from Zoo:

If you're not home by twelve-thirty no later than one, you won't like the way I cut up. Taking a deep breath, I tried not to let Zoo worry me. Pulling up at Applebees, I tried not to laugh when Zoo's words popped up in my head. I didn't mind getting something off the two for twenty menu yet Zoo had to make it seem like it was the worst thing in the world. His plan to purposely ruin my date was working.

Dell was doing everything right like opening the door for me, so I tried not to let Zoo's actions play a factor in how I viewed him. After being seated, I tried to make small talk, sensing Dell's discomfort.

"You look nice," I smiled, checking him out.

"You look beautiful as well. I forgot to mention it once you came to the door because of the interrogation." He tried to make light of the comment, yet I could tell he was serious.

"Thank you." I smiled, brushing off his comment about Zoo.

"So, what's the deal with the guy at your house?"

"The deal?" I tried to control my facial expression. This was our first date. We didn't know a thing about each other, yet instead of trying to get to know me, Dell wanted to talk about Zoo.

"Did y'all used to date?" Dell asked.

"Never! Like, I already explained to you Zoo is my best friend. Dating is new for me, so he's a little overprotective. He's just looking out for me." I lied. I knew that wasn't the reason for Zoo acting out, but I wouldn't tell him that.

"Yeah, well that's understandable. I see why he's overprotective. You're beyond beautiful.

"Thank you." I blushed.

"Hey, I'm Les, and I'll be your server today. Can I start y'all off with drinks?"

"Sprite for me." I smiled at the waiter.

Picking up the alcoholic beverages menu, Dell looked through it for a couple seconds. "I'll have a Raspberry Cosmo."

Yet again, I found myself trying to control my facial expression as I listened to this man give our waiter his drink order. I couldn't believe that this overgrown man was sitting here ordering this girly drink like it was okay. I was thankful Zoo and Luchi wasn't around to witness this. They would've given me hell.

Moving on from the conversation of Zoo, I was trying to ignore the fact that this grown ass man was sipping a fruity drink, which was a huge turn-off. Conversation wise, I thought he was cool and funny. He seemed to be into me, which I really liked. After dinner, we went to the movies, and Luchi blew up my phone most of the time; Zoo texted me every half hour reminding me how much time I had left. I constantly apologized to Dell about the buzzing of my phone explaining that it was my son leaving out the fact that Zoo was blowing me up as well. He was quite understanding letting me know he fully understood the feelings, because he had two kids as well.

I was thankful the movie ended around twelve, because I didn't feel like dealing with Zoo. He had already started blowing up my phone calling back to back, and it was only eleven fifty-nine. Pulling up in front of my house a little after twelve-thirty, Dell got out to open the door for me, so he could walk me to my front door.

"Alright, brah, I got it from here?" Zoo said, appearing out of nowhere, startling both Dell and me.

"Really, Rah? You went out with a scary ass nigga." Zoo's cocky ass chuckled, amused.

"Why do you keep popping up?" Dell asked. I could tell he was irritated by Zoo's presence.

"Dude, because this is what the fuck I do. I pop the fuck up where I please when I damn well want to. Now, say goodnight, Ramsey."

"Zoo, must you always be so rude?"

"I must, now tell this nigga goodnight; it's cold as fuck."

"Good night, Dell. Sorry about this. I had a good time, and if this fool didn't scare you off, give me a call tomorrow. I would love to go out again." By the look on Zoo's face, I could tell he was getting pissed off with every passing minute, but I didn't care. Nobody told him to be here when I got home.

"He didn't, beautiful. I'll hit you tomorrow."

"Yeah-yeah-yeah, get ghost, nigga."

"May I get a hug good night?" Dell paid Zoo no mind.

Now, I was stuck between a rock and a hard place with this request. I didn't want to be rude by telling him no. I also didn't want to tell him yes, because that would be a sign of disrespect in Zoo's eyes. Thinking about him and Amber fucking around while I was in the same house as them had me leaning into Dell for a hug. It was innocent, but I could feel Zoo's eyes burning a hole through me.

"Good night, Dell." I smiled, weakly, walking away from both.

"Good night, beautiful." Dell called out before walking over to the driver's side hopping in.

"Good night, Zouk." I stopped Zoo with my hand from entering once I opened my front door.

"Rah, don't play with me. Fuck your little date. I sleep here every night. Tonight won't be any different."

"You haven't been lately." I said, smartly.

"That's because your petty ass haven't been answering the phone. I know you see the bags and shit forming under my eyes. A nigga is barely sleeping.

"What? Amber doesn't bring you peace and comfort?" I asked still being smart.

"Only when she's giving me head." Zoo smirked. I could feel my body getting hot. Not only was I getting mad, because he was being disrespectful, but the thought of Amber pleasing him had me seeing red.

"You're so damn disrespectful."

"Do you want to talk about respect after you were just cuddling with a nigga in front of my fucking face?"

"Tell me what's it to you?" I challenged. Zoo loved to play like he was my man until I called him out on it.

"Man, I'm going to bed. Before you come lay next to me, take a shower. That nigga's cheap ass cologne is all over you." Zoo said, before walking away.

"Shouldn't you be worried about what Amber's doing right now?"

"Amber ain't my bitch."

"Neither am I, yet you're here."

"Just shut your smart mouth and shower."

Done going back and forth with Zoo, I made my way into the bathroom stripping out of my clothes. After a fifteen-minute shower, I exited the bathroom. Zoo was already sleep. Seeing my phone vibrate and light-up on the nightstand, I was wondering how it got upstairs, but my question was answered when I read the text from Zoo replying back to a message from Dell.

Dell wrote me a long message telling me how much of a good time he had and how beautiful I was, but Zoo ruined the nice message replying back saying, *Nigga, that was cute and all, but she's sleep, stop texting.*

Right now, I wanted to smother him with a pillow in his sleep. Zoo was really blocking hard. Texting Dell apologizing for the hundredth time tonight, again, I told him how much fun I had and hoped we could do it again. I was glad he wasn't letting Zoo scare him away. Although I had a good time with Dell, that didn't stop me from curling up next to Zoo. I felt at home when he wrapped his arms around me pulling me closely. I quickly drifted off to sleep.

Chapter Twelve

Ramsey

I went back to ignoring Zoo the following day after my date with Dell. Dell and I had been on a few dates since our first, and I could honestly say I liked him. I wasn't ready for him to meet my kids yet, but we agreed to see where things could go between us. I knew that, in order for Dell and me to have a normal relationship, I needed to make ground rules for Zoo.

Like now. I was staring in the face of Zoo, because he showed up at my house unannounced trying to chill. Taking a deep breath, I prepared myself for what was about to go down. I knew that Zoo wouldn't like what I had to say, but it had to be done.

Walking over to my coffee table, I picked the remote up, then clicked the power button turning the TV off.

"Come on, Rah, with the bullshit. I'm trying to watch TV and chill."

"Yeah, I understand all of that, but I need your undivided attention, because we need to talk."

"About what, man? You sound serious. So, what's up?"

"Look, Zoo, I really enjoy our new-found relationship, but I have a dude, now, so you can't just drop by whenever you please."

"And why is that?" I could tell Zoo was ready to go off.

"What do you think my dude would say?"

"I don't give a fuck what your dude may think, but here's what I think. You and your little boyfriend can do your thing, but it won't be done here. Every nigga you meet don't need to be around Luchi and Luna. Do your thing on your own time."

"Zoo, you don't dictate what goes on in my household."

He let out a hearty laugh. "That's cute; since when? This new nigga really got you feeling yourself. Believe it or not, I do. I been running shit, and I won't stop now. So you heard what the fuck I said. You better tell that fuck nigga to take you out, because ain't no laying up over here. Think smart, it's cuffing season. Don't let a motherfucker think they're about to just lay up over here, and the only thing you're getting out of the deal is fucked.

"You know what, Zouk, get out. I can't deal with the way you speak to me. You're so disrespectful. You think you have everything figured out. Well, tell me this. How would you feel if Luna grew up and met a man who talked to her the way you talk to me? I'm pretty sure she would think this shit is normal, because it's all she sees, and I feel sorry for the poor little thing who runs across Luchi. At six, his attitude is already like yours. I could only imagine how reckless he'll be at sixteen or seventeen. I'm Luna's mother. I should set the example of how a woman is supposed to carry herself. I don't want Luchi to think how you talk to me is how he's supposed to speak to women. Continuing to allow you to talk to me any kind of way, I know after a while, I'll start to look weak in my babies' eyes. Shit, they probably already think I am. I can't do you and your attitude anymore. I'm setting a poor example for my kids having you around.

"Now, you're taking shit too far. This nigga really got you feeling yourself, so that's how you really feel? It's all good, Ramsey. Fuck you, I'm out your hair." Zoo yelled, before storming out of my house and out of our lives.

I sat in the same spot for several minutes thinking about how I would explain to my kids that Zoo wouldn't be around anymore. I found it hard to find the right words. I knew that, no matter the way I explain it to my kids, they would still be angry about my decision so I decided to wing it.

"What's wrong with you?" Jen asked, walking into my living room. I was so spaced out I didn't hear her walk through my front door with Luchi and Luna. "You live in a decent neighborhood, but it's not like that where you could just leave your doors unlocked."

"Hey, babies, go put your things away," I said, kissing the twins on the cheek as they hugged me tightly, making me feel loved. I wondered if they would still show me so much love once when I told them I banned Zoo from seeing them.

"Why was you in here zoned out, looking like you lost your best friend?" Jen asked, walking over to sit next to me on the couch.

"Zoo and I just got into it. I told him, he couldn't come around the twins and me anymore." I said, feeling heartbroken.

"About damn time you cut his rude ass loose." Jen smiled in excitement like she hit the jackpot.

"You did what? "Luchi asked from behind me. For some reason, I was startled by his tone. It was crazy how much this boy embodied everything about Zoo.

"Luchi, go in your room; we'll talk about this later." I said, not quite ready to explain myself. I could hear him mumble something under his breath, but I couldn't make out what he was saying.

"So what happen?" Jen asked, once Luchi made his way back upstairs to his room.

"I told him things were official with Dell, so he couldn't stop by whenever he wanted anymore." I said, getting up from my seat on the couch making my way into the kitchen to get something to drink. Jen followed behind me to the kitchen. I could tell that me telling her that Zoo would no longer be around was the best news she heard in a while. "He was being his normal rude self, thinking he was running shit, talking crazy, and I just couldn't take it anymore. I know my kids are going to hate me for this, but what type of example am I setting for them?"

"I'm proud of you, girl. That nigga deserves the boot." Jen danced around the kitchen. "So, you really must like Dell to pick him over Zoo?"

"Jen, it's not even like that. Of course, I would like to see where things could go between me and Dell, but he has nothing to do with the decision I made when it came to Zoo. If he can't respect me, there's no need to be around."

"Well, congratulations for growing some balls finally." Jen hugged me tightly.

"Thanks for watching the kids for me; I'll call you tomorrow." My tone was kind of rude, but I didn't care. I was ready for her to go.

"I see you're not just dismissing Zoo today. You're making moves all around the board, huh? I didn't plan on staying much longer, anyway, while you're trying to put me out." Jen rolled her eyes before leaving out my kitchen. Moments later, I heard my front door slam shut.

"If one more person slam my shit." I said, walking to my front door, locking it up. Now, it was time to have the dreadful talk with the twins. I knew I would get a different reaction from each of them. I knew Luna would be heartbroken, and I had already gotten a glimpse of how Luchi was going to take it; his mood would be angry.

Luchi

While my mama ran her mouth to my Aunt Jen in the kitchen, I snuck past them into the living room to get Ramsey's phone off the coffee table. Running back upstairs, I made my way into the bathroom, locking the door behind me. Pulling the toilet seat down, I sat down before calling Zoo on Facetime. After calling him twice, and getting ignored, I grew angry. I tried three more times, getting the same results.

I wasn't going to give up; I needed to talk to Zoo. I called one more time, and I got excited when he answered on the first ring. That shit quickly changed when he started going off yelling. "Rah, stop fucking calling my motherfucking phone. We ain't got shit to talk about."

"Yo, chill, it's me."

"Luchi, what's up? Does your mama know you're talking to me?"

"Naw, I overheard mama telling Jen y'all beefing. Jen's down there hyped being a bitch about the shit."

"Yo, Luchi, chill out on that shit. I won't keep telling you to watch your fucking mouth." Zoo said, running his hands over his face. I could tell my attitude and cussing was getting him worked up.

"What happened?" I asked brushing him off.

I was getting tired of everyone always telling me to watch my mouth. It wasn't going to happen, so I felt like they were wasting their breath by telling me to stop cussing. I was always going to say what I wanted.

"Luchi, that's a conversation your mama need to have with you and Luna. Just know, no matter what, I got you and Luna. If you need me, you know my number."

"I know, so with that being said, can you buy us an iPhone, so we can FaceTime you whenever we want?"

"Luchi, you stay asking for the most off the wall shit. I honestly think you forget you're only six, but I'll see what I can do."

"You'll see?" I looked at him crazy. "Naw, that's not good enough. I see I have to send in the big guns." I laughed, unlocking the bathroom door. "Come here, Lulu. Come ask Zoo to buy us a..." my words were cut short as I walked out the bathroom walking smack dead into Ramsey.

"What are you doing with my phone, Luchi?"

"Talking to Zoo."

"Say goodbye."

"But mama."

"Say goodbye, Luchi!" She said, raising her voice.

"Don't take your fucking anger out on him." Zoo yelled.

"My anger not against him; it's with you. Now say goodbye, Luchi."

"I got you Luchi on that, and remember what I said."

"Okay."

"Okay." Zoo said, before ending the FaceTime.

"Go get Luna, and come in my room so I can talk to you."

"Man," I said, walking off in search of Luna.

"Come on, Lulu. Mama got some bullshit to drop on us."

Luna followed behind me as we made our way into my mama's room.

"There's something we need to talk about."

I could tell she was nervous, trying to find the right words to explain what happened with her and Zoo.

"What's up, mama? What's going on with you and Zoo?" I asked. I wasn't going to make breaking whatever news she had easy for her.

"Listen, I know how much y'all love Zoo, but we made an agreement that he won't be around as much anymore." She spoke, nervously.

"Why?" Luna looked so sad and heartbroken. Seeing my twin upset pissed me off.

"Luna, mama just thinks it's best." Ramsey's voice softened like she was sad for us only pissed me off more.

"Best for who? You or Us? Because that's not what we want." I asked, while Luna cried next to me. "This ain't what Zoo wanted. This is all you, because you have a new nigga. You ran off Zoo."

"Luchi, you better watch your damn mouth and show me some respect before I beat your ass."

I was trying to control my anger, but I felt myself getting pissed by the second. Zoo was the closest thing I had to a father, and I wasn't trying to lose him, because Ramsey was in her feelings.

"Luna," She called out to my sister. She knew trying to talk to Luna would be easier than trying to make a point with me.

"Can I call Zoo, Mommy?" Luna cried.

"No, Luna." Ramsey quickly shut Luna down. Taking off, Luna ran out the room.

"Luchi, listen…"

"Man, whatever, I hate you." I said, storming out the room. This is some bullshit." She had to know I was about to go to my room and talk bad about her.

Zouk

I felt better after hanging up with Luchi, although Ramsey was still on her bullshit. Not only did I feel some type of way about Ramsey telling me she found herself a nigga, but she also tried to tell me I couldn't be around Luna and Luchi, anymore. I was ready to fuck shit up, but truth be told, she was right. Hell, the way Luchi spoke about his aunt let me know the way I felt about Jen was rubbing off on him. Ramsey was right. I was Luna's heart. In her eyes, I did no wrong. She saw the way I talked to her mother, and I didn't want her to think the way I behave was acceptable. She was also right about the fact that I would body any little nigga who stepped to her the same way I stepped to Ramsey.

Needing someone to talk to, I pulled up to Zo's house. Grabbing my phone from my cup holder, I dialed his number and waited for him to answer.

"House of beauty, this is cutie. How may I help you?" Zoe spoke into the phone once he answered.

"Nigga, open the door." I yelled into the phone, bringing my brother down off his high horse.

"Eewww, nigga, you don't have to be so rude." Zoe whined. I'm pretty sure he was rolling his neck like some bird. Hanging up on him, I hopped out my car.

"What do your rude ass want? You only stop by when you're going through something, so what's up ugly?" Zoe asked, greeting me at the door.

"Man!" I said, making my way into his living room, sitting down on the couch. I ran my hands over my face frustrated. "Ramsey claims she's cutting me off from being in their life."

"About damn time." Zoe clapped. "If I didn't know any better, I would think Ramsey was some lonely, weak bitch for putting up with a nigga who talked to her the way that you do, but I'm for certain sure she tolerates your ass because she's in love with you."

"Man, I don't know about all that." I ran my hand over my face again.

"Tell me what happen."

"I showed up trying to chill, and her dumb ass had the nerves to tell me I can't show up whenever I pleased, because she has a boyfriend now. She had a problem with me saying I didn't want different niggas around the twins. She had the nerves to ask me when did I start running shit at her house? Dude got her feeling herself."

"Or, maybe dude talk to her like he has some sense instead of the way you speak to her, and that made her look at things and you differently." Zoe added.

"Okay, she can feel how she want to feel, but that shouldn't stop me from seeing my kids." I yelled at Zoe, frustrated, like he was the cause of my problems.

"Zoo."

Zoe looked nervous as he sat next to me. I could tell he was worried I would have another breakdown.

"I can't go through this shit again." I said, feeling a sense of abandonment.

"Zouk, how did it get to this point where she felt like you shouldn't be around the kids anymore? I feel bad for you. I know how much you love Luna and Luchi, but I never heard you claim them as you own."

"She basically said I'm a fucked-up role model for the twins. She claims I'm disrespectful. She believes I'm the reason Luchi is out of control. I guess she fears that Luna will grow up and find a nigga like me, one who disrespects women, because that's how she sees me treat Ramsey."

"I know you probably don't want to hear this brother, but she does have a good point. That girl is crazy about you, although she never says it. You can tell by her actions. You're a pain in that girl's ass, you talk to her like she ain't shit. Y'all did all that tonight, but I bet if you went over there right now, she would welcome you with open arms."

"I don't think so; she was pretty pissed."

"Why don't you give it a try, but leave big bad Zoo in the car.

"I'll pass. I'm just about to take my ass home."

"Okay, whatever. You're going to lose that girl because of your ego."

"Trust me; it's not my ego." I said, making my way out the door.

I sat outside of Zoe's thinking about my next move. Truth be told, I wasn't willing to stay away from Ramsey and the twins, even if I wanted to. Starting up my car, I made my way back over to Ramsey's. I just couldn't help myself. We needed to get shit squared away.

Ramsey

After having the talk with the twins, listening to Luna cry, and Luchi tell me how much he hated me, I was ready for the day to be over. I couldn't get any sleep, thanks to Luchi's words haunting me. I never wanted to hear those words come out of my kids' mouths, but I somewhat expected it. I was finally able to get some sleep, but that was short-lived, thanks to the ringing of my phone.

"What Zouk?" I answered, without looking to see who was calling. I knew it was him, because this was normal for him to call this late, not caring that it was almost three in the morning.

"Come open the door." His demanding voice flowed through the phone.

"No, did you forget what we talked about already?"

"Come open the door, please. I swear, I'm not on no bullshit."

Letting out a frustrated sigh, I relentlessly climbed out of bed to open the door for Zoo.

"Man, what I tell you about that shit?" Zoo looked me up and down shaking his head as he followed me up to my room after locking the door behind him.

"Man, what I tell you about thinking you running shit?" My attitude matched his. "You show up at my house unannounced. I was sleeping comfortably in my bed. If you didn't want to see me dressed like this, you could've FaceTime me to speak your peace or waited until a decent hour." At this moment, I had nothing to offer but attitude seeing that I hated being woken from my sleep.

"Alright, man, I didn't come over here to fight. I just want to talk."

"So, whatever you had to say couldn't wait until morning to be said?"

"No, it couldn't. I wanted to get what I had to say out tonight."

"I'm listening." I said, rolling my eyes, climbing back into bed to get comfortable.

"Are you going to give me attitude the whole fucking time?" I could tell by Zoo's tone he was frustrated, but so was I.

"If you're going to continue to cuss at me, you can leave." I said, pointing toward the door.

"Man, I'm here so we can work this shit out for the sake of the twins. I didn't come here to beef with your ass." Zoo ran his hands over his face. "Okay, you have a dude now, cool. All I ask is, out of respect for me, you don't have this nigga trying to play daddy. I'll try to give you your space. Just don't take my twins away from me."

"You'll try?" I laughed, sarcastically, shaking my head. Zoo was a piece of work.

"Brah, can you try to meet me halfway? All I want is to continue to have a relationship with the twins."

"Okay."

"If you want to have this nigga around the twins. I need to properly meet him first. "

"Really, Zoo? Are you kidding? Don't you think you're doing a little much?" I laughed. I wanted to say I was shocked by his request, but I wasn't. This was normal Zoo; he needed to feel like he was in control of every situation.

"Ramsey, do I often kid? No. So, why would I start now?"

"Okay, whatever Zoo."

"Okay good. I'm glad we have an understanding." Zoo spoke removing his clothes.

"What are you doing, Zouk?" I asked, laughing. It was clear he didn't have it all.

"It's three in the morning; what does it look like I'm doing? I'm going to bed."

"Now, you care about the time? Is this your way of trying to give me my space?"

"Starting tomorrow." Zoo said, climbing into bed, pulling me close to him.

"This is inappropriate."

"How, when it's not even like that." Zoo's eyes were already closed.

"Where you going?" he asked, as I pulled away.

140

"Can I turn the light out, Zouk?" I questioned, shaking my head. Sometimes, he could be a big baby, and when he was tired, was one of them.

Turning the light out, I cuddled back under Zoo. By habit, his hand made its way up to my head. Playing in my hair was something that calmed us both.

"Zouk," I called out. I wanted to know how he really felt about me dating. I wanted to know was it really only all about the twins with him.

"Zouk," I called out, again, since he didn't answer me the first time. I realized he was sleep when I noticed the pattern of his breathing had changed.

It was just my luck that, when I finally built up the nerves to ask the question I wanted to know for months, he falls asleep on me. I was taking that as my sign to leave well enough alone.

Chapter Thirteen

Ramsey

Christmas and New Year had come and gone, and Dell and I had been dating for close to two months. I was finally ready for him to meet the twins. Luchi and Luna weren't too fond of the idea, but I knew it was all because they weren't accepting another man in our life but Zoo.

Speaking of Zoo, he was doing a poor job at giving me my space. He still liked to come and go as he pleased. We spent Christmas and New Years with his family. Zay hosted Christmas, and Zoe hosted New Years. I could tell Dell was somewhat intimidated about the role Zoo played in our life. I knew this, because he had no problem voicing his thoughts and concerns on the matter. I tried to explain to him how my relationship with Zoo came about, and why it was so important to me, although Zoo was a pain in my ass.

Dell had asked me did I love Zoo, and I could say I was stuck by his question. I had brushed it off by making light of the situation. I wanted him to understand that to deal with an attitude like Zoo's some love had to be there. I could tell Dell didn't like it, but respected the relationship Zoo and I had. I explained to him Zoo's role in the twins' life as well. His role in the twins' life made his role in mine seem small. I cared for Zoo, but I really didn't want to let go of the bond he built with my kids.

Zoo wanted to have a sit-down with Dell before I introduced him to the twins, but I wasn't having that. I knew he would take the meeting overboard. Just like Dell felt threatened by Zoo's presence in our life, I knew Zoo felt the same way. He was selfish when it came to the twins and me, the thought of Dell coming into our life making a lasting impression pissed Zoo off.

I agreed to meet Dell at the skating rink. I wasn't trying to force him on my kids by having him all in their space. I knew they weren't really feeling the whole playdate. Dell had a seven-year-old son and an eight-year-old daughter, so we thought this would be the perfect time for everyone to meet.

On our way to the skating rink, Luchi and Luna's iPhone that they shared rung. The only person who called them was me, Cari, Lil' C, Zoo, or Nanna, so one of them had to be calling.

"What's up, Zoo?" Luchi asked.

"What are y'all doing?" Zoo asked. I heard him, because Luchi had him on speaker phone.

"Nothing important." Luchi had the nerve to say.

"Zoo, can you come get us?" Luna asked.

I was glad we were at a red light. Reaching in the backseat, I snatched the phone from Luchi before Zoo could answer.

"Hey!" I tried to sound like I was happy to talk to him.

"Where are y'all going?" Zoo asked, ignoring my greeting.

"I'm taking them out for a little fun." I said, leaving out what was really going on. I was trying to give Zoo less information as possible.

"Why you didn't invite me?"

"Zoo, can I call you back? I'm driving." I tried to avoid his question.

"Ramsey, I didn't call you. I called Luchi and Lulu. I don't even know why you're on the phone."

"Zouk, I'll have them call you back later."

"Ay!" Zoo called out before I hung up on him. I knew he either had more questions or he wanted to talk to the twins, and I didn't trust them enough not to tell him where we were going and who we were going with. I knew, if Zoo knew where I was taking them, he would raise hell.

Looking through the rearview mirror, the look on the twins face told it all; they had an attitude. Trying to ease the tension, I sparked up a conversation.

"Hey, are y'all excited about meeting Dell and his kids Star and Kordell?"

"I want to pretend like I'm excited just for you, Rah, but I can't. I'm really not feeling this shit."

"I'm sorry, mama, but I agree." Luna added.

"Can y'all just give him a chance for me?"

"I can't promise you anything. I'm not feeling this. I'm only here because I want to go skating." Luchi let it be known.

"I agree." Luna voiced.

Letting out a frustrated sigh, I continued to drive in the direction of the skating rink. I was torn right now. I wanted to be happy in a relationship, but I wasn't willing to sacrifice my kids' happiness for mine. I didn't want to, yet I was willing to end things with Dell if it meant keeping my kids happy.

Pulling into the skating rink parking lot, I smiled when I noticed Dell and his kids standing near the doorway waiting for us. Getting out the car, the twins dragged their feet behind me. It was clear that they were going to give me a hard time today.

"Hey." I greeted Dell with a hug.

"What it do, beautiful?" Dell leaned in for a kiss on the lips, and I quickly turned my head, so his lips could meet my cheek. This was all about baby steps, and as crazy as it may sound, I didn't want Luchi to cut up.

The look of disappointment that crossed Dell's face didn't go unnoticed. I decided not to address it, because I wanted this day to go by smoothly.

"Hello, I'm Ramsey." I smiled, introducing myself to Dell's kids.

"Hi, I'm Star." Dell's daughter introduced herself with so much sass as she smacked on her bubble gum.

"Nice to meet you, Star, and what's your name handsome?" I asked Dell's son.

"The name is Kordell." He spoke, rudely.

"Watch it, nigga." Luchi's attitude matched Kordell's.

"Chill out, fellas." Dell laughed. I didn't find anything funny. By the way my kids were acting, and the way Dell's kids were acting, I could tell this was going to be a long playdate.

"I'm Dell; it's nice to finally meet you, Luna and Luchi."

"Yeah, sorry, brah. I can't say the same." Luchi's tone was so even and nonchalant. Luna giggled, amused by his rudeness. I, on the other hand, was embarrassed by their behavior.

"Luchi, don't start." I wanted to tell him if he didn't behave we would leave, but I knew that would only make him happy.

"Let's skate." Dell laughed Luchi off. He often asked questions about my kids. He knew how outspoken Luchi was. He was convinced he had the power to win him over. So far, he wasn't doing too well.

"What are you doing?" Luchi asked, as I reached into my purse, pulling out my wallet, so I could pay our admission.

"We're about to skate." I answered, confused by his line of questioning. He knew we were about to go skating.

"That nigga ain't paying our way?" Luchi asked upset.

The look on Dell's face let me know he was taken back by Luchi's words. Choosing to ignore him, I paid for our admission. I should've known Luchi wouldn't make this meet and greet easy. This child of mine was Zouk all over again. Although Luna didn't say much, I knew she was feeling the same as him. She allowed her brother to be her voice. She stuck by his side like glue as we made our way over to get our skates.

"Can you help me put my skates on, Ramsey?" Star asked, after we received our skates, finding a seat.

"Yes, sure sweetie." I smiled, gently pinching her cheeks. Star was such a cute little girl. She had a lot of Dell's features. "Sit next to me, Lulu, so I can help you as well.

"It's okay, mama. Luchi is going to help me." Luna walked over to sit next to her brother.

"So, Ramsey, your hair is cute. Is it weave? If so, who did it? It looks so natural." Star smacked her gum.

I was somewhat taken back by her questions. "Um, no, it's not a weave." I quickly answered tying her skates.

"I just turned eight, and I wanted to get a weave for my eighth birthday, but my daddy said it was too grown for an eight-year-old. My mama said she didn't mind, my daddy said no." Star rolled her eyes twirling her gum around her index finger.

I was trying not to show how displeased I was with Star's mama's approval of her eight-year-old getting a weave. "Your daddy is probably right, sweetie." I forced a smiled lacing up her other skate.

After lacing up my skates, I made my way over to Luchi and Luna. "Y'all ready to skate?"

"Yes!" Luna cheered.

"Y'all need to help, Mommy; I haven't done this in a while." I grabbed both their hands.

The skating rink was pretty busy today, because it was Saturday. Four different birthday parties were taking place, so kids were everywhere.

Once my skates hit the floor, my skills came back to me. Skating was one of my sisters and I favorite pastime when we were younger. We were at the skating rink every Saturday night for Champs skate and dance. That was a first time I laid eyes on Lance, but that's a story that I won't get into.

I was shocked to see that Luchi was a pretty good skater; Luna was good enough to keep it together. Luchi held her hand just to make sure she didn't fall. Star tried to hold Luchi's hand as well, but he wasn't having that. My boy was so rude. He went as far as skating away from

Star and I with Luna. I was embarrassed by his behavior, but not surprised.

Grabbing Star's hand, I skated around with her. Dell and Kordell weren't too far behind. Kordell was having trouble keeping his balance. I smiled as I watched how patient Dell was with him. Star pulled away from me, so she could skate to the middle of the floor. She joined the other kids who stood around dancing. I quickly moved catching up with the twins.

"Are you having fun?" I asked, grabbing their hands.

"Yeah, we have to do this more often." Luchi moved back and forth to the beat of the music.

"Yeah, we should." Dell said, skating up to us.

"Naw, what you should do, is keep a better eye on your daughter. Look how she's over there dancing. Luna, I wish you would ever try to dance like that." Luchi mean mugged Star. She was in the middle of the dance floor popping her behind while two little boys watched.

I could see the fire in Dell's eyes as he skated over to Star.

"Zoo!" The twins yelled, causing my heart to skip several beats. What the hell was he doing here?

Zoo

Call me crazy, but when Ramsey hung up on me, I waited twenty minutes before tracking the twins' phone. Luna and Luchi wanted me to spend time with them, so I was going to make it happen. I knew I said I was going to give her space, but I lied. If anything, I wanted to be around them more.

Walking into the skating rink with Cari and Lil'C by my side, I let them get their skates before we looked around for the twins. Looking around the skating rink, I spotted the twins at the same time they spotted me.

"Zoo!" They called out, causing me to smile. The look on Ramsey's face was priceless.

Cari and Lil'C made their way over to the twins as they made their way over to me. Luna was excited like she hadn't seen me in years, and it had only been a day or two. Luna was moving so fast, she fell, but Lil' C, Luchi, and Cari were right there to pick her up. I smiled, proudly, because I knew my little niggas would always be right there to protect my baby.

Looking over at Ramsey, I was trying to figure out why she wasn't on her way to greet me as well. I tried to keep my cool when I saw her so-called boyfriend all in her face with his hands wrapped around her, holding her close. Knowing Ramsey well, the awkward smile on her face let me know she was nervous.

Focusing back on the kids, I let Ramsey and her lame ass nigga have their moment. I was here to spend time with the kids.

"Zoo, come skate." Luna hugged my legs.

"Lulu, baby, skating ain't my thing." I smiled, picking her up.

"Please, Zoo-Zoo, I won't let you fall. I'll hold your hand." Lulu begged.

"Lulu, I don't skate."

"Just do it for me, your favorite girl." She said, showing off her pretty smile.

"Okay!" I was too cool to be busting my ass on some damn skates, but I came to spend time with them, so   I guess that meant putting skates on.

"You know Dell's lame ass is here, right?" Luchi sat next to me as I laced up my skates.

"Fuck I tell you about cussing?"

"Man." Luchi stretched his word.

"Man, your ass, nigga. I'm not going to keep telling you to watch your damn mouth. You're not grown."

"Alright."

I wasn't about to address Ramsey's nigga. Shit, Ramsey better hope I acknowledged her ass. I asked her to do one fucking thing, and her sneaky ass couldn't do that. That's why she was trying to rush me off the phone. She didn't want to tell me where they were going, because she was meeting up with her nigga.

"Let's skate." I said, grabbing Lulu's hand.

I can't remember the last time I went skating. It wasn't my thing, because I was never good at it. The moment I stepped foot on the rink, I felt like a dumb ass. I know I probably looked like one. I felt like a newborn giraffe just now learning how to walk. Luchi, Cari, and Lil'C were amused about the fact that I didn't know how to skate.

Luchi skated around me laughing. "Don't pay them any attention, Zoo, I got you." Luna held onto my hand, tightly. I don't know what she thought that would do; if I was going down, she was going down with me.

Hearing her say that only made them laugh harder. I wanted to reach out and smack one of them, but I didn't want to risk falling, giving them something else to dog me about. After a few slow laps around the skating rink, I was starting to get the hang of it.

Ramsey and her nigga were too busy watching us; they were barely paying attention to each other. I didn't have shit to say to her, and if she wanted to keep the peace, she should do the same and not say shit to me, either. My feet were starting to hurt, so I was done skating. Changing out of my skates, and turning them in, I watched as the kids enjoyed themselves. I saw how some little girl followed them around trying to get Lil' C's attention. I was getting hungry and ready to go.

"Ay!" I called out as they skated past. "Come here."

"I'm about to go; y'all riding out with me?" I questioned.

"I am." Luna was the first to answer.

"Go get your things; I'm ready."

Rushing off, they went to return their skates. Once they returned their skates, we set off to find Ramsey. She wasn't too far out of sight, watching our every move like a hawk. Walking over to her, I stood in front of her and her nigga.

"We're out." I let her know.

"Um, we were going to take them to get something to eat." Ramsey spoke, nervously.

"Ramsey, I'm having a good day." I smiled.

"That's good."

"That means don't piss me off. Stop trying to force your forced relationship on them. They're not feeling it."

"Listen, man." Ramsey's dude tried to add his input, but I stopped him in his tracks.

"You listen; you're not the main man in this story, so fall back and play your role. You're here for the moment, so keep quiet and enjoy your time." I said I wasn't going to address this nigga, but him trying to come at me pissed me off. "I'll probably keep them overnight. Y'all say goodbye to you mom, so we can dip."

"Zoo!" Ramsey whined.

"Look, man, I'm not here for the dramatics today. Save whatever you have to say."

"Come give me a hug." Ramsey stretched her arms out waiting for a hug.

"He got it like that?" Dell asked. I could tell by his tone he was upset.

"You already know what it is." I laughed. "We're out. Be expecting a call from me."

"She'll be busy." Dude smirked.

This nigga was a joke to me. I couldn't help but laugh in their faces. "So, you'll be busy, Rah?" Ramsey tried to avoid eye contact, "Rah!"

"Bye, Zouk."

"I said be expecting my call."

"Tell him you'll be busy." Dude added.

"Just stop. I can't take both of y'all's ego at once."

"All I know is, when I call, you better answer." I said, before grabbing Lulu's hand, walking off. I wasn't about to keep going back and forth with this nigga, when I already knew that, when I called her ass, she would answer.

Ramsey

Dell had been going on and on about Zoo since we left the skating rink. After he had dropped his kids off, he showed up at my doorstep. I should've known my day wouldn't turn out like I planned. Zoo showing up was just as a shock to me as it was to Dell. For some reason, he didn't believe me. He wanted to argue about the situation. The fact that Zoo took the kids and talked shit before doing so didn't help. Dell wasn't convinced that me and Zoo weren't sleeping around, so we spent most of our night going back and forth.

When Zoo called like he said he would, Dell started to raise hell. I couldn't even answer the phone, because Dell snatched it up before I could answer. He constantly declined Zoo's call every time my phone rang. I know, not only was I hearing Dell's mouth, but I was going to have to hear Zoo's as well. I wouldn't be surprised if Zoo showed up banging on my door as well.

"Look Dell, I'm not feeling too well. I think you should go."

"That nigga must be on his way over." Dell's tone was unpleasant.

"Nobody on there…." Before I could finish my sentence, vomit made its way everywhere.

"Shit, baby, are you okay?" Dell asked concerned.

"Yes, I'm fine. I just want to lay down, so come on, so I can lock up."

"Are you sure you don't want me to stay? I can take care of you."

"I'm fine; I got it covered. I just want to rest before the kids return tomorrow."

I could tell he wanted to protest as I ushered him to the door.

"Are you sure?"

"Yes, I'm fine." I said, feeling dizzy. He needed to go, because I was ready to lay down.

After cleaning up the mess I made, I stripped out of my clothes. I downed some Nyquil before climbing into the shower. I couldn't stay in the shower too long, because I kept getting dizzy spells. Not too long after getting out the 'Quil started to kick in, and before I knew it, I was passed out.

Zoo

I was growing more pissed off by the second, as I bang on Ramsey's front door. I've been knocking for ten minutes and blowing her phone up all day, getting no answer. If her new nigga had her tripping acting like she couldn't answer my calls, I was going to raise hell. This wasn't like Ramsey to not answer her phone. I wouldn't be surprised if her nigga was monitoring her calls. Dude felt like he had something to prove; he wanted to be the man, but I wasn't letting that happen.

Finally after banging for ten minutes, the front door quickly opened. Ramsey stood there wiping the sleep from her eyes.

"Why are you sleeping in so late? You got that nigga in here?" I asked pressing my way inside. She was acting like she wanted a nigga to stay on the porch. The twins hugged her before running past.

"No, Zoo, and can you lower your voice?"

"No, I can't." I said, looking around. I wanted to see if I saw any signs of her nigga.

"Well, thank you for dropping the kids off; you can go now." Ramsey spoke, covering her mouth yawning. Paying close attention to her, I could tell something was wrong.

"What? You got a hangover? What's going on with you?"

"Since last night, I've been feeling dizzy and nauseous, as well as having aching bones. That's why I been sleep all day; I don't feel well."

"I know your ass didn't allow this nigga to knock you up?" I could feel myself ready to explode.

"No, Zouk!" she yelled. By the look on her face, I could tell she was embarrassed, but I didn't give a fuck. "I'm not pregnant, Zouk. Just human. I know you probably think I'm superwoman, but I'm not. I, too, get sick sometimes. How have the twins been? Please tell me it hasn't been a rough day? All I want is peace and sleep. I swear, it's no break to this shit. No days off. I pray that they make my job easier tonight."

"The twins have been the twins; ain't shit changed."

"Whatever, Zoo. Have Luchi lock up behind you. I'm going to lay back down." She said over her shoulder, as she walked away.

"Luchi, come get your coat out the middle of the floor." He wasted no time going into the living room turning the game on the moment he walked through the front door, leaving his coat and shoes all over the place. "Go hang your coat up, then get ready for bed."

"Zoo, I'm trying to play the game."

"No game; it's time to get ready for bed. Mama doesn't feel good, so everyone is going to call it a night a little early."

"Zoo-Zoo ,can you stay?" Luna asked, excitedly.

"Yes, come on, so you can get ready for bed as well."

"Can you read to me after I get out of the shower?" Luna asked.

"Let's see how getting ready for bed goes first. I'm going to make your mama some soup. I want y'all to lay out an outfit for school, and I'll come check it."

"Okay, Zoo-Zoo." Luna took off running upstairs.

"Quietly, Lulu."

Going into the kitchen, I placed a pot on the stove to make Ramsey some soup. Going into the cabinet, I took out everything I needed to make her some tea. While her soup cooked, I went to check on the twins. Luchi was already in his pajamas, sitting on the top bunk of his bed drawing in his sketchbook. Luna was still in the shower, so I made my way down the hall to peek in on Ramsey. She was passed out in bed with her mouth hanging slightly open, snoring. Shaking my head, I quietly shut the door. Luna was exiting the bathroom dressed in her pajamas.

"Are you ready to read me a book now?"

"I'll be right in after I give your mama her soup."

"Okay." Luna said, before running into Luchi's room.

After placing Ramsey's soup and tea on a tray, I carried it up to her room. "Wake up, Rah?"

"What, Zoo?"

"Here, I made you some soup and tea. Sit up and eat. I already got the twins ready for bed. I'm about to go read Lulu a story. I'll be back in here to get your tray after you're done."

"Thank you." Ramsey smiled.

"What book do you have for me?" I asked Luna, once I walked into Luchi's room.

"I picked this new Amelia Bedelia book mama just bought me."

"Okay, move over."

Moving over, Luna allowed me to get comfortable before resting her head on my chest. Luchi climbed down from the top bunk, with his sketchbook still in his hand, and got in bed as well.

"Amelia Bedelia, by Peggy Parrish." I read the title and the author's name. That was a requirement of Luna's whenever someone was reading to her.

Luna laughed throughout the whole book as we took turns reading. Amelia Bedelia moved throughout her boss' house doing her work chores all wrong. These were the moments I lived for, making memories with the twins. Knowing they enjoyed the simple things, like me just reading them a book, did something to a nigga's heart. Luna convinced me to read them two more stories before I finally went to check on Ramsey.

Once I entered her room, she was back under the covers fast asleep. The bowl was empty, and she drank most of her tea. Going into her bathroom, I cleaned the tub out before running her a hot bath, then adding Epsom salt.

"Come on." I said standing over her.

"No, Zoo, I'm not going anywhere. I'm tired." She whined.

"I ran you a bath, so come on before your water gets cold."

Ramsey wore a shocked look on her face as she rose up in bed. I guided her into the bathroom, and once I saw that she was straight, I removed myself to give her privacy. Going back into her room, I picked up a little. She had used tissue all over her nightstand, and clothes were on the floor. Grabbing my lighter out of my pocket, I lit the two candles that decorated her dresser. She had her room all dark and gloomy.

Walking down the hall, I peeked in on the twins, and they were passed out together. Walking over to Luchi, I took the sketchbook out of his hand. That was how he fell asleep most nights. Covering Luna up, I kissed her cheek before turning off the TV. Going into the hall closet, I grabbed a washcloth and towel and my body wash. I was ready to call it a night as well. Getting the kids up for school would roll around quick as hell. Once I was finished with my quick shower, I made my way back into Ramsey's room. Walking over to the bathroom door, I knocked before walking in.

"Ay Rah, you good?" I asked.

"Yes, this water felt so good, I fell asleep." She lightly giggled. "I'm about to wash up and get out." She said, turning the hot water on, refreshing her bath.

Nodding my head, I closed the door behind me. Going into Ramsey's nightstand, I reached all the way in the back for my weed stash. As I was rolling up, I felt vibrating. Looking around, I found Ramsey's phone tucked under the pillow. I saw it was her nigga calling, so I answered. Continuing to roll my blunt, I waited for dude to speak.

"Hey, baby. I was just calling to see how you're feeling?"

"She's forever good as long as I'm around."

"Man, why are you always there?"

"Because, nigga, I been here, and I'm not going anywhere. You being in the picture don't mean shit. Learn to play your role."

"Nigga, it's clear I got the role that you want." Dude chuckled.

"Nigga, fuck out of here." I let out a hearty laughed; this nigga was a joke to me. "Nigga, you don't have shit I want, and if you did, I don't have a problem taking shit. But, then again, I don't need to take what's already mine."

"Man, just put Ramsey on the phone." He spoke. I could tell he was pissed by his tone.

"Naw, call her back tomorrow; she needs her rest."

"Man, put Ramsey on the phone." I guess he thought raising his voice would move me.

"Okay, hold on. Wait for it." I said before hanging up. Placing her phone on the nightstand, I got comfortable before lighting my blunt.

"That bath was what I needed." Ramsey emerged from the bathroom with a towel wrapped around her body. I watched her as she moved around the room, beads of water rested on the top of her breasts. I had the urge to get up and explore her body. I had to tell myself to chill; I was only thinking about fucking her right now just to prove the point that I could.

"I've been so tired today. Everything just hit me out of nowhere." She spoke, pulling me out of my thoughts as she bent over to get pajamas from her drawer. I chuckled when she disappeared in her closet to change.

After she had dressed, she walked out of the bedroom, I'm assuming to check on the twins, but moments later, she returned, climbing in bed next to me. Grabbing her phone off the nightstand, she scrolled through it.

"Damnit, Zoo! What did you say to Dell?" Ramsey rolled her eyes and neck like a ghetto bird.

"What? He called himself telling on me like some little ass kid?" I laughed.

"Zoo, you can't say things that will cause unnecessary problems in my relationship. Stop making Dell feel like it's more going on between us than it is."

"Man, shut the fuck up and hit the light. Text that nigga back and tell him I'm only here to get the twins ready for school, since you're so concerned about easing the nigga's mind."

"Thank you! I appreciate you getting them ready for bed for me."

I didn't acknowledge what she said, because I felt like it was my job to take care of the twins as well. I rolled over as she texted away on her phone. I wanted to snatch it from her, but I didn't want to hear her mouth about privacy and boundaries.

"I'll give you your privacy. I'm going to sleep on the couch."

"Zoo, you don't have to leave."

"Yes, I do. Goodnight." I said, shutting the door behind me. I could hear her whining telling me to stop, but I kept it moving. I had to remind myself I was only here for the kids. Ramsey was someone else's girl.

Chapter Fourteen

Zouk

I didn't feel how Ramsey had her door open where anyone could just walk on in like I was about to do. I could hear Luchi yelling once I crossed the threshold. Rushing into the living room, I didn't like what I saw.

"What the fuck is going on here?" I asked, feeling my anger rise.

"Zoo, tell him to get the fuck off me!" Luchi yelled with tears running down his face.

Giving Ramsey's bitch ass boyfriend a look, he let Luchi go already knowing what was up. "Why the fuck do you have your hands on him for nigga?"

"The little nigga need to watch his mouth." Dell mugged me. I could tell he wasn't feeling how I was coming for him.

"Nigga, I don't give a fuck if he spit in your face, don't put your fucking hands on him. Rah, why the fuck you just standing here watching the nigga do the shit?"

"Zoo, Luchi was cussing. You discipline him when he cuss; why can't Dell?" She asked.

I wanted to jack her ass up for asking such a dumb ass question. These two motherfuckers had been on some other shit since the night I stayed at Ramsey's to help her get the kids ready for school. This nigga had been attached to her hip every second of the day. The twins turned eight a few weeks ago, and this nigga thought he had some kind of clap to include himself in the planning, but I quickly shut that shit down. The day of the party, this nigga tried to play loving father to the twins, and it took everything in me not to fuck this nigga up. Off the strength of wanting the twins to enjoy their day, I kept what little cool I had. Now, this nigga thought he could put his hands on my young one. Shit was about to go left and quick.

"My nigga, the difference between me and this nigga is I take fucking care of them. All this nigga do is sit around sucking up free cable, and eating up all Luchi and Luna's fucking snacks and shit. This nigga don't have any fucking clap around here, and I don't appreciate you making him think he do. Nigga, you ain't got shit going, so make sure you keep your fucking hands to yourself. If it's any problem when it comes to Luchi or Luna, you come to me with it, and I'll discipline them how I see fit. Don't put your fucking hands on him, anymore. I don't give a fuck if he called your mama a bitch."

It took everything in me not to beat the shit out of Dell. Seeing the frightened look in Luna's eyes, stopped me for turning into Floyd Mayweather in the middle of Ramsey's living room.

"Luchi and Lulu, go pack your shit." I said, never taking my eyes off Ramsey and Dell. Ramsey held her head down low knowing she fucked up big time letting Dell rough Luchi up. Dell looked like he wanted to say some slick shit not wanting to look like a punk in front of Ramsey, but he knew me talking crazy to him was less damaging to his ego than me beating his ass.

"Where are y'all going?" Ramsey asked, refusing to make eye contact with me.

"Don't question me, Rah. I would gladly appreciate it if you didn't say shit to me at all."

"She has the right to know where you taking her kids." Dell finally found his voice.

I let out a little chuckle; I could tell the smirk on my face threw Ramsey for a loop. "Yo, Luchi and Lulu."

"Coming." They yelled at the same time running down the steps.

"Bye, mama," Luna yelled running right past Ramsey to the door.

Luchi, on the other hand, said nothing to his mama or Dell. Before walking out the room, he turned around to give Dell the finger.

"Luchi!" Ramsey yelled.

I laughed, as we made our way out the door. Normally, I would've gotten on Luchi about his behavior, but I myself didn't respect Ramsey's lame ass boyfriend, so I wouldn't tell Luchi to do the same. I could tell that nigga was intimidated by my role in Ramsey and the twins' life. I would have to have a talk with Ramsey to let that fuck nigga know to, either get with my program, or get lost.

"Can we stay with you tonight?" Luna asked from the backseat.

"I'll do you one better, Lulu. You can stay the weekend. I might even let y'all stay until Monday."

"We have school on Monday. The bus don't come to your house, Zoo-Zoo"

"Lulu, what the fuck you think cars are for? It's nothing for him to drive us. Plus, I need a break from Ramsey and Dell as a unit. Zoo, that nigga got mama's head gone."

Hearing Luchi say Dell had Ramsey's head gone had me feeling some type of way. "Luchi, you need to really chill on all that cussing. I'm not going to keep telling you about your fucking mouth. Don't think you can cuss like a fucking sailor just because I'm not around to smack you. The same rule apply with both me and your mama. If she say watch your mouth, Luchi, I need for you to do so, because if that nigga put his hands on you again, it's going to be some serious problems. Do you understand?"

"Yes, I understand. He better be lucky you showed up when you did, because I was about to be a serious problem." Luchi said mocking me.

"The serious problem was going to be a panic attack from you crying so hard." Luna laughed.

Looking through the rearview mirror, I laughed at Luna and Luchi. I laughed so much in one day with them that I have over the past few years. They brought so much meaning back into my life.

"Shut up, Luna, before I make you cry. Only reason why I was crying was because of Dell lame ass... I mean, butt, was holding me back from showing him what was really up. He knew the deal."

"Did he hit you?" I asked, getting pissed all over again.

"Naw, he knows better; that nigga scared of you. Always crying to mama about you being around." Luchi smirked looking out the window. "Soft ass nigga." Luchi mumbled under his breath, but I still heard him.

Shaking my head, I laughed at my mini-me. I knew I had fucked this little nigga up. He was already giving grown niggas hell at seven. I could only imagine how he would be in ten more years.

"Y'all trying to go to Sky Zone?"

"Hell, Yeah!" Luchi screamed while Luna screamed yeah.

"Luchi." I tried not to laugh.

This little nigga was so much like me sometimes it was scary. No matter how many times I smacked him or yelled at him for cussing, he wouldn't listen. He had that "can't nobody tell me shit" attitude just like me. Seeing that I had someone looking up to me, I knew I had to tone down my ways.

Ramsey

I had been sitting outside of Zoo's house for two hours now waiting for them to come home. I knew he was beyond pissed at me, because he placed me on his block list, which I thought was childish. Seeing the headlights of Zoo's car pull up, I climbed out the driver's seat of my car.

"We need to talk." I said, not wasting any time to get right to the point of why I was there.

"I was just about to call you. Lock up your car and get in. We need to take Lulu to the hospital. She's burning up."

Rushing back to my car, I quickly grabbed my purse from the back seat before locking my doors. Hopping into the backseat of Zoo's car, I saw that Luchi was holding his sister in his arms.

"What's wrong with mama's baby?" I asked Luna, as she climbed into my lap burying her face in my shirt. I could feel the heat radiating off her tiny body. "What happened?" I asked Zoo, but Luchi answered.

"Baby sis ain't feeling too hot."

"We wasn't at Sky Zone a good hour, before Lulu started throwing up. Shit just started getting worse from there. The way her body feel, I know she have to be running a high fever."

I rocked back and forth rubbing Luna's back trying to soothe her. I could feel Zoo watching us through the rearview mirror the whole way to the children's hospital. Pulling up at the entrance, Zoo turned around to face me. "Go get Lulu checked in; me and Lucci gon' park the car.

Doing as I was told, I walked inside up to the nurse's desk so I could get Luna signed in.

"Hi. Are you trying to be seen in the emergency room?" The nurse sitting behind the computer asked.

"Yes."

"What's the date of birth of the patient we'll be treating today?"

Reading off Luna's birthday, I watched the nurse type away.

"What's the patient's name?"

"Luna Scott."

"What will she be seen for today?" the nurse asked, continuing to type away at her computer.

"She's running a fever." I said, not really knowing what was going on with Luna.

"Okay, have a seat; someone will be with you shortly." The nurse said after placing Luna's information bracelet around her arm. I found an empty seat in front of the television just in case Luna was up to watching TV. Sitting in front of me, was a young girl rocking her son back and forth with an irritated look on her face.

"Agh, how much longer. I'm ready to go; I got shit to do." She said to nobody in particular.

I tried not to roll my eyes, but I didn't see what could be more important to her when her son was clearly not feeling well. His nose was running, the cough he had sounded terrible, and you could tell he was very tired but was too uncomfortable to sleep. Minding my business, I turned my focus back to my daughter. Feeling her head, I placed tiny kisses across her forehead.

Five minutes later, Lucci and Zouk walked into the emergency room. Luchi kissed Luna's forehead before walking over to the touchscreen tablet that was mounted on the wall for kids to play on.

"What they say?" Zoo asked, sitting next to me. Hearing his voice, Luna raised up to look for him. Reaching her arms out, she whined for him to pick her up.

"She's only been checked in so far."

"Your daughter is cute." The girl sitting across from us spoke flirtatiously, rudely cutting our conversation off to grab Zoo's attention. She was smiling so hard I knew her damn cheeks were hurting. She looked my way then rolled her eyes. The look on Zoo's face was priceless. I knew some bullshit was about to fly out of his mouth.

"Your son nose is running." Zoo said with his lip turned up.

"Clearly, he sick; that's why we're here." The girl spoke annoyed.

"Clearly, you need to focus on him," Zoo spoke annoyed as well. "And just cause he's sick, don't me you can't wipe his damn nose. No wonder why y'all here. He look like he's dying; it's obvious he can't breathe."

"Zouk, stop." he was so blunt. I could tell he was getting under her skin.

"Luna Scott!" the nurse yelled throughout the waiting room.

"Come on, Luchi."

"Excuse me; how did they get called before me and I been here longer?" The girl yelled being ghetto as hell.

"Honey, your son has already had his vitals taken."

"Aw, is that what you're doing?" the girl said feeling stupid. You could see it all over her face.

"Excuse me, ma'am. Fuck what she's talking about. What room are we going in?" I could tell Zoo was ready to explode.

"The first room on your left, sir, but first I need to get her weight." The nurse said, escorting them to the scale out the room.

After getting her vitals checked, just like Zoo suspected, Luna was running a high fever. We had to go back into the waiting room until we were escorted to a room. The emergency room was packed tonight, so the young girl with the baby was still there once we returned. This time, the look she gave Zoo was anything but nice.

"Keep walking. Sit over there. This bitch and her snotty nose son is not about to get on my damn nerves."

"Okay, come on, Zoo. Please don't act a fool up in here."

Finding some empty seats, I pulled out my phone to check it. Dell had been blowing me up since I told him he had to leave, so I could go check on the twins. He swore up and down it was about Zoo, so now we were going back and forth texting. I was already tired of explaining myself to him. He did a lot of playing hard around Zoo, but constantly whined to me. Dealing with a guy like Zoo then going to a guy like Dell was a challenge. Although Zoo and I were never together, I now compared most men to him. Dell's attitude was unpredictable. Some days, I felt like he was too damn feminine for my liking, then other days, he acted like big bad Dell. Tonight, he was trying to be big bad Dell, and I wasn't in the mood.

Luna's fever was a hundred-and-four, and that was my main focus. I had told Dell about Luna's fever, and instead of asking how she was doing, he wanted to make it about Zoo. He was slowly making his way to my block list. We were in the emergency room well into the middle of the night. Luna had strep throat that caused her to have a high fever. We were released once they got Luna's fever down.

Luna and Luchi still wanted to go home with Zoo, so I let them. Since it was late, I went as well. I know Dell wouldn't like it, but I didn't care right now. I was tired and ready to go to sleep.

Chapter Fifteen

Zoo

Luna was on medication, so the doctor gave her the okay to return back to school. After dropping them off at school, I decided to go check on Ramsey. I was getting tired of telling this hard-headed girl the same thing over and over again. I didn't know if she was excited about being kid-free, but it never failed. It seemed like, every time I come over to check on her, Ramsey's monkey ass left the door unlocked.

"Rah!" I yelled roaming throughout her house. I knew she was home, because I spotted her purse on the kitchen counter along with her keys. "Rah!" I called out again, but received no answer as I took the stairs two at a time. I checked Luchi and Luna's rooms out of habit. As expected, it was empty since they were at school.

Making my way to Ramsey's room, I found her sound asleep in her bed without a care in the world. Taking the back of my hand, I gently slapped her cheeks a few times to get her attention.

"Ramsey, wake your ass up." I was trying to control my anger; this dumb shit was normal for her. "Ramsey, wake your dumb ass up." I yelled tapping her a few more times.

"What Zouk?" She replied, never opening her eyes to look at me.

"How many times do I have to tell you to stop leaving your damn front door unlocked? You won't be satisfied until someone come in here on your dumb ass."

"Someone do. You! Now, stop yelling." Her tone was so nonchalant. Her calm attitude was pissing me off.

"I'm not fucking playing, Rah." I said towering over her.

"I hear you, Zoo."

"You say that shit all the fucking time, yet you keep doing the same dumb shit on the regular."

Rising up from the bed, Ramsey still had her eyes closed as she reached for me. I could tell she was tired, but I didn't care. I needed her to understand she couldn't keep leaving her door unlocked.

"It won't happen, again, Zouk, now stop yelling and come lay with me." Ramsey whined, pulling my shirt over my head.

"Rah, I didn't come over here to sleep. I'm trying to get my day started. I have shit to do." I spoke, but she paid me no mind, as she pulled me into the bed with her.

"Just for a little while?" she whined, pushing me down, then curling up under me.

"Ramsey, I have shit to do. Call that nigga. Ain't that what you got him for?" My jealousy showed, and that pissed me off even more.

"He's not here, you are. Plus, I miss this." She said, grabbing my hand, then placing it in her hair.

Staring down at her, I thought she was so beautiful. I didn't like that another nigga got to hold her at night, but what could I say or do? I wasn't ready to commit to her. I didn't know if I would ever be.

"Zoo." Ramsey whined, bringing me out of my thoughts. She started moving my hand around wanting me to play in her hair.

I hated to admit it, but Ramsey did something to me. I came here pissed off at her, and now all I wanted to do is baby her. I was willing to say fuck my plans for the day to lay up next to her. I had no problem with lying next to her watching her sleep. This shit wasn't my job, but I would rather do it, than her calling her weak ass boyfriend to lay next to her.

"Yo, do you be fucking that nigga in the very same bed you're begging me to lay in?" I yelled, quickly raising up. I didn't mean to. I was moving so quick, I pulled her hair along with me.

"Zouk!" She yelled, rubbing her scalp. "No, I have a three-month rule. He doesn't even know what my room looks like." I could tell she had an attitude by the way she rolled her eyes and neck.

"I'm sorry; I didn't mean to pull your hair."

"What was that?" Ramsey asked with a shocked look on her face.

"What? I said sorry for pulling your hair."

"Am I hearing you correctly? Are you okay? Are you sick, you have to be?" She laughed, moving closer to me to check me out.

"Back up off me, man. I'm fine." I smacked her hands away.

"I kind of miss spending time with you." she smiled, pushing me back down so she could lay her head back on my chest.

"Nobody told you to start dating a fuck nigga and switch up on me."

"Everyone is living their life how they like, so why shouldn't I?" she asked, lifting her head up to look up at me. I knew she wanted to hear me confess my feelings for her, but I didn't have it in me. I was willing to watch her deal with another man than telling her what's real.

"You're right." I said trying to end this conversation.

Looking at me intensely, she shook her head.

"You want breakfast?"

"Are you cooking?" she smiled.

"Yeah, I feel like you should, though, since you're making a nigga spend time with you."

"Zoo, stop acting like I'm making you do something you don't want to do. When I don't want you around, you're stuck to me like glue."

"I'm here for the kids."

"Boy." She laughed. "The kids ain't here, so keep telling yourself that." Ramsey laughed like she knew something I didn't.

I wanted to cuss her ass out for being right, but instead, I got up to start breakfast.

"What were your plans before I made you spend time with me?" Ramsey asked, walking over to the refrigerator, grabbing the strawberries. I watched her as she hopped on the counter. I don't think she meant to make her biting into the strawberry look sexy but she did. Walking over to her, I stood in between her legs. Grabbing a strawberry, I rubbed it against her lips, and she stared at me intensively as she bit into the strawberry in my hand.

"Zoo, what are you doing?" Ramsey moaned, as I lightly kissed her lips to taste the strawberry juice left on them.

"You made the strawberry look good; I wanted a taste." I spoke in between kisses.

"Zoo, we can't do this. You have Amber, and I have Dell."

"Ramsey, stop playing with me. Amber is just something to do, just like Dell is something to do for you." I said, sliding my hand in the front of her boy shorts. Just like I expected, she was super wet. I wanted nothing more right now than to fuck her.

"Zouk, we don't need to cross this line." She moaned into my ear, while she moved against my fingers.

"Okay." I kissed her, again. Her tongue tasted just like strawberries.

"Do you taste like strawberries?" I asked, moving my fingers faster in and out of her.

"Zouk!" Ramsey whined.

"Ramsey, let me…" Before I could finish my sentence, the doorbell ring several times, snapping us both back to reality. I was about ready to stick my dick inside Ramsey. I knew that shit would be everything I expected it to be. I also knew shit wouldn't be all sweet whenever shit was all said and done.

"Move, Zoo, I need to get that." Ramsey looked embarrassed, as she jumped down from the counter.

She was already at the door with it open by the time it hit me that she was answering it only in her tank top and boy shorts that barely covered her ass.

The look on Dell's face matched the look on mine… menace.

"What's going on in here?" Dell asked mean mugging me.

"Nothing." Ramsey quickly answered.

"Why the fuck are you standing around with no fucking clothes on?"

"I ummm," Ramsey stumbled over her words.

I stood there waiting to hear how she would answer his question. I stayed muted because I didn't give a fuck about helping her save her relationship.

"I was coming down to get some things out of the dryer the moment you rang the doorbell." Ramsey lied. She was a terrible liar, but by the look on this nigga's face, I could tell he was buying it.

I laughed, because I guess he didn't notice her hard nipples and wet spot between her legs.

"I'm up. I'm about to go check up with Amber."

I could see anger flash across Ramsey's face at the mention of Amber's name. Walking past Dell, I purposely bumped him hoping he jumped stupid so I could knock his ass out.

"Zoo."

"Stop fucking talking to me."

"Nigga, watch how you're talking to her." Dell tried to check me.

"Nigga, if you don't like how I'm talking to her, do something about it." I stood there for a minute, waiting to see if he wanted a problem. "Yeah, I thought so. Lock the fucking door."

I wasn't really about to pull up on Amber. I just said that to piss Ramsey off. I was about to take my ass to work. She asked me to spend the day with her, and I was horny and frustrated. I could've gone over to let Amber suck me off, but I didn't like how fucking clingy she was getting. So, I was going to take my ass into work and make some fucking money.

Chapter Sixteen

Ramsey

I felt guilty about what happened between Zoo and I. I know Dell wasn't blind to the fact that something took place between us. I was now so weak for Zoo, I often craved his touch. I knew the feeling wasn't mutual; that's why I kept my distance, focusing on my relationship with Dell. I was tired of being alone. I wanted to have someone of my own. I wasn't looking for forever; I was looking for right now. I also didn't trust that I wouldn't start doing crazy shit like trying to beat Amber's ass, because I felt entitled to Zoo.

Things between Dell and I weren't so great, and my kids still hated him and his kids as well. I felt bad about the fact that I didn't like having Dell's daughter Star around because she was a fast little girl. Her mother dressed her like she was eighteen, not eight. She danced like she worked at one of the many strip clubs on Seventh Street, and her mouth was slick as hell. Luchi and Kordell fought every chance they got. The relationship was somewhat all over the place, but we were trying to make it work.

I was getting private phone calls, and I knew for a fact they were coming from Star's mama Tamia. The first few times when I answered, she would only breathe into the phone. After she had realized it didn't bother me too much, she started to talk shit. She threatened to beat my ass on sight, and I had never met this woman in my life. She hated me that much. Dell tried to assure me that she was just running her mouth, but that only caused an argument between him and me. Something wasn't adding up. Tamia was still claiming Dell, he brushed her off as a crazy baby mama, but I was no dummy. There was some truth to her claims.

Sometimes, she would even go as far as texting me crazy shit and sending me pictures of Dell sleeping at her house from his phone on many of late nights. That would cause a fight, because I didn't understand why he was always there when he claimed him and Tamia didn't get along. He would pull the Zoo card; he tried to justify his actions by comparing them to Zoo's. He claimed he was always at his baby mama's house, because he was there with his daughter, yet Tamia was singing another tune. She had no problem telling me Dell was still her nigga. This situation was stressing me out, because this was the same shit I went through with Lance and vowed to never go through again, yet here I was.

Dell had been working overtime trying to make things better between us, so we had been spending damn near every waking moment together. Today, he wanted to take me and the twins out to do a little shopping, which the twins wasn't too happy about, yet I dragged them along, anyway.

After doing a little shopping, we went to Hooters for lunch. Luchi had been a pain in the ass most of the day, with his attitude, but being at Hooters fixed his mood real quick. He spent most of his time flirting with every waitress that walked past, causing a good laugh. That boy was something else. I wanted to say our outing ended on a good note, but that would be a lie.

Dell's baby mama and Star were leaning up against his car waiting to cause hell. "So, you lied and kept telling me you're on your way, but you out pretending with this bitch and her kids."

"Tamia, what are you doing here?"

"I was riding down Dixie when I spotted your car. I wanted to come inside and fuck shit up, but you know this is my favorite spot, and you had the nerves to bring this hoe here."

"Mia, leave, and I'll meet you at your house."

"No, I'm tired of you just fucking me, but out here in these streets playing family with this bitch." Tamia yelled, causing a scene.

"So, you lied to me? You have been sleeping with her?" I asked. I was no dummy. I wasn't surprised. I just wanted to hear Dell say it.

"Yeah, bitch, what did you expect? Somebody had to do it. Your boring *Sister Act* ass wasn't busting it open." Tamia yelled, and I didn't notice a crowd until I heard bystanders laughing. It was crazy how people were drawn to drama.

"Come on, Dell. I'm ready to go. I have my kids with me, and I don't have time for this."

"Bitch, you can leave, but not before I deliver this ass whooping I promised. Bitch, didn't I say on sight?" Tamia yelled.

"Mia, man, just go on about your day."

"Naw, fuck that, nigga. You stay trying to lay in my bed, but as soon as this bitch calls, you go running." Tamia yelled in Dell's face. This shit was so embarrassing. I was pissed that I didn't drive my own car. Pulling out my cell phone, I stepped away from the madness holding hands with the twins, so I could call a cab.

As I finished up my call with the cab service, Tamia turned her attention back on me.

"Bitch, what you calling for? Back up?" Tamia yelled, charging toward me. I didn't have enough time to react before her fists were connecting to my face. I know I looked like a punk as I tried to back away, but I wasn't trying to be fighting outside a Hooters in front of my kids. Tamia continued to charge toward me, so I had no choice but to defend myself. I could hear Luchi yelling and cussing up a storm. Dell tried to break us up, but his crazy baby mama was strong as hell.

When I heard Luchi yell, "Get off my sister," that's when I lost my shit, growing the strength of the hulk. Someone had their hands on my daughter, and that was a huge hell no. Grabbing a fist full of Tamia's hair, I pulled her head back to get a perfect shot of her face, hitting her twice. She stumbled back, letting go of the grip she had on my hair. When we broke free from each other, I couldn't believe my eyes. Star was fighting Luna. Luchi didn't care about Star's gender, as he punched her in the face, causing her to let go of Luna's puff ball.

"Ay, little bitch ass nigga." Dell pushed Luchi away from his daughter. Dell was about to charge Luchi until I bolted over to Luchi standing in Dell's way of getting to my son.

"Don't you ever in your life put your hands on my son again?" I yelled pointing in his face.

"That little nigga just hit my fucking daughter."

"And your fast ass daughter was acting just like her ratchet ass mama. She shouldn't have had her hands on my daughter.

"Bitch, I will kill you." Tamia yelled, as Dell held onto her while she jumped around wildly.

This was like Déjà vu. I did so much fighting over Lance, I promised myself I would never fight over another man again, and here I was fighting, looking just as crazy as Tamia. Grabbing both my kids' hands, I quickly removed myself from the messed-up situation.

"It ain't over, bitch." Tamia yelled.

Once I realized I was in the clear on the other side of Hooters, I checked to see if Luna was okay.

"I'm so sorry, Lulu." I hugged her tightly, as she cried in my arms. My baby was too sweet and didn't deserve for anyone to put their hands on her. She cried so hard in my arms, I knew it was more about her feelings being hurt.

"I'm about to call Zoo." Luchi said pulling out his phone. I could tell by his body language Luchi was about to become unruly.

"No, Luchi!" I yelled, snatching his phone. I didn't need to hear Zoo's mouth right now.

"Man, Dell's ass needs to be handle. Luna, don't ever let a bitch put her hands on you without you fighting back, do you understand me?"

"Luchi, enough!" I yelled frustrated.

"Ay, Ramsey, you good?"

Looking up, Zay's friend Boston had pulled up in front of us. "I peeped shit from the light, but traffic is crazy. I had a hard time getting over here."

"No, I'm not okay, but I will be once our cab shows up, and we get the hell away from here."

"Let me give y'all a ride home." He offered.

More than ready to go, I accepted his offer to give us a ride home. The ride was a silent one; I was glad Boston wasn't trying to ask me any questions or spark up a conversation, because I wasn't up for one. The only time we spoke was when he asked for directions, and I would give them.

Pulling up to my house, I thanked him for the ride before saying my goodbyes. I haven't fought in so long my body was already starting to feel it. I wanted to talk to the twins before I showered. I felt like I owe them an apology for putting them in harm's way.

"I'm sorry about what y'all had to go through. Y'all don't have to worry about seeing any of them ever again."

"I'm only mad Kordell wasn't there to get fucked up." Luchi paced back and forth.

"Listen, Luchi, I like that you protect your sister, but I don't want you putting your hands on females."

"Man, when it comes to my twin, I can't promise you anything."

I wasn't in the mood to argue with Luchi. Kissing their cheeks, I told them I loved them before going to take a hot shower. I was ready for the day to be over.

Zoo

175

I had just finished my day at the barbershop, and I had stuck around to bullshit with Zay and the rest of the niggas chilling around the shop.

"Bruh, look at this shit." One of the regular's named Jerry announced laughing. "Two bitches are real deal brawling outside a Hooters. Crazy shit is, their little shorties is out there brawling as well." He laughed, walking over to Zay, handing him his phone.

"Zoo!" Zay yelled. His concerned tone didn't sit well with me, and that let me know it was about to be some shit.

"Damn, Luchi!" Zay laughed.

Hearing the mention of Luchi's name caused me to quickly jump from my seat, grabbing the phone from Zay's hand. The video was ending, but what I did see was Dell bucking up to Ramsey with a deadly look on his face. Playing the video over, I watched it from the beginning. I was pissed to see Ramsey fighting; that shit wasn't even in her character. I was thinking murder as I watched this little bitch put her hands on Lulu. Luchi did the same shit I would've done it I was there, little girl or not. I didn't condone him hitting girls, but anything goes when it came to Lulu.

"This shit embarrassing! Look how many views it got. I'm about to fuck Ramsey and this nigga up."

"Y'all know them?" Jerry asked.

"Yeah, that's Zoo's girl and kids." Zay answered.

"Aw, shit." Jerry shook his head. Handing him his phone back, I bolted out the door. I was ready to fuck Ramsey, Dell, and his daughter up. Hopping in my car, I damn near sped to Ramsey's house. The fact that I constantly called both her and the twins phone nonstop, but getting no answer only pissed me off even more. I needed to know Luna was okay, and they weren't answering the fucking phone.

I breathed a little easier once I pulled in front of Ramsey's house. Hopping out of my car, I banged on the front door like I was the

Louisville Metro Police Department. I was trying to get my thoughts together, because I already knew I was about to flip out on Ramsey.

"Who is it?" I heard Ramsey yell from the other side of the door.

"Open the fucking door before I kick this bitch in." I yelled back. My blood was boiling.

"What, Zouk?" she yelled swinging the front door open.

"It's taking everything in me not to smack the shit out of you." I yelled pushing her back roughly.

"Stop, my body already hurts!" she yelled inches away from my face.

"I would fucking imagine. You're out here fighting with bitches. You want to be out here looking stupid fighting over this nigga, cool, do you, but don't be having my daughter out here fighting. You know your stupid ass is going viral." I yelled in her face causing her soft ass to flinch with every word that came out of my mouth.

"I didn't have MY daughter fighting. You know I'm not even like that." I peeped how she put emphasis on the word my.

"Lately, I don't know shit. Wait, I know this nigga got your head gone. Got you out here looking like a weak bitch, now y'all bring my daughter into this shit?"

"Why you keep yelling about your daughter? Since when?" she asked, trying my patience.

"Since when?" I asked, laughing.

"Yes," she asked with her hand on her hips.

"Since I started providing EVERYTHING she needs, since I started doing shit that fathers do, like staying up with her all night when she's sick, running a fever of hundred and four. Since I started walking around wearing fingernail polish, because I'll do anything to see her smile and happy. She's been my daughter since the moment I met you, and I always loved her as such. That's why I keep yelling about my fucking daughter. Look at your face! You're not fucking with that nigga no more. That shit is done, Rah." I softened my tone gently rubbing her cheek.

"I blame this all on you, Zoo." She whined, as I ran my thumb across the bruise on her cheek.

"How is it my fault?"

"I guess my actions aren't good enough. What? You need me to say it?"

"Say what, Rah?" I played dumb. We had been doing this back and forth shit for a while, and Ramsey never had the balls to say how she felt because of fear of rejection. I knew she wouldn't find her voice tonight.

"If you don't know, I'm not going to tell you." She said with an attitude jerking away from me.

"Don't fucking walk away from me." I pulled Ramsey into my arms. She whined from the pain that ran through her body. "I see you, Ramsey." I whispered in her ear before kissing her neck. Pulling her head back, I kissed her lips.

Turning around to face me, she ran her hands under my shirt. Standing on her tip toes, she tried to kiss my lips only for me to push her away.

"Back the fuck up. I just got pissed all over again about my daughter being out here fighting."

"Agh, I hate you; you're so fucking bipolar. Just get out, Zoo." Ramsey jerked away from me, this time I let her go.

"Where are my kids?" I called out.

"Fuck off." Ramsey, causing me to laugh.

Ramsey was in the kitchen slamming shit when I walked past to go upstairs. "Bring y'all ass here." I yelled to the twins.

"Shit, we're busted. We got caught ear hustling. Luna. I told your ass to move faster."

"Fuck I tell you about cussing?"

"I hear you talking." Luchi laughed. "It's hard to take you serious, though, when every other word out of your mouth is a cuss word."

"I'm grown, nigga."

"So, since you claiming us, can we call you Daddy?" Luchi asked. Luna's eyes lit up while she waited for me to answer his question. I wanted to say yes, but I didn't know how strong I was to hear someone call me daddy again. Ramsey stood in the doorway waiting for my answer. "I wouldn't have it any other way."

"Can you and mommy finally get together, now, too?" Luna asked.

"Yes, me and mommy can finally get together too." I told Luna, causing Ramsey to choke on her drink.

"Oh, shit, you good, mama?" Luchi asked concern.

"Luchi," Ramsey and I spoke at the same time.

"My bad, my bad. Come on, Luna. Let's give them a moment. By ma's shocked expression, I'm pretty sure they have some shi... I mean, stuff to talk about." Luchi and Luna took off running.

"Wait, Lulu, come here." I stopped her.

"Yes, Daddy." Hearing her call me that was bittersweet.

"Are you okay?"

"Yes, I'm fine; the girl just pulled my hair."

"I'm glad you're okay." I kissed her cheek.

"I love you."

"I love you, too, Lulu."

"Okay, y'all talk." Lulu winked at Ramsey before running out the living room.

"Yo, your kids are crazy."

"Your kids now?" Ramsey smiled straddling my lap.

"What you doing?" I asked, gripping her ass.

"What I been wanting to do since I peeped how fine you were when you walked into the hospital."

"Wait, before we go there. I want to talk to you about something."

"Look at you wanting to talk and shit without me trying to force it out of you."

"Come on." I kissed her lips before standing up. "Make sure everything is off down here then meet me upstairs."

"Wait." She stopped me in my tracks. The kiss she laid on my lips was so passionate. Pulling her close to me, I gripped her fat ass with both hands. "Do as I said." I smacked her ass hard while pecking her lips one last time before walking away.

Checking Luna's room, I realized that it was empty. Going across the hall, I checked Luchi's room. Luna was on the bottom bunk with her *Home* cover watching *Monster High,* while Luchi chilled on the top bunk drawing.

"What are y'all doing?"

"Nothing, just chilling before bed. We about to turn this TV off in ten minutes."

"Luchi, you're not anyone's daddy."

"Do you want to sleep in your own room?"

"No."

"Okay, then, well you'll follow my rules."

Looking at my watch, I saw that it was going on 8:50, so I allowed them to argue, because it was pointless to interfere. Luchi already knew they both would be knocked out by nine.

"Good night, Luchi and Luna."

"Night, Daddy." They both spoke at the same time.

Grabbing some clean boxers from the bottom drawer, I made my way to the bathroom to take a quick shower. I needed a moment to clear my mind and get my thoughts together.

✸✸

I was now facing my second blunt waiting for Ramsey to get out the shower so we could talk. She looked so beautiful when she walked out the bathroom wrapped in a towel. Her hair was wet, styled in a sloppy bun at the top of her head. The fog exited the bathroom at the same time she did causing my dick to jump. Her chocolate skin looked amazing with the water glistening against her skin.

"It was so hot in there." Ramsey said fanning herself with some mail that sat on top of the dresser.

"You're so beautiful, Rah." I admired, taking her all in.

"Thank you." She blushed turning away from me.

"Don't act shy now, come here." I motioned for her to come to me with my finger.

"Can I put some clothes on first?"

"No, come here."

Crawling over to me, she straddled my lap. I pulled on her towel causing her to grip it tighter.

"What are you hiding?" I laughed.

"Nothing." She looked nervous.

"Okay, so let go of the towel. I want to see you naked."

"No, so what do you have to tell me?" she tried to change the subject.

"Let go of the towel." I demanded. Whining, she did as she was told.

"This is cute." I smirked.

"Oh, this old thing?" Ramsey looked nervous trying to cover up her tattoo with her hands.

"Old, yet it's still healing." I laughed removing her hands. "A monkey, a giraffe, a tiger, a zebra, and two elephants making a heart with their trunks. Is this a zoo tattoo?" I asked a question I already knew the answer to.

"You live to embarrass me." She whined covering her face.

"I like it, plus Luchi already put me up on game." I laughed pulling her to me by her neck, kissing her lips. Moaning, Ramsey added some tongue to our kiss.

"What did you want to talk about?" she asked, nibbling on my bottom lip.

"I really want to thank you."

"For?"

"If you be quiet. I'll tell you."

"Okay, sorry."

"I want to thank you for allowing me to be in you and the twins' life. My attitude so fucked up, and I purposely push people away. You being one of them, yet you've never given up on me. I feel like God told me to drive down your street the day of the fire. I feel like God sent me you as my second chance.

"Second chance?" Ramsey asked confused.

"Yes, second chance. Love was my first chance. We were together for four years and had two daughters." I felt this uneasy feeling wash over me, as I talked about my first love and my daughters. "Zola was four, and Za'Kiya was two. They, along with Love and her mother died in a house fire two years ago. That was the worst day of my life. I stopped caring about a lot of shit that day until I met you. I know I've been stubborn as fuck when it comes to my feelings for you, and it has a lot to do with Love and my daughters. Meeting you made me come to terms that Love is really gone. I didn't want to love anyone else but you made that shit so hard." I spoke nervously for the first time in a long time.

Looking up at Ramsey, waiting to hear her thoughts on everything I was saying, I realized she was silently crying.

"Baby, what's wrong?" I asked concern.

"I just feel for you. I often lay awake at night wondering how that night would've played out if you would've never shown up to save our life. I often thank God for you when I say my prayers. I've wondered why you're so angry and hated me."

"I've never hated you. Since I laid eyes on you, I've been drawn to you. Before I met you, I was a ticking time bomb. It's like, since I've had you and the twins in my life, the time stopped ticking. For a while, I been wanting to tell you I love you and I want to be with you, but I been talking myself out of it telling myself I wasn't ready."

"And you feel like you're ready now?"

"I do. You didn't hear me say I love you? I love the twins, and I want to be a family."

The way Ramsey was looking at me pissed me off. I didn't like how confused she look like I was speaking French or something.

"What, Rah, man. I say I love you, and you act like you don't have shit to say."

"This is just a lot."

"So, you're saying you don't want to be with me."

"I haven't said much of anything."

"So, say something before I flip the fuck out." I was getting nervous that she didn't want me.

"Zouk, you just told me you have two kids and a girlfriend. I'm just trying to process it all."

"Okay, I get that you need to process it, but at least, can you tell me if you love me or not."

"Is that something you really have to question?" she smiled kissing my lips.

"So, tell me, then."

"I love you, Zouk Taylor."

"Show me." I let my hands roam her body.

Ramsey passionately kissed me while leaning forward a little. I felt her hand in my boxers, and seconds later, she was pulling my dick out, sliding down on it. I threw my head back, cuz her shit was heaven. Her moans were so loud and sweet. She bounced up and down on my dick moaning my name, telling me how much she loved me. I felt my nut rise. I wasn't ready to come, so I quickly flipped her over, placing her on all fours. Her ass looked amazing from the back. Smacking her ass hard as fuck, I watched it jiggle while she cried out. I roughly pulled her by her hair, pulling her head back, so I could kiss her lips. I was being rough, but by the way Ramsey moaned, I could tell she liked it.

"Fuck me harder, Zouk!" Ramsey yelled out.

"Shut the fuck up before you wake the twins." I said, but still did what she asked. She continued to moan loud as I beat away at her spot. Soon after, we were both coming together.

"Good night." Ramsey kissed my lips before climbing to the top of the bed. Catching her by her foot, I stopped her and pulled her back toward me. "You got life fucked all the way up. Since when have you started calling the shots? Did I say I was done?" I asked, whispering in her ear, as I thrust back inside of her.

I was already in love with the way she whined, while I was deep inside of her. I knew on a different occasion that shit would get on my nerves, but right now at this very moment, the shit sounded sexy as hell. We went at it for hours before I let her get a quick nap in, and I do mean, quick. After I finished rolling up and smoking my blunt, I was waking her ass right back up.

Going down to the kitchen, I grabbed a beer from the refrigerator, and just when I was about to sit on the couch, the doorbell started going off like crazy. Looking at the huge clock that hung on Ramsey's living room wall, I grew pissed when I saw that it read damn near two-thirty.

Storming over to the door, I pulled it open without asking who it was. I really didn't give a fuck who it was. I just wanted to know what was their purpose of ringing the doorbell like that at this time of night like it wasn't two kids in here sleep.

Dell hopped back a little once I came face to face with him.

"Brah, you better have a good fucking reason why you're ringing this doorbell at two in the fucking morning."

"Nigga, what are you doing here?" I could tell he was drunk by the way he slurred his words.

"Bitch, nigga, stop acting dumb. Ain't I always here?"

"Yeah, and that's the fucking problem. Every time I look up, you're in my girl's face."

"Well, it's no longer a problem of yours, because you and Rah are finished. Warn your bitch and your little bitch that they on my hit list for putting their hand on my fucking daughter."

"Nigga, don't disrespect my family. You want to be something you're not so bad. You wish them kids called you daddy." Dell laughed.

"They do, and so does Ramsey. Plus, I just got done busting in her a couple times, so in a couple more months, I'll have another one of her young ones calling me daddy. Your lame ass is finished here, now get the fuck off my girl's porch and lose her number."

"Let me hear Ramsey say that shit, nigga."

"Nigga, you heard it from me. You already know what I say goes." I laughed, knowing that would piss him off even more.

"I want to hear Ramsey tell me we're done." This nigga threw a fit like some little bitch.

"You heard him loud in clear." Ramsey appeared behind me dressed in her robe.

"Ramsey, you told me you wasn't fucking this nigga." Dell yelled sounding heartbroken like a scorned woman.

"Nigga, you better lower your voice. Speak to her with an indoor voice at all times. I don't give a fuck how angry you are."

"You told me you wasn't fucking him." He repeated, this time following my rules by lowering his voice.

"You told me you wasn't fucking Tamia; she's just your crazy baby mama. You should know firsthand people lie." Ramsey stood there unbothered with her arms folded under her breasts.

"What's good, Daddy? You want me to handle this nigga? I never liked him, anyway." Luchi asked, popping up out of nowhere.

"Naw, Luchi, we good. Go back to bed." I laughed. Dell was so soft, I believe Luchi could take him.

"Alright, well you handle him, because you already warned him what would happen if he felt bold enough to put his hands on me again." Luchi reminded me Dell pushed him earlier during the fight.

"Dell, you need to go." Ramsey stepped in like she knew my next move. I was about to rock Dell's shit until Ramsey stepped in blocking my way.

"Ramsey, I can't believe this shit. The first time we hit a huge bump in the road, you run to the same nigga you try to convince me you wasn't fucking."

"Brah, just move around. She's trying to save your life by telling you to leave. You should've known the shit wouldn't work. I'm trying to respect her wishes by not fucking you up. You standing here still pleading like a little bitch is going to make me change my mind. Go home, nigga; it's over." I said, before moving Ramsey out the way, so I could slam the door in his face. I was over the conversation with this nigga.

"You're done with that nigga, understood." I pointed in Ramsey's face.

"I was done with him anyways, Zoo." Ramsey said, wrapping her arm around my waist. She started off with slow pecks on my lips that led to us damn near fucking each other in the living room.

"Did y'all forget a nigga was standing right here?" Luchi asked pissed. "I'm going back to bed. Try to keep shit down this time." Luchi said, running back upstairs.

"Carry me back upstairs on your back."

"Fuck no, what's wrong with your legs?" I questioned walking away.

"I don't know why I thought us being together would tone down your rude attitude." She rolled her eyes. Paying what I said no mind, she jumped on my back. "Being nice to me will get you plenty of sex and your dick sucked on the regular." Ramsey sucked on my earlobe.

"You know who the fuck I am. You're going to give me that regardless."

Grabbing a fist full of Ramsey's hair, I kissed her roughly. I realized that she loved that rough shit. The way she moaned when I slammed her roughly on the bed further confirmed what I knew. Crawling over to me on all fours, she pulled my basketball shorts down. Taking me into her mouth, she sucked me up while staring up at me. I massaged my fingers through her hair as I moved her head up and down on my dick.

"You right," she smiled before spitting on my dick, massaging it with her hands.

"Yo, who the fuck are you right now? Where is sweet baby Rah?"

"Ain't shit sweet when that bedroom door close and these clothes come off." I watched her untie her robe letting it drop to the floor in front of her. My dick was on brick just looking at Ramsey's body. Sliding back into her pussy, I knew I made the right decision to make shit official.

Chapter Seventeen

Ramsey

Things between Zoo and I were going well. I sat on the couch across from him, and we were supposed to be watching a movie together, but I was too busy watching him.

"Babe, chill the fuck out on that creep shit." Zoo looked over at me with his handsome smile on display. "Stop watching me, watch TV."

"I can't help it. I'm just so happy that you're finally mine." I smiled brightly moving closer to him.

"You love me?" Zoo asking, pulling me into a tight hug. I deeply inhaled, taking in the scent of his cologne. I felt like he was asking me a silly question, because without a doubt, he knew I loved him, but I decided to answer, anyway.

"Do you think I would put up with your attitude if I didn't?"

"Ramsey, you and the twins make me feel whole again."

"I'm just as happy to have you, Zouk." I said in between kissing his lips while straddling his lap. My kisses traveled down his neck as I unbuckled his pants.

"Babe, chill, the twins are upstairs running around. They could come down at any moment catching your horny ass in the act." he explained to me. Everything in me wanted to ignore his warning, but I knew he was right. I don't want the twins to catch me with my pants down nor could I resist being in Zoo's presence without being all over him.

"Agh, what time is it? It's not bedtime, yet?" I whined, resting my head on his chest. Sex with Zoo was amazing. I wanted it every chance I could get it. I couldn't get enough of him.

"I thought I knew you." Zoo smirked before pecking my lips. "Your innocence is what pulled me in with you. Now, I find myself thinking who is this girl? I didn't think you had this level of freaky in you." Zoo smiled, gripping two handfuls of my ass, as I ground up against his hard dick.

"Let's go upstairs. There's something I want to show you." I wanted him badly.

"Ramsey, we're supposed to be watching a movie." Zoo laughed me off.

"Zoo, stop being stingy." My mood quickly changed; my bitchy attitude was starting to kick in.

Zoo's laughter filled the room. It was clear he took me as a joke. "Rah, baby, you have a problem."

"You're about to have a problem, too, if you don't give me my way."

"What are you going to do to me?" Zoo continued to laugh at me like I was putting on a comedy show for him.

"I'll take it." I said, pulling his dick from his boxers, then sliding down on it. I pulled the blanket we used to cuddle with over our bodies to cover us. "I'm taking some pointers out of your book. It's either my way or no way." I whispered in his ear, running my tongue up and down until I reached his earlobe. I sucked on it as I moved up and down on his dick the way he liked it.

"If we get caught in the act, I'm putting your ass on punishment."

"Punish who?" I asked, bouncing up and down on his dick, while tightening my pussy muscle. "You would give this up?" I hungrily kissed his lips, as I picked up my speed. "Huh? You're really willing to give this up?" All I got from Zoo was moans. "I didn't think so; you love my pussy just as much as I love the way your big dick hit my spot as I'm riding you."

"Your mouth is so damn filthy." Zoo moaned.

"Tell me the same thing when I hop off your dick to catch your cum." I moaned, switching up the rhythm of the way I was riding Zoo's dick.

"Fuck, Rah." Zoo laid his head back on the couch with his eyes closed. I could tell my baby was in heaven, and I loved the fact that I was taking him there. I loved how I could break his mean ass down and bring him peace. I loved having sex with him, because he had no problem with my freaky ass being in control. Zoo liked to play hard to get knowing that would make me freakier. I know who ran our relationship so it excited me when Zoo let me think I was in control.

"I'm about to cum, babe; do your thing." he said after roughly kissing me.

Although I wanted to continue to ride him until it felt like my body was seizing, I hopped off his dick. Sliding under the covers, I took him in my mouth inch-by-inch. Grabbing a fist full of my hair, Zoo fucked my mouth while I quickly rubbed my clit. Pleasing my man, while pleasing myself had me on a high. You would think it was life on death the way I was handling my business. Listening to his moans hype me up, my fingers were moving at the same speed as my mouth causing us both to explode at the same time.

"Fuck, Ramsey! Have I told you how much I love you?" Zoo asked out of breath.

"You don't have to tell me, because I know. I'm about to take a shower. Join me?"

"You're not pregnant, yet? Who would've thought old timid ass Ramsey would be a fucking nympho."

You know what they say, all you need is to find that one who brings the freak out of you. Come on." I said, grabbing his hands, pulling him off the couch. We took a moment to fix our clothes before making our way upstairs to shower together.

"Daddy, can we go to the Hibachi buffet?" Luna asked, popping her head out of Luchi's room.

"Yeah, get dressed; we're about to do the same."

"Get dressed, too. Don't be in there on no other shit, either." Luchi called out from the top bunk.

"Nigga, who you think you talking to? Who's the daddy, me or you?" Zoo asked.

"You got it." Luchi brushed him off, focusing back on his drawing.

"Your ass better be ready." he said, pulling me away from Luchi's bedroom.

"I'm done telling his ass to stop cussing; it's clear that the little nigga going to do what he want to do."

"Well, can I get my way now?" I asked, attacking his body.

"Sorry, babe, I gotta put you on hold. My kids are hungry."

"Zoo." I whined.

"Come on, let's shower, and I do mean just shower."

"Okay." I said, rolling my eyes, walking away. I was going to let him think showering was the only thing going down. Zoo didn't have a chance; the moment we stepped into the shower together, it was on. Even quickies with my baby were amazing.

Zoo

"Tell me about your family." Ramsey turned on the light before rolling over, wrapping her arms around me.

"Why, when you already know my family. I have a gay little brother and an older brother who thinks he's my damn daddy and my mama and pops." I ran my hands through her hair.

"Not your brothers and parents. I want to know about your daughters, and your ex-girlfriend Love."

191

I tensed up a little. I didn't like using the term ex when it came to Love. My daughters and Love had been a topic that's been off limits since their death. I no longer talked about them. It hurt too much. I thought about them a lot, but I couldn't bring myself to speak on my thoughts and feelings.

Taking a deep breath, I ran my hands over my face. "Rah, I can't…"

"Zouk, I love you. I just want you to let me in."

I could hear it in her voice. She was pleading with me. The room grew silent, as I thought about where to start. Getting my thoughts together, I started with my relationship with Love.

"I met Love when I was eighteen through a chick Zay was fucking with. When I first met her, I had a girl, but I was eighteen, so I felt like what could it hurt to take other girls' numbers. I could never have too many. Right?" I chuckled. I used to be a young, wild nigga.

"At first, I didn't take Love too seriously. I felt like I was too young to be in anything serious, but we always fucked around. She was a part of my rotation. Love wasn't too into that, so she did everything she could to make herself my girl, and eventually, after years of staying down, it worked."

"We started to officially date, and soon after that, my heart Zola came along. Zola was a daddy's girl. I would do anything for her, and she learned that early on. Since birth, she had me wrapped around her finger." I laughed, thinking about my Zola. "If you saw Zoo, you saw Zola. I remember when she was first born, and I was running the streets heavy. I thought it was funny, but Love hated how Zola wouldn't close her eyes until I stepped foot through the door. She wasn't going down until she felt my presence. The older she got, the worst she got. Somedays, Zola would fall asleep in her breakfast. She would be so tired from staying up all night waiting for me." I laughed at the memories that ran through my mind of my beautiful baby girl.

"I remember countless times when I would come into the kitchen to kiss her goodbye for daycare before she left and find Love cussing up a storm, because Zola's long pigtails would end up in her bowl of cereal."

"Za'Kiya was my wild, sassy child. At two, she had so much attitude. She acted more like Love, both were huge divas and so damn slick at the mouth that sometimes them two gave me a real deal headache. Za'Kiya marched to the beat of her own drum. She felt like she was her own boss. She got over on me a lot, because although she was bad as hell, she was beautiful. Her little butt had mastered her puppy dog face that broke me down every time. She had the biggest pretty brown eyes with long, pretty eyelashes, and she would beat them a few times, and all was forgiven."

"I remember one time, her bad ass colored on a pair of my brand-new Jay's. The look on her face when she showed them to me was so proud. Her little caramel face lit up with joy. She thought she was doing something that would make me happy, but I would never forget the look on her face when I yelled at her scaring the shit out of her." I laughed, wishing someone had captured the moment. "I didn't know if I wanted to kick her ass more or Love's for not watching her. Still, 'til this day, I believe Love put her up to it. She was known for taking a joke too far. They were my babies, man, and everyday, I wish I could bring them back. They were my world, and every day, I wish I was there for them more. I was grinding so hard to get to where I am today, I was neglecting my family."

Love would always complain, and I would just brush her off. I loved my family, but I felt like nobody was going to stop my money flow. I had four mouths to feed, and I wanted them to have everything they needed plus more. A few days before the fire, Love and I had a big blow up. She told me she was done with me, and that she was going to stay with her mom until she figured out her next move. I was just as stubborn back then as I am now, so I let her do her thing. I knew I was

Love's world, so she wouldn't be gone long. I was giving her time to be in her feelings. This was her routine when she didn't get her way. She always threatened to leave me. Once she walked out the door with my girls, I never thought she would leave me forever. The day they died, I died with them. For years, I had just been a robot moving through life. It's crazy how God brought you and the twins into my life the same way he took Love and my daughters away. The moment I met you, my healing process began.

"Why did it take you so long to let me in?"

"Admitting my feelings for you would mean I had to face what I'd been in denial about for years. I haven't talked about Love and my daughters to anyone since their death. I just wasn't ready. I'm still not, but how could I ask you to be with me and ask you for one hundred percent if I'm not doing the same? My daughters and Love are a sensitive topic for me. I want to know that you will move at my pace when it comes to me opening up about them."

"I can respect that. Are you sure this is something you're truly ready for?"

"Yeah, but I will be honest with you. I'm still learning how to deal, although it's almost been three years. I should be asking you is this something you're ready for, because some days, I could be hard to deal with. The mood swings that come along with grieve is crazy unpredictable."

"I'm ready. I know we can make this work, and I can make you happy, again."

This was one of the reasons why I loved Ramsey so much. She had so much faith in me. From the jump, I was hurt and angry, but no matter what, she stuck by my side, even when she didn't have to. I was praying that my fucked-up ways didn't make me lose her.

Chapter Eighteen

Ramsey

It had been a few weeks since I talked to Rory on Skype, so I was happy to see her face. She was even able to get Jen's mean ass on the line.

"Hey, Loves." Rory cheered.

"Hey, Beautiful. How have you been?" I asked her before she could ask me. Every time she called, she made everything about me. I wanted to know how she was doing for once.

"Ramsey, nothing is new on my end. Same shit, just a different day. Jen, how have you been?"

"You know me, mostly partying and bullshitting. "Jen smiled, proudly. I wasn't mad at her; she was twenty-one, with no kids, living her life.

"That's nice." Rory smiled. I could tell it was fake, which caused me to giggle.

"So, Ramsey, what's up with you? Since you feel like you can't call your sister on the regular and fill her in on the updates in your life." Jen's bitchy attitude appeared.

"I'm pretty sure you know me and Dell broke up; that's what you're referring to, right?" I asked my attitude matching Jen's. I wasn't about to take her shit today.

"Right, why did I have to see a viral video to know what's going on with you?"

"Wait, what video?" Rory asked confused.

"Someone recorded me fighting Dell's baby mama. I hate this damn generation."

"Why were you fighting Dell's baby mama?" Rory asked.

"Because Ramsey's been fucking Zoo the whole time." Jen said, before I could say anything. She stayed acting like a bitter bitch.

"Come on, Jen. Don't play. You know damn well I don't even get down like that."

"Well, that's what Dell told us." Jen was doing a lot of eye and neck rolling.

"So, you're going to take this nigga's word over my character?"

"I mean, your character has been a little sketchy lately."

"Bye, bitch! Your whole existence is really starting to work my soul."

Rory laughed, but I was dead serious. Jen's attitude got on my damn nerves. The fact that she was taking this nigga's word over mine was blowing me.

"So, what happened?" Rory asked through laughter.

I explained what took place, while Jen hung on to my every word, yet did a whole a lot of eye rolling as well, as if I was lying. Whatever Dell told her, she believed.

"Zoo and I are in a relationship now." I announced. I couldn't hide my smile.

"Yes! Finally!" Rory yelled. She was more excited than I was. This is why I loved Rory. As long as I was happy, she supported me.

"Ramsey, you're so stupid." Jen said, shaking her head.

"Why am I stupid because I'm with a nigga who loves me and takes damn good care of me and my kids? Jen, shut your hating ass up." I spoke, fed up.

"Bitch, don't get beside yourself, because you gave Dell's baby mama a few good licks. My hands work different from hers. Trust me, this ain't what you want. Ain't shit changed."

"Jen, now you know your words don't move me. Bitch, your bark is bigger than your bite."

"Will y'all stop arguing?" Rory tried to play peacemaker.

"I'm so tired of her, I swear. She don't like my nigga, cool! She don't have to be around him, but what I'm not about to be is any more of her stupid and dumb bitches. She's so team Dell like she didn't hear me say this nigga was a cheater, his baby mama was crazy ass fuck, like I didn't say his ratchet as daughter didn't fight Lulu and like I didn't say Dell tried to fight my seven-year-old son! This nigga tried to fight my seven-year-old fucking son, yet never jumped bad with Zoo. If anybody in this equation is a stupid bitch, it's you, because apparently, you don't comprehend well."

Whatever was all Jen said, because she knew I was right.

"So, how's the kids?" Rory asked, trying to change the subject.

"Good!" I said, keeping it short. I really wanted to talk to my sister because I missed her, but I was tired of looking at Jen's face. I was ready to end this Skype call.

"What's up, baby?" Zoo asked, entering my bedroom.

Although I was upset, a smile graced my face, because I was happy to see him for the first time today. Walking over to me, he aggressively grabbed a fistful of my hair, pulling my head back so our lips could connect for a kiss. I didn't want to moan seeing how my sisters were still on my tablet watching, but I couldn't help myself. Zoo passionately kissed me.

"Aw, shit now!" Rory cheered, causing Zoo to break our kiss to look down at my tablet that I held in my hand.

Pecking my lips, Zoo spoke to Rory ignoring Jen. Picking up my phone, I checked my notifications. I shook my head when I realized the only thing I had was a text message from Luchi telling me to meet him in the living room in twenty minutes. This boy and his damn cell phone. Acting like a big kid, Zoo climbed in bed next to me resting his head on my breasts. He gripped my other breast like he normally did when he got sleepy not caring that my sisters were watching. I tried to move his hand, but he wasn't having it.

"Awe, y'all are so cute together." Rory smiled, causing me to do the same.

"Tell him to leave; we're talking." Jen bitched.

"Rory, I mean no harm, but-" Zoo tapped my screen disconnecting the call.

"Zoo, why did you do that?" I asked pissed.

"I was tired of hearing Jen's mouth, already."

"Fuck, Jen. I don't get to talk to Rory like I would like because of her busy schedule, so when I do, I cherish it even if that means I have to deal with Jen's mouth."

"I'm sorry." Zoo kissed my lips.

"That's why she don't like you now." I laughed.

"I don't give a fuck; the feeling is mutual. That's why I hung up on her ass." Zoo said. Picking up my tablet, he called Rory back.

"I'm sorry." He apologized once she answered.

"It's understandable, but nigga, don't hang up on me ever again."

"I got you, sis."

"Aww shit, this shit is for real. I'm happy y'all finally made things official. I was tired if her crying about wanting you."

"Shut up, Rory!"

"Why do she need to shut up for? It's not like she's telling me anything I don't already know. I know you been gone off me since day one."

"Whatever, boy; you're not like that."

"So, you don't love me and everything about me?"

"Yeah, you're alright."

"Zoo, don't act like the feelings aren't mutual." Rory added.

"You're right. I never said they weren't. As a matter of fact, are y'all done talking, because I'm trying to fuck."

"Zouk!" I yelled embarrassed.

"What? We're all grown here. She already know what we do."

"Sister, handle your business. I'll call you back later." Rory laughed. Unlike Jen, Rory was never offended by the stuff that Zoo said.

"See Rory, that's why I fuck with you." Zoo nodded his head at my sister in approval.

"Alright Bro, go ahead and enjoy all that sexy chocolate." Rory laughed.

"Oh, I plan to." Zoo licked his lip at me, causing me to blush. He was so damn sexy, and he was all mine.

"Bye, crazy girl. I love you." I blew my sister a kiss.

"I love you, too. Bye, Zoo."

"Bye, sis, stay safe."

"Will do. Sister, I live through you since ain't shit going down over here. Enjoy the dick for me as well."

"Oh, my goodness! But will do." I laughed, these two were so embarrassing.

"Bend that ass over." Zoo announced the moment Rory ended the Skype. Doing as I was told, I got on all fours tooting my ass in the air.

**

"What's everyone doing here?" I asked, walking into my living room after showering from Zoo and I sex session. I guess they had got the same text message from Luchi as I did. Luchi had the family sitting around the living room waiting for him. Cari was spending the weekend with us, and we were waiting on the arrival of him and the twins. We didn't know what they were up to.

"What the fuck is going on?" Zoo asked no one in particular.

"No telling with Luchi. That nigga so above his time I wouldn't be surprised if he was sitting us all down to announce he's about to become a father." Zay laughed. Zo laughed as well. The look on Zoo and my face let them know we didn't find anything funny.

"Zay, I don't find that funny." I rolled my eyes, before throwing a pillow from the couch at him.

"I'm just fucking with you, sis." Zay laughed, throwing the pillow back at me, but it hit Zoo. "Nigga, stop looking at me like that. I said I was only fucking around."

"Yo family, may I have your attention." Luchi said, walking into the living room with Cari and Luna at his side. "Before we start, I need to collect the admission fee."

"Admission fee?' we asked at once, confused.

"Yes, we gathered everyone here today to show off some of Cari and my artwork." Luchi announced. "Luna," he said, looking over at his twin.

Pulling a small bucket from behind her back, Luna stood in front of Zoo. "Fifteen dollars, please!" she smiled, brightly, batting her curly eyelashes at Zoo.

"Wait, let me get this straight. Y'all called us over here for an art show?" Zay asked.

"Right." Luchi and Cari answered.

"Okay, cool, but the catch is we have to pay y'all to be here?" Zay looked from his son to Luchi.

"Look, Pops, one day Luchi and I will be making mad paper."

"And motherfuckers will be begging to see our shit, so we're giving it to y'all for the low price of fifteen dollars." Luchi spoke. My baby was so cocky, sometimes it was scary.

"Luchi, drop!" Zoo's voice boomed throughout the living room.

"Fuck," Luchi mumbled under his breath dropping down to the floor to do push-ups.

"I heard that, nigga, so add twenty more, which makes sixty, now go."

"Come on, man." Luchi complained.

"Nigga, shut up. You know the deal. It's a dub for each cuss word, now knock them out."

"Lulu, collect our money." Luchi said, while doing his push-ups.

"Fifteen dollars, please." Luna smiled, pushing the bucket in her hand closer to Zoo.

Reaching into his pocket, Zoo peeled off two bills placing them in the bucket. "There's a little extra for being my favorite girl." Zoo never took his eyes off Luchi, making sure he didn't cheat on his push-ups.

"Ooouuu, thanks for the big faces!" Luna squealed, bouncing up and down moving on to Zay and Zo.

"Wait, what? Lulu, come here. Let me see what I gave you." Zoo looked away from Luchi.

"What do you have for me, Unc?" Luna cheesed, ignoring Zoo.

Looking in the bucket, Zay laughed at the two hundred dollar bills Zoo accidently gave Luna.

"I'm not balling like your daddy, so…" Zay laughed, going into his pocket pulling out a fifty, dropping it into the bucket.

"That will work." Lulu smiled, looking over her shoulder at Luchi and Cari, giving them a thumb's up.

"What about you, beautiful?" Luna showed off her perfect smile. I laughed at my baby hustling them out of their money. She buttered Zoe up by using compliments.

"I see why she has Zoo wrapped around her finger. So cute, but I still only have fifteen dollars for you." Zoe spoke, while going in his purse, placing fifteen dollars in the bucket.

Luna smiled at Zoe before turning away. The moment she did, her smile dropped, and she mumbled "cheap" under her breath.

"No, ma'am, Miss Thang." Zoe acted shocked, being overly dramatic.

I couldn't help laughing, because my kids were a mess. Luna wasn't as bad as Luchi, but she had her moments.

"Now that y'all done made two sixty-five off of us, let's see this art." Zay leaned forward.

"Two sixty-five," Luchi and Zoo repeated at the same time; their tones were different. Luchi hopped up from the floor beaming. And Zoo wore a pissed off look on his face.

"I knew you were the person for the job." Luchi hugged Luna the moment she reached his side.

"I divide two hundred and sixty-five by three, right, Daddy?" Cari asked, pulling out his phone. I laughed at the fact that he was breaking down their cut of the money. The three kids standing before us were too smart and a force together. It was clear that they had their role and played them well.

"Right!" Zay beamed, proudly. Cari was extremely smart for his age, and Zay was the reason. He took his fatherly duties seriously. Education was at the top of his list. "What did you get?" Zay asked him.

"Um…." Cari focused on his phone, "… we get eighty-eight dollars apiece," Cari spoke, but continued to type away on his phone. "It's a dollar left over. I guess Luna can have it since she earned it." Cari smiled, pulling her in for a hug.

"That's my boy." Zay extended his fist out, so Cari could pound it.

"Okay, let's get started! I'm Luchi Scott." Luchi introduced himself as if we didn't know him.

"And I'm Ba'Cari Taylor."

"And I'm their lovely assistant, Luna Scott. Welcome! Today, I'm going to show you all some pieces from Scott and Taylor's art gallery," I giggled, because Luna was reading from cue cards, which I'm pretty sure was Cari's idea.

"The first masterpiece was created by The Goat Luchi Scott," Luna used her hands as air quotes causing us to laugh. I'm quite sure Luchi made her say that. "This piece is called *Angry Black Man.*"

The room fell out when Luna revealed a picture that looked like Zoo. Zoo was the only one not laughing, which only made it funnier.

"This next piece is by Ba'Cari Taylor, and it's titled The King and I." I smiled at the picture that Ba'Cari drew of him and his father. What he named the picture is what really tugged at my heart. It was beautiful to see young men look up to their fathers in a positive light.

"I love it, son." Zay smiled, proudly.

The presentation they put together was so sweet and cute. The fact that they took the time to draw a nice picture for everyone that was present in the living room was nice.

"Why don't you ballers treat us out to eat?" Zoe suggested to the twins and Cari.

"Alright, O'Charley's on us." Cari agreed.

I smiled, truly happy, because not only do I have a crazy yet amazing boyfriend, I received his family as well. For the first time in my life, I felt like I had a real family.

Chapter Nineteen

Ramsey

Today was my off day. The kids were in school, and Zoo was at work. I didn't want to sit in the house bored, so I decided to pop up on Zoo while he was at work. Walking into the barbershop, I chose not to speak to anyone, as I made my way over to Zoo. He had his back to me making it possible for me to sneak up behind him. Wrapping my arms around his waist, I let my hands roam.

"You're just going to grab my dick while I'm at work?" Zoo smirked, looking over his shoulder at me, shaking his head.

"What? I was just saying hi." I smiled, innocently, letting my hands roam up his shirt, so I could feel his ab muscles.

"You couldn't use your words?" he asked, looking at me through the mirror on his barber station.

"That's kind of a boring greeting, don't you think?" I questioned, wiggling in between him and the workstation, stopping him from setting up for his next client. "Plus, I see these thirsty things that's lurking around here. "I cut my eyes over to the two chicks sitting close by. "I just had to let it be known, you ain't out here hoeing anymore. This dick is property of Ramsey Scott." I smiled, sweetly, grabbing his package again. "Grab my ass so these niggas know what's up." I giggled, wrapping his arms around my waist. Like a magnet, Zoo's hands firmly gripped my ass.

"Stop being silly. Niggas know what's up, and so does these bitches." Zoo reassured me by placing his hand gently under my chin pulling me in for a gentle kiss. Wanting more, I closed in any space that was left between us. Wrapping my arms around his neck, I roughly tugged on his bottom lip before running my tongue across his lips, letting him know a gentle peck wasn't good enough.

Remembering he was at his place of business, Zoo pulled away trying not to overdo it. Kissing my neck a few times, he squeezed my ass a few more times before patting it and pulling away.

"Why does it feel like you want something?" Zoo smiled. I loved seeing my baby smile, and knowing that *I* was the reason behind his smile turned me on.

"No I don't. I can't just stop by to see how my man's day is going?"

"I guess." He kissed me again. "You look good by the way."

"Thank you. I picked this outfit out just for you." I blushed.

"What do you want, Rah?" Zoo looked at me laughing. Walking over to me, he wrapped me in his arms pulling me close. What he had to say was for my ears only. "Don't tell me your ass rode down here for some dick, because I just blessed your horny ass three times before I left not even three hours ago." Zoo whispered.

"No, but I'll take it, if that's what you're offering. "I leaned back so I could see his handsome face.

"Have I told you…"

"You love me?" I smiled, finishing his sentence. "All the time, but you don't need to, because you show me with this." I gripped his dick again. Just as I was about to lean in for a kiss, the sound of Bean's voice stopped me.

"Damn, I could tell your ass was freaky as fuck. I'm mad I missed out on that shit." Beans licked his lips staring at me with lust filled eyes. I could feel Zoo's body tense up.

"Nigga, I don't know how many times I have to tell you to stop addressing my fucking girl. I been wanting to take off on your ass for disrespecting, but Zay saves your ass every time. Zay can't play bodyguard forever. Stop fucking speaking to her, nigga. You'll never have her, because I have that heart on lock." I held onto Zoo's arm. I didn't think Beans was worth the drama.

"Nigga, I'm not worried about her heart; that's soft shit. I'll leave that up to you. I'm trying to see what that pussy is like." Beans laughed, looking around to see if anyone agreed.

By the look on everyone's face, it's like they all knew what was about to happen next. I could read Zay's mood from across the room. He knew this day was coming because Beans couldn't let go of his fixation on me. Zay stood back calmly watching as Zoo hit Beans with a quick right hook then a left. I could admit, I felt like Beans deserved everything coming his way. Every time I was around him, he had something slick to say about my body or was always claiming I was the one who got away. I knew my baby felt disrespected, and I was surprised he lasted this long without them coming to blows.

"Baby!" I screamed, watching Beans and Zoo go at it.

"One moment, baby. Let me handle this nigga." Beans laughed taunting Zoo. Bean wasn't a soft nigga, and neither was Zoo, so watching them go blow for blow frightened me.

"Zay!" I yelled praying that he would break it up.

"Sorry, sis, I can't help you. Let them fight that shit out. You don't disrespect a man's family." Zay spoke to me, but kept his eyes on the fight.

"Zouk!" I ran over to him trying to get his attention.

It was too many niggas standing around watching as Beans and Zoo fucked the shop up. Realizing nobody was going to break it up, I realized it was up to me. Standing closer, I quickly jumped back. Zoo was beyond pissed, and not only was he landing powerful blows, but Zoo was slamming Beans, breaking shit.

"Watch out ,sis!" Zay pulled me back, so I wouldn't get knocked down.

"No, if no one else is going to break it up, I will!" I screamed, trying to rush past Zay. Thanks to the tears running down my face, I knew my once flawless makeup was now ruined.

"Bitch nigga, lusting over pussy that will never be yours. Get your shit, nigga, and get the fuck out! If it wasn't clear by your fucked-up face, you're fired. Have your shit packed and out my shit within the next hour." Zoo yelled, as Zay and Crash dragged him into his office.

Zoo's temper was the worst. Just because Beans wasn't around doesn't mean Zoo was done fighting, as he punched a hole in the wall in his office.

"All I have is y'all and my fucking respect, and this nigga just tried both!" Zoo yelled, giving the wall a combination of punches.

I didn't know what to say to calm him down without making the situation worse.

"I never should've came down here." I cried, feeling bad that I was the cause of this.

"Fuck you mean you should've never came. You should be able to go any motherfucking where freely without a nigga coming at you. You came in our shit to see your man. I don't see a problem in that, and neither should you. I'm going to beat that nigga's ass every time I see that hating ass, secret feeling ass nigga."

"All I wanted out of this day was to get pretty for my man, come down here, and butter you up with love and kisses, so you could take me out on a date while the twins were at school. My day was so promising." I whined.

"You did your part, baby, so I got you. "I could tell he was still pissed but force a smile for me. "Go wash your face, beautiful. You want to see a movie? I got you."

"I'm not even in the mood anymore."

"Too late; we're going. You look too pretty not to take you out and show you off."

Wrapping his arms around me, Zoo pulled me close, kissing up and down my neck. I knew where things were heading the moment he picked me up, placing me on the desk. Things begin to move so fast I didn't realize I was naked until I was bent over the desk.

I wouldn't be surprised if the entire barbershop heard me the way I was screaming and moaning. I knew my baby was frustrated, so I allowed him to take his anger and frustrations out on me. I knew we wouldn't be making it to see a movie, and I was fine with that. I just wanted to be with my man.

Chapter Twenty

Ramsey

Life had been moving fast, and I was loving my relationship with Zoo. Our bond was crazy. Although we were total opposites, we just worked together. The weekend before was a crazy one. It was Zoo's twenty-sixth birthday, and they partied hard from Thursday to Sunday. A whole lot of partying wasn't really my thing, but I would be a fool not to be by my man's side, especially with Amber's thirsty ass still around. She didn't respect the fact that Zoo and I were together. This bitch would try her hand with Zoo when she felt like I wasn't looking, but I wasn't worried; I trusted Zoo.

I was thankful I was off this weekend, because after Zoo's birthday weekend, and a full workload, as well as getting the twins ready for school and tending to their needs after, I never made a full recovery.

The twins were spending the weekend with Nanna, so I was at Zoo's house, and my plan was to sleep in peace. After eating some leftovers and taking a quick shower, sleep quickly took over my body. It felt like I only slept for ten minutes before I jumped from my sleep. Strangely, an uneasy feeling came over my body.

"Baby, you scared me. Why are you standing over me?" I asked, holding my chest.

"You're beautiful. I was watching you sleep."

"That's sweet but kind of creepy." I lightly giggled still tired.

"Ask me do I give a fuck," Zoo said stripping out of his clothes.

"I missed you today." I said, dozing off again.

"Did you?" he questioned, climbing on top of me kissing my neck.

"Yes." I let out several moans.

"Well, show me how much." he said, sliding my panties down. He wasted no time sliding inside me.

"Wait, baby," I moaned.

"Wait for what. I ain't had none since yesterday, Ramsey. I need you." He bit down on my ear as he blessed me with nice, long strokes. "Baby, do you love me? Tell me you love me."

"No questions asked, you know I do." I cried out.

"I love you, too, Ramsey. I want you to have my babies."

"I want to have your babies, Zoo. I love you so much. Nothing would make me happier! Fill me up." I continued to cry out, meaning every word I spoke.

"Is that what you want?"

"It's what we want." I said, fucking him back. After getting mine off, I was extremely tired and ready to go back to bed.

After showering together, I had dressed in my skimpy pajamas while Zoo did the opposite, dressing in street clothes.

"Where are you going?" I asked, climbing into bed.

"I'm going to spend time with my baby." Zoo smiled.

Rolling my eyes, I fluffed my pillow. "You and this damn car is not about to get on my nerves."

"Don't be jealous." He leaned over, kissing my lips.

Zoo bought himself an Infiniti for his birthday. Nobody was allowed to ride in it but him. He was so in love with that damn car. I was jealous, but right now, I was sleepy, so I was going to let him go on about his business, since it didn't involve him messing up my sleep.

Zoo

I had been riding around in my new baby blazing up for about three hours, and now I was making my way through my front door. I was expecting to smell an amazing aroma to be filling the air. I was hungry and horny. Making my way upstairs, Ramsey was stretched out in my bed.

I was so proud to call her mine. Taking her hair wrap off, I ran my hands through this beehive style she called a wrap. I know me messing up her hair would piss her off, but I didn't give a fuck; I did what I wanted. Right now, I wanted some pussy.

"Baby, are you sleep?" I smirked, knowing I was waking her from her sleep, which she hated.

"Really, Zoo, you know better." Her attitude was clear.

"What? I was just trying to see if you were awake."

"That's a dumb ass question. Don't you see my fucking eyes closed?" I tried to hold my laughter in. By the way she was cussing at me, I knew she was beyond pissed.

"Damn, baby, you're feisty. Shit making my dick hard." I laughed, smacking her ass.

"Leave me alone, Zouk. I'm tired." Ramsey whined, pulling the cover over her body.

"But I need to tell you something." I said, pulling the cover back off her so I could continue to enjoy the view of her curvy body.

"What, Zouk? It can't wait until I wake up?"

"Naw," I said, while climbing in bed next to her. Rubbing her ass, my hands found their way between her legs, rubbing on her clit. It took me no time to get the little fabric of the thong that covered Ramsey's pussy super wet.

"Well, what Zouk?" Ramsey moaned my name. Her voice when she was horny was like music to my ears. It held so much passion.

"Damn, I forgot!" I said, leaning forward to suck on her neck.

"Are you fucking serious? I don't know who's worse, you or Luchi. Y'all hate to see me happy, enjoying a nice sleep." Ramsey rolled over pushing me away from her.

"Baby?"

"Don't baby me, Zouk. I'm tired. Let me sleep." Ramsey side-eyed me before rolling back over, turning her back to me.

"Baby…"

"I swear, Zouk. I got you. I'll wait until you're in a good sleep too then I'm going to fuck shit up."

"Baby," I said, getting up to take off my clothes. I was going to get some if she liked it or not.

"It's not going to happen, Zoo. Leave me alone." She said, placing a pillow over her head.

Her body looked amazing. All she had on was a tank and a thong. I wanted to see her ass jiggle again so I smacked it several times. I was caught in shock as I watched Ramsey quickly leap from the bed, attacking me. "You know how I feel about my fucking sleep, so why are you playing with me?" She yelled going crazy.

"Ay, Nigga! Chill out before I beat your ass." I laughed trying to control her arms. She was swinging at me wildly. I could tell she didn't care where she hit me. She just wanted me to feel pain. "Rah, calm your ass down."

"No, I'm sleepy, and you keep messing with me." She continued to fight me. "You wanted my attention, now you got it, so square up!"

"Ramsey, I said calm your little ass down. You ain't weighing in to square up with me." I said, playfully slamming her on the bed, pinning her hands above her head.

"All I want to do is get some sleep, and you won't let me, so look what that got you." She moved her body around, swinging wildly.

"Baby, you must not know what losing look like, huh?" I laughed, biting down on her neck. "If you're so tired, you better stop using what little energy you have trying to fight me, and instead put forth this same amount of energy riding this dick.

"You would like that, huh?"

"Hell, yeah."

"Just like I would like some sleep. Guess both are not happening." she said, trying to fight her way out of my grip.

"You got me and life fucked up." I said, sliding the front of her thong to the side, so I could play inside her wetness.

"No, Zoo." She tried to fight the way I was making her feel but failed.

I played with her until I felt like I had her right where I wanted her. "Bend your ass over." I said, grabbing her up by a fist full of her hair. One thing I loved about Ramsey is she never questioned me. She always listened, so when I demanded her to bend over, that's exactly what she did, giving me a perfect view of what I wanted.

"I love you, so I'll let you get some sleep, but first, I want to feel my pussy.

"Zouk." She whined.

"Hush that whining shit up, unless you're whining because this dick is getting that pussy right." I slid in without warning.

"Oh, Zoo." Ramsey cried out moaning.

"Yeah, this is the only time I want to hear you whining." I drilled at her spot just to hear her moan and cry out my name over and over again. I talked shit while I handling my business. Once she started throwing it back, it was my turn to do the moaning, sounding soft and shit.

Regaining control, I flipped her over, spreading her legs as wide as they could go. Grabbing her ankles, I buried my dick deep inside her.

"You feeling this shit?" I asked, picking up my pace.

"Yesss."

"When I'm done making you come, and I bust my shit off inside you, I want you to go make me something to eat, do you understand?"

"Yes!"

"Tell me you understand."

"I understand, baby." she cried out, placing her hand on my chest. "Ease up, baby. You're too deep." she whimpered

"Shut up and take it." I said, going harder. I continued to hit her spot until we both came.

I roughly kissed her lips before biting on her neck. "Get up and do as you're told."

"Zoo, you promised I could sleep."

"Okay, and I thought we had an agreement that you were making a nigga a meal."

"Zoo, I will agree to anything when your dick is deep inside me."

"Well, if you want to keep getting this dick inside you, you better get in that fucking kitchen and make me something to eat. After you do, I won't bother your ass anymore, tonight."

"You promise?"

"Yeah, I'll take fried chicken and fried potatoes."

"Zoo, I didn't take any chicken out."

"I did before I took my baby out for a spin. Now, stop making excuses and go."

Throwing my shirt over her head, I smacked her ass as she walked past me. Watching her ass sway back and forth, I wanted to fuck her again, but since she made a nigga promise to leave her alone, I was going to ignore her ass for the rest of the day.

Chapter Twenty-One

Ramsey

I gave Zoo a look once I saw him walk into his room going straight into his closet roaming through his clothes like he had plans to go somewhere. He must've felt me watching his every move by the way he turned around giving me an evil look that only made my pussy jump. Only Zoo had that kind of effect on me.

"What?" He questioned.

"That's what I want to know." I turned the TV off. "What are you looking through your clothes for, Zouk?"

"Why else do people put on clothes? To go out." he spoke smartly.

"Zouk, who did you ask?" I questioned, rolling over to the other side of the bed, hopping up walking over to him.

"Man, you sound silly as fuck. Who did I ask?" He looked at me crazy before letting out a light chuckle.

"Yes," I said, standing in front of him blocking his way, preventing him from going through his clothes.

"Move, Rah. I'm a grown ass man. I don't have to ask a motherfucker to do shit. I'm about to go out with my brother, man." He moved around me, grabbing the hanger of the outfit he wanted out of the closet.

"Is that what you think?' I challenged.

"That's what I fucking know." His facial expression matched his words, as he laid his clothes across the bed. I stormed out the room once he removed his shirt.

The twins were with Nanna, so I thought Zoo and I would spend some quality time, but I guess he had other plans. I knew he was being a smart ass from earlier. Losing my attitude, a bright idea popped up in my head. Rushing into the guest bathroom, I quickly stripped down turning on the shower. Grabbing a washcloth from the closet, I entered the shower quickly washing up twice before getting out, then brushing my teeth.

Not caring to dry off, I made my way back intoZoo's room. If I wanted my plan to work, I needed to move quickly. Moving around the room, I lit all the candles I had spread throughout the room. I needed to set the mood before going in the bottom drawer that housed my underwear. After finding what I was looking for, I laid it next to Zoo's outfit.

Drying off properly, I moisturize my body before putting on the lingerie I had lying on the bed. Checking myself out in the mirror, I thought I looked great. I wanted to do my makeup, but knowing it wouldn't be long before Zoo exited the bathroom, I only added lipstick. Styling my hair in a deep, side part, and throwing most of my hair to the right side, I made it look wild yet sexy. Hitting the lights, I grabbed the remote to the stereo. I felt like the mood wouldn't be one hundred percent right without some slow jams.

Hearing the shower turn off, I quickly hopped on Zoo's king-sized bed. Lying on my stomach, I made sure he had a perfect view of my ass in this black laced teddy. I loved the gold chain that hugged my exposed sides. The fabric barely covered my ass, which I knew Zoo would love.

Watching the bathroom door open, I was greeted with steam from the shower, and moments later, Zoo stepped out of the bathroom peeping my set-up. A huge smile spread across his face before busting out laughing.

"Rah, you on a whole lot of other shit." He continued to laugh, looking around the room at all the candles I had lit.

Slowly crawling over to the edge of the bed, I smiled, seductively. So far, my plan was working by the big grin on his face.

"What?" I tried to sound innocent walking over to him but stopped before I got too close to him. I wanted him to take me all in. I wanted him to see how sexy my body looked in this lingerie. Turning my back to him, I bent over to touch my toes, giving him a pussy shot. Looking back, I bit down on my bottom lip as I got a glance of the tent in the towel wrapped around Zoo's waist.

I giggled when I felt his fingers rub up against my clit.

"Rah, you really going to do a nigga dirty like this?" he asked, watching me move toward him closing in the space between us.

"I ain't never did nothing you didn't want me to do." I said, sucking on his neck before trailing the tip of my tongue down his chest, then licking off beads of water.

"Ramsey, I never knew you to not to play fair." His voice was so smooth. I was turned on by the way his voice dripped with so much lust. One of his hands palmed my ass, and the other cupped my chin, gently guiding my lips to his. We passionately kissed, as I removed the towel from around his waist, and his dick shot up like a missile.

Wrapping both my hands around his tool, I slowly jerked him up and down as we continued to passionately kiss.

Breaking our kiss, I kissed down his neck trailing down his chest until I reached his dick. My mouth watered at the sight. Licking my lips, I looked up at Zoo. He looked down at me biting his bottom lip anticipating my next move. Smacking the head of his dick in my slightly opened mouth, I let my tongue graze his dick a little, teasing him, causing his dick to jump twice. Smiling, he roughly grabbed a fist full of my hair causing me to cry out.

Taking him into my mouth, I worked my hands and mouth at the same speed. I loved watching Zoo while I gave him head. I had him under my full control, with no shit talking. My head always made his knees buckle. I drained that nigga's soul every time my lips were wrapped around his dick. I didn't stop until I swallowed every drop.

"Get up. I'm not about to play with your ass." He finally found his voice, pulling me up by my hair.

My lips crashed into his, the moment I stood to my feet and we came face to face. Picking me up, he carried me over to his bed, gently laying me down. Climbing on top of me, smiling, Zoo shook his head.

"You look sexy as fuck, baby." Zoo sucked on the side of my neck.

"Thank you, I had this baby tucked away for nights like this." I laughed, running my hands up and down his back.

"Aww, yeah?" Zoo asked, biting my nipple.

"Mmmhm." I moaned.

"You love me?" Zoo flicked his tongue around my hard nipples, driving me crazy. He knew how much I loved my nipples played with. They were sensitive to his touch.

"Yes!" I managed to get out.

"You sure?" He rubbed his dick up and down my opening, while still paying my nipples attention. I was so wet, I knew the sheet had a puddle.

"You sure you love me?" he asked again when I didn't answer fast enough.

"I mean, I really don't know right now. I think I do, but then again, it could just be the way you play with my pussy and nipples that got me feeling like it's love. I might think I love you for all the wrong reasons."

"You know where that shit talking always get you, right?" He flipped me over so fast.

"Baby, you know I live for this shit." I giggled, turning my head to the side, so I could get a decent view of him. He now had my head pushed down into the pillow, and my ass tooted up in the air.

"I know you do." he said, roughly smacking my ass before entering me without warning, causing me to let out a loud weep. I was thankful we were here alone I cried out so loud.

"You like this shit, Rah?" he asked, pounding away quick and hard with no mercy.

"Umm." All I could do was let out several moans.

"Rah, I said do you like this shit?'"

"No, I don't like it." I moaned, looking over my shoulder at Zoo. My baby was so damn sexy.

"You don't?" he asked, smacking my ass hard as hell. I was for certain it would leave a bruise.

"No, I don't like this shit, baby. I love it." I loudly moaned fucking him back.

"That's what the fuck I like to hear. Now, throw that ass back on this dick, and don't let up until I come." Zoo pumped in and out of me gripping my hair with both hands. He knew I hated that shit, because it felt like he was trying to rip my hair from my scalp. At the same time, it was weird, because the pain from my hair being pulled, and the amazing "D" I was receiving brought me great pleasure.

I threw my ass back until I felt Zoo's body tense up letting me know he was about to come.

"I love you, Zouk." I moaned, reaching my high.

"I love you, too, Ramsey." He groaned, releasing his load inside of me. "But I'm still going out." I could hear the smile in his voice, although I wasn't looking at him. Pulling out of me, Zoo smacked my ass again, before making his way into the bathroom laughing.

"Ugh, well that failed." I whined once I heard the shower come on.

Lying there, I took a moment to regroup and another plan popped up in my head. I was going to let him go out with his brother.

Zoo

"Nigga, you're in a good mood. Fuck you done got into?" Zay asked, looking from the road over at me.

"Nothing, just over here thinking about Rah's sneaky ass and the shit she pulled before I left."

"What she do?" Zay asked, lowering the music.

"I didn't tell her ass I was going out, because I didn't feel like I needed to. Her little ass tried to boss up on me, once she saw me getting dressed. That shit didn't work, so little baby tried to seduce me to stay home." I laughed, thinking about the candles and shit lit the moment I walked out of the bathroom and remembering the way her ass sat up in her sexy ass teddy.

"No lie, that shit almost worked. Baby pulled out all the stops. I wasn't expecting that shit, and that's what I love about Rah. You see how she got a nigga over here looking stupid cheesing and shit. Her ass was on a mission. She knew doing that shit would make me stay home or make me think about her ass the whole time my ass was out." I laughed feeling like a sucker.

"I'm glad you have Ramsey and the twins. I love seeing you happy again. It seems like she makes you crazier. You will knock a nigga out over her ass, but you're more upbeat since she's been in your life. You're still rude as fuck, but it's clear she's making you better."

"Yeah, that's my baby, and I can't wait until she gives me babies." I smiled, thinking about Ramsey having my kids. I didn't understand why she wasn't pregnant by now. I stayed busting inside her.

"Babies?" Zay smiled. I could tell he was shocked.

"Yeah, babies. I love the shit out of that girl, and I want her to be the mother of my children. I watch her with Luna and Luchi, and she's the real deal. I mean, Luchi is bad as fuck, but my Luna is perfect." I chuckled, thinking about my little family.

"Damn, bro, I'm truly happy for you. I know you been struggling these last few years, and I'm happy that you could finally move on."

I knew Zay didn't mean it the way I was taking it, but his words rubbed me the wrong way. I didn't want it to feel like I was replacing Love and my daughters; that's why it took me so long to let Ramsey in. Nodding my head, I didn't reply back, because I wanted the conversation to end. Thinking about Love and my baby girls put me back in one of my moods. I was glad we were pulling up to the club; I needed a few drinks. After parking, Zay and I hopped the line. We knew security, because Zay cut Big Bo's hair.

Shit was jumping, and after greeting a couple bitches and niggas, I made my way to the bar. I wasted no time getting faded. Zay and I kept a blunt in rotation tossing back drinks enjoying the music.

"So, y'all just going to leave a bitch out? That's for us?" Zoe walked up yelling over the music.

I let out a frustrated sigh.

"Don't breathe heavy, nigga. What? You're not happy to see me?" Zoe asked, rolling his neck, giving me more fucking attitude than I needed right now.

"Hell no, I'm not happy to see you, because you always have this bitch Amber with you." I mean mugged Amber.

"Nigga don't act like that because you loved seeing me when I was deep throating your dick." Amber shot back.

"You were a thirsty bitch then, and you're a thirsty bitch now." I spoke, harshly.

"Shut up, Zoo. Zoe, I'm going to get a drink."

"Zoe, why do you keep bringing that bitch around." I leaned over to yell in my brother's ear.

"She was my best friend before you stuck your dick in her mouth. Just because you quit her, doesn't mean that I have to."

"Whatever, just keep that bitch away from me. I'm not trying to hear my girl's mouth."

"Is Ramsey here?"

"Naw, she's probably back at home looking silly." I smiled, thinking about how I played her after I got the pussy. I didn't feel bad about pulling a hit and run. Her ass wanted to play with fire, so she got burned.

"Here, nigga!" Zay handed me the bottle. I probably should've slowed down, but fuck it. As long as I didn't do anything to disrespect Ramsey, I was going to enjoy myself.

"Aye, bitch, that's our song." Zoe yelled, dancing over to Amber, as she approached us with two drinks in here hands.

Looking over at me, she started smiling before bending over twerking her ass to the beat. I shook my head at her thirsty ass, but that didn't stop me from watching her ass cheeks clap together.

I laughed, because somehow my mind drifted off to the way Ramsey bounced her ass on my dick. Lost in my thoughts, I didn't realize some shorty had walked up on me, dancing, and she was clapping her ass against my dick.

"Ay, shorty, you need to back the fuck up off me," I leaned forward, whispering in her ear so she could hear me over the loud ass music. Everything in me wanted to push her ass off me, but shit like this was normal in the club. Bitches just loved to dance.

"Good, boy, but I'm mad you don't recognize your own lady." Ramsey smiled. "No more drinks for you." She wrapped her arms around my neck.

"Your ass is determined to be all up under a nigga, huh?" I cheesed. Ramsey was doing too much, but I loved every minute of it.

"You damn right. If you would've stayed home with me, I wouldn't have to do the most."

"Give me a kiss!" I yelled in her ear. Leaning down, our lips connected. Grabbing her ass, I realized how short her dress was. "Ramsey, this motherfucker is barely covering your ass." My attitude was visible.

"I know; I wore it just for you. Easy access, I know how you get with Henny in your system."

She ran her tongue up and down my ear. Kissing her again, I turned her around, so she could bounce her ass on my dick. I threw the bottle back while she bent over popping her ass. She already knew what I was going to do to that pussy. Henny made me horny as fuck.

"Tell your bitch stop looking at me crazy before I ruin everyone's night." Ramsey said, turning around looking deep into my eyes.

"You're the only bitch of mine in this club, so I don't know what the fuck you're talking about. I'm not thinking about that bitch. You, she, and I all know that. Don't let some head from some hoe stress you." I checked Rah.

"Alright," she rolled her eyes, kissing my lips. Stepping away from me, she began to walk away.

"Ay, where you going?"

"I just came to say hi," she smiled.

"Man, you're not going no fucking where."

"Zouk, I didn't come here with you." she whined, walking back over to me. I quickly grabbed her pulling her closer to me, I wrapped her tightly in my arms.

"Who did you come with?"

"My sister, and she's waiting for me."

"You're out your fucking mind if you think I'm letting you out of my sight with this short ass dress on."

"I'll stay in sight." She laughed, pulling away from me.

"Rah!" I yelled after her.

"I'll be over here, baby. Have fun with your brothers, and keep these thirst buckets out of your face." She said, walking past Amber looking her up and down.

Zay and Zo laughed at Rah, but I didn't find anything funny. Amber looked like she wanted to jump bad as she mean-mugged Ramsey. She had envy written all over her face. Although Ramsey stayed in my view the whole time, I didn't like how she was cutting up with Jen. I saw other niggas watching her, but that shit didn't bother me too much, because she couldn't keep her eyes off me. The more I watched her, the more I wondered what the fuck I was doing in the club. I could've been at home in my girl's face instead of in a club watching her every move.

"Alright, Zay, I'm out." I gave my brother a brotherly hug.

"I was wondering when you were going to dip out. Over there torturing yourself watching her give you a private show."

"You see how she plays?" I laughed. "She stay trying to seduce a nigga. I should've just stayed my ass in the house. She won." I laughed, looking over at Ramsey. She must've known what was up by the way she was looking at me smiling.

"Yes, plus get your girl out of here, because I don't like the look in Amber's eyes. She's been watching sis harder than you have."

"That bitch can jump bad if she want to. That bitch will catch a bullet behind fucking with my girl." I spoke heated thinking about someone trying to harm Rah.

"I hear you, bruh." Zay slurred.

"Come on, nigga. I'm not letting you drive yourself home."

"I'm good, bruh."

"I know, because you're leaving with me." I didn't give him time to protest, dragging him over to where my baby brother was bent over shaking his ass like some damn female. "Zo, we're gone. You're done on the alcohol, don't drink anymore. I love you, call me if you need me."

"Okay, love you, too." He stopped, dancing to hug us goodbye. I didn't like the thought of leaving my brother in the club by himself. I wanted to tell him to leave with us, but I didn't want to ruin his fun being overprotective. Motherfuckers knew not to fuck with my brother, but that didn't stop the evil stares motherfuckers gave him. I didn't want to take the chance of something happening to him just because a hating ass nigga didn't like the choice my brother decided to make in his life.

"Call me if you need me," I stressed.

"I'm good, Zoo. Love y'all, drive safe." Zoe brushed me off. He wasn't worried, because he could fight but I was, because coward motherfuckers weren't throwing their hands nowadays, and they most definitely wasn't going to take an L from a gay guy.

"Okay, call me when you get home. I'll be waiting on your call."

"Be waiting on mine, too," Amber flirted.

"Don't you get tired of playing yourself?" Zay asked. "Bitch, fall back. He got a girl. That's why you can't let thirsty bitches suck your dick." Zay yelled pissed like Amber was coming onto him.

The look of embarrassment was written all over Amber's face, but I didn't give a fuck, and neither did Zay. Zoe was always yelling best friend, best friend, but he wasn't going to go against the grain, so he didn't say shit to defend her.

"Call me, Zo." I stressed, again, before pulling Zay's drunk ass away from Amber. He looked like he wanted to punch her ass out.

"You ready?" I asked Rah, wrapping her in my arms.

"Yeah!" she cheesed like she won a prize. "Bye, Jen. I'm gone."

"Whatever, bitch. You're fake as fuck." Jen's rude ass shot me a look that could kill. I hated her ass just as much.

"Jen, don't act brand-new. You know I came here on a mission. Mission complete, so I'm gone." With that being said, I pulled Ramsey away before a huge unnecessary scene broke out. Knowing Jen, I knew it was coming. Walking out the club, hand-in- hand, I stopped to talk to Big Bo.

"Ay Bo, do me a solid and look after Zo."

"Zoo, you know I got you. Y'all drive safe."

"Good looking," I dapped him up before walking away.

"Where did you park your car?"

"I parked your car over there." She whispered, but I still heard her. "Rah, did you ask to drive my shit?"

"Man, you sound silly as fuck. Did I ask to drive your shit?" Ramsey hit me with the same look I gave her earlier when she asked me the same question before laughing. "I'm a grown ass woman. I don't have to ask a motherfucker to do shit." she mocked giggling.

"Keep playing." I followed her to my car. Zay was a few steps behind trying to text and walk. Dude was so fucked up he stumbled from side to side.

Opening the back door for him, I climbed on the passenger's side leaning over to open the door for my baby.

"Thank you, Daddy." Rah leaned over to kiss me.

"Now I'm daddy?" I asked in between kisses.

"It's only right since I swallow your kids." Ramsey smirked.

"You on some other shit." I grabbed her face with both hands, running my tongue across her bottom lip then biting down on it.

I broke our kiss, once Zay hit my backseat passing out immediately. "Is he serious?" Ramsey asked looking back at Zay laughing.

"Zay, nigga shut my fucking door." I turned around, smacking his dumb ass.

"Baby, stop and just shut the door." Ramsey laughed, stopping me from smacking him again.

"I opened it for his dumb ass. The least he could've done was shut it his damn self. I offered this nigga a ride, not to be this nigga's damn chauffeur."

"I know, baby. I know." she giggled, trying to pacify me so I could shut up.

Once I shut the door, she pulled off like she wasn't driving my brand-new fucking car. "Rah, if you don't drive my shit like you got some damn sense, I'll fuck your ass up. You're driving like this while I'm in my car, I can only imagine how you drove my shit here."

"Relax, baby, I got this." She brushed me off running through a yellow light that turned red seconds later.

"I said chill out." Rubbing between her legs, this little ass dress she had on was rising up causing her thong to show.

"Stop Zoo." She whined scooting over toward the door, trying to get away from my reach.

It was only so far she could go. Leaning over into the driver's seat, I parted her legs. She tried to squeeze them shut, but my strength outweighed hers.

"Stop, Zoo, before you make me wreck. "She whined, as I rubbed against her clit. It took me no time to get her thong wet.

"Stay still then." I sucked on her neck.

"Zoo, please just let me focus on getting Za'Cari home." She closed her eyes enjoying the feeling of my fingers and lips. Thank God we were at a red light.

"I thought you wanted my attention. Ain't that what you been fighting for all night?"

"I do, but once we get home."

"Fuck that, I'll let you get Zay home, but I can't promise you that I won't fuck your fine ass in his driveway."

"Okay, well that's all I ask." Ramsey said, sounding relieved.

The ride to Zay's house seemed long as fuck. Really, it was only a fifteen-minute ride. Shit felt like hours. I guess I was just horny as fuck. I kept trying to play in Ramsey's pussy, but she wasn't having it. I was getting pissed, because she acted like she couldn't multitask.

Getting out of the car, I pulled the back door open. "Zay, wake your drunk ass up." I yelled, smacking the shit out of my brother.

"Watch out, Zoo. I have him." Angel appeared out of nowhere.

"Bitch, you almost got snuck, sneaking up on me." I yelled in Angel's face.

"Zoo, don't talk to her like that. You're being disrespectful."

"Rah, I don't give a fuck! She should've made some fucking noise before walking up on me!" I yelled, smacking Zay again. "I'm horny as fuck, and this nigga need to get the fuck out of my car."

"Zoo, stop smacking him in his fucking face. I said I'll get him out your car." Angel yelled frustrated.

Looking at Angel crazy, I brought my hand up halfway, pausing to make sure I had her undivided attention before smacking the shit out of Zay again.

Ramsey sat in the front seat laughing shaking her head.

"Bitch, hit me again here." Zay said coming to.

"I'll give you a few seconds to get out of my shit."

Knowing me well, Za'Cari started putting a little pep in his step with the help of Angel, who look like she wanted to lay hands on me.

"Thank you." I stood outside my car until Angel got Zay safely in the house.

"Get your ass in the backseat."

"Zoo!" she whined.

"What did I say?" I asked, hopping in the backseat undoing my pant. Pulling my pants down, taking my shit out, I began to massage my dick waiting for Ramsey to hop in the back with me.

"Take that thong off before you get back here." I wanted her to slide right down on my shit.

Doing as she was told, Ramsey hopped in the back and right on. Although she was on top, I didn't let her do much work as I held onto her hips pumping in and out of her at a quick pace.

"Baby, you have some good dick." She cried out, as I bounced her up and down. Working at her spot, the faces she was making were so damn sexy.

"The best dick for the best pussy." I stared intensively into her eyes. It was no denying that I loved the hell out of this girl.

I never broke the glance the whole time I was serving her ass dick. The way she squeezed her pussy muscles around my dick had me ready to nut.

"Fuck." I called out feeling like a bitch shooting my huge load deep inside her. "Facts baby. That was my son I just put inside of you." I said, as I felt her body shaking moments later.

Chapter Twenty-Two

Ramsey

I had some errands to run, so I was dropping Luchi off at the barbershop with Zoo. Luna was spending the day with Jennifer. Despite how much my sister got on my last fucking nerves, she had always been a great aunt to my kids. I appreciated the help. I could do what I needed to do without yelling at my kids or them slowing me down.

"What's up, sis?" Za'Cari greeted me as I walked through the door.

"Hey, Bro." I said, walking over to him giving him a hug.

"Hey, Hey beautiful." Zoe sat in Za'Cari's barber chair about to get his hair cut.

"You look cute as always." I hugged Zoe.

"What's up, young one?" Za'Cari spoke to Luchi.

"What's up, Unc?" Luchi walked over to Zay dapping him up.

"What's up, Unc?" Luchi did the same with Zoe.

"Boy, you mean what's up, Auntie? Don't play." Zoe joked.

"Yo, chill on that shit." Luchi gave Zoe a look before shaking his head.

"Luchi," I reached out to smack him, but he was too quick, already making his way in Zoo's direction.

"Dude is bad as fuck." Zay laughed.

"I swear, that's why I say shit to fuck with him." Zoe laughed.

"He's bad, because of y'all." I laughed walking off.

"What's up, Daddy?" Luchi walked up to Zoo. Briefly looking up, Zoo smiled at Luchi giving him a head nod before focusing back on the client and his chair."

"Yo, what's good, little man? Damn, my little nigga. I can't believe how much you've grown."

Chills ran down my spine as I listened to a voice that I hadn't heard in years.

The look on Zoo's face let me know it was about to be some shit. Placing the clippers down, Zoo looked at Lance.

"My nigga, do I know you?" Luchi addressed Lance looking him up and down. "Daddy, who is this guy?" Luchi asked Zoo confused.

"Ramsey, you really got my son out here calling the next nigga daddy?" Lance asked, pulling the barber's cape from around his neck, jumping up from the chair moving toward me.

Zoo was like superman the way he flew in front of me blocking my body with his. "Nigga, you better back the fuck up off my girl." Zoo pointed his finger inches away from Lance's face.

"Nigga, this has nothing to do with you." Lance backed up a little.

"Nigga, this has everything to do with me, when you're talking to my girl and addressing my son. I'm his only daddy lame ass nigga."

"Is this nigga for real right now Ramsey? You seriously got my kids calling him daddy." If I didn't know any better, I would've thought that Lance really cared about my kids the way he stood in front of me putting on.

"What else are they supposed to call him? He's the only man around here taking care of them. I don't see anyone else here helping me with the day-to-day when it comes to them, but Zoo, so miss me with the shits. Don't play with me about my fucking kids, because that's the quickest way to take me all the way there. Either, you sit the fuck down and finish getting your hair cut and do like you've been doing, acting like me and mine don't exist, or get the fuck out causing unnecessary problems. Lance, don't get your feelings hurt trying to play like the loving, devoted father that we all know you're not." I yelled going off.

"Talking about you can't believe how much he has grown. Nigga, what the fuck did you expect to see? The two-year-old that you walked out on several years ago?" I questioned, trying to move around Zoo to get to Lance. I wanted to put my hands on dude so bad, but Zoo wouldn't let me get close to him.

I could tell by the look on everyone's face they were shocked to witness me flip out on Lance like that, but I felt he had it coming. Him getting a tongue lashing from me was long overdue, and the fact that he tried to check me about how I raise my kids was a huge no-no.

"Baby, say the word, and I'll fuck this nigga up." Zoo mean-mugged Lance. I could tell Zoo was itching to take off on him. It was clear by the look in his eyes.

"Naw, fuck him. Luchi is right here." I was saying the opposite of how I truly felt.

"Daddy, don't spare this fuck nigga on my account. This nigga don't mean shit to me." When Luchi spoke, his attitude reminded me so much of Zoo.

"Is this how you're raising him? To disrespect adults? His father?" Lance yelled.

"Nigga, you ain't never been shit to me." Luchi yelled ready to take off as well.

"This shit is crazy." Lance shook his head at Luchi "I could only imagine how Luna acts. She's probably running around here twerking acting like a little hoe."

My eyes grew big, shocked at the way Lance spoke on my daughter. I couldn't say I was surprised as I watched Zoo rock Lance with body shots like he was a punching bag. I knew if anything sent Zoo over the edge it would be someone speaking ill about Luna. What I was shocked about was Luchi jumping in trying to help Zoo fight Lance. Sadly, nobody tried to break it up, not even me. Za'Cari and Zoe stood around laughing at Luchi. Once I saw that Zoo and Lance were going toe-to-toe, I pulled Luchi out the way, so he wouldn't get hurt.

"Alright, niggas, that's enough! This is a business, not a boxing ring." Za'Cari yelled, pulling them apart with the help of a few of the barbers.

"Ramsey, I got you. I'll see you in court about my kids." Lance yelled, as he was being pushed out the door.

"Nigga, I will kill you, before I let you get ahold of what's mine!" Zoo yelled out trying to charge Lance but failed because his brothers were holding him back.

"You been gone, so stay gone. We got a daddy." Luchi added.

"Like I said, I'll see y'all in court." Lance yelled, before storming out the door.

I was startled by Zoo kicking over a trash can before storming into his office. "Zay, can you keep an eye on Luchi?" I said, before rushing after him. I shut the door behind me.

"On everything, I will kill that nigga if he try some shit." Zoo yelled, pacing the floor.

"Baby, calm down. I would bury that nigga in court before I let him take my kids."

"I will bury that nigga alive before y'all even make it to court. I'm not sharing my fucking kids."

**

The rest of the day went by awkwardly. Luchi and Zoo were quiet, which was uncommon. Both were in their own world. I knew it bothered Zoo to hear Lance threaten to take the twins. I, on the other hand, paid Lance no mind. He used to pull the same card back in the day when he realized he could no longer control me anymore. It was never about my kids with Lance; it was about me. He hated that I was no longer a fool for him. He hated that I was no longer a weak little girl who hung on to his every word.

The last time Luchi laid eyes on Lance, he was two years old. He never talked about him, but I knew, before Zoo entered our life, Luchi yearned for his father to be a part of his life. I tried to talk to Luchi about how he felt about seeing his father, and sadly, he also picked up the behavior of shutting down about his feelings from Zoo as well.

I normally didn't call Rory. I waited for her call, because her schedule was so busy, but I needed someone to talk to, and Jen was out of the question. South Korea was fourteen hours ahead of Louisville time, so it was now evening time for Rory. Praying she was free, I Skyped her.

"What's wrong, Ramsey? Is everyone okay?" Rory asked concerned.

"Yes, everyone is fine. I ran into Lance today at Zoo's barbershop. They fought in front of Luchi."

"Did Zoo kick his ass?"

"Yeah, and Lance threatened to take me to court."

"Okay, what's new?" Rory laughed. "You know his sorry ass always tries to pull that card when he feels defeated. How does Luchi feel about seeing Lance?"

"Girl, his crazy ass tried to fight Lance with Zoo, but he's been extremely quiet since."

"Ramsey, fuck Lance. Don't let him pop up and start shit in your life. Keep living and being happy with your kids, even if he did try to fight you for the twins, no judge is going to give him custody of kids he don't even know. They were two when he last saw them, and even then, he was barely around. Something seems off about him randomly popping up after five years. Did you ask Zoo was he a regular at his shop?"

"No, but that's a good question. See, that's why I called you. It's like Lance can sense when I'm happy. It's taking me years to move on, and when I do, he wants to pop back up pretending like he's the world greatest dad, questioning me as a mother. When are you coming home? I need a strong drink."

"Fuck, Lance. He has no room to question anyone's parenting skill. Be happy with your family. Fuck that nigga. Now, he wants to play daddy, because he sees another nigga handling a job he wasn't man enough to do," Rory went off. She hated Lance just as much as my nanna did.

"Sister, I didn't call to fuck up your day like he did mine." I said, feeling bad about calling her with my problems.

"What you mean? That's what big sisters are here for. Say the word, and I'm on the next flight with my Smith and Wesson. I have no problem teaching Lance's bitch ass a lesson. He knows I'm nice with them things. I don't know why this nigga even playing with you, knowing I don't play about you. Did he forget about me chasing his ass out of nanna's that one time he tried to get tough with you after you had the twins." Rory laughed, causing me to laugh with her as I strolled down memory lane. It wasn't funny at the time, because Rory's crazy ass was running through my nanna's house shooting at Lance. She wasn't thinking about my one-month-old twins. All she saw was Lance, not only disrespecting me, but disrespecting my nanna's house as well, and she lost it.

"I didn't have time to remind him. Zoo was too busy kicking his ass." I laughed.

"Ramsey, baby, I hate to cut our conversation short, but duty calls. I promise to call you tomorrow."

"Okay, I love you. Be safe." I said, sad to see her go."

"I love you more. Kiss the twins for me."

"Will do." I said, blowing her a kiss before hanging up.

Zoo and Luchi had been playing the game together since we arrived home. It was now going on two in the morning, and they were in the living room still going at it.

"Good night, Luchi. It's bed time." I announced, entering the living room.

"Daddy?" Luchi looked to Zoo. I was telling him one thing, but he was looking to Zoo to tell him another.

"Good night, Luchi. I told you last game two games ago." Zoo said backing me.

"Okay!" I could tell by the look in Luchi's eyes he was tired yet fighting his sleep. "Good night. Love y'all." He said, before taking off running up the stairs.

Turning the game off, Zoo got comfortable on the couch, flipping through the channels.

"Do you want to talk?" I asked.

"No, not really." He spoke, nonchalantly, looking at me for a brief second before focusing back on the TV.

"Can I ask one question?"

"Shoot."

"Is Lance a regular at your shop or was that your first time dealing with him?"

"Never saw that nigga before today."

"Interesting." I spoke more so to myself than Zoo. Knowing how Lance worked, I knew he was up to something. I could feel it.

Chapter Twenty-Three

Ramsey

It had been a month since the run-in with Lance at Zoo's barbershop. Like I expected, Lance was just talking when it came to fighting for custody of the twins. Things between Zoo and I most times were hot and cold. Like he warned me they would be in the beginning. Sometimes, he woke up in a bad mood, which I tried hard to be understanding about. Some days, it was hard to handle, but because I loved this man so much, I tried to stick it out. If I was being honest with myself, I knew he loved another.

He was dealing with not having closure. I felt selfish and often kicked myself, because I wanted to feel sensitive to his thoughts and feelings, yet a huge part of me wanted Zoo to let go and move on. I didn't want another woman to live in his heart, because that's where I wanted to be.

I was going through the motions with him, so it felt like I lost Love and his daughters as well. Wanting to be a loving and supportive girlfriend, I listened to him when he felt like he wanted to talk about his life with Love and his daughters. The conversations were rare, but when they did happen, all I could do was listen and be his shoulder. Sometimes, I felt jealous of the love he still showed for Love, but how could I show it. I didn't want to be *that* girl. I also couldn't shake how I felt… like, I was the second choice, because he lost what he truly wanted.

I knew Zoo loved us, but I couldn't help being bothered, wondering were we just in his life to fill a void he was missing from losing Love and their daughters. I guess you could say, with all my questions of our relationship, I should've seen what took place today coming.

Lulu was sad about, not being able to attend the boys' weekend at Zay's house, so Zoo took us out-to-eat to cheer her up. While we were out, we decided to stop at Target to do a little shopping for household items for both households. While Zoo went to shop for personal hygiene products, Lulu pulled me away to look at the toys. I thought she had too many toys as is, so I wasn't up for getting her anymore. I had already given her the rundown telling her no toys before we got out the car, so I didn't understand why she was trying it now. I guess she thought me seeing all the toys would change my mind. The plan was to buy new movies, so we could have a movie night. Instead, she had two Barbies in her hands trying to convince me she needed them.

"Please, Mama, can I have just these two? I promise I won't ask for anything else."

"No, Lulu. No toys. Movies, popcorn, and candy. That's all. Now, let's go find your daddy."

I was making my way over to Zoo at the same time another woman was approaching him. I was never one to cause a scene, nor did I feel threatened by this woman's presence, so I was going to let this scene play out.

"What's up, Armani?" Zoo spotted her walking up to him. She reached him before I did, but I was close enough to hear their conversation.

"Hey, Zoo, how have you been?" She asked, greeting him with a hug. Nothing seemed sexual about it, so I continued to keep my cool.

"Daddy, Mama told me to ask you can I have some new toys?" Luna called out, grabbing their attention.

"No, what I said was no more toys. Not ask your Daddy." I said, walking up, standing next to Zoo.

"Did I miss something?" The girl asked in a nasty tone, looking back and forth between Luna and me.

"Umm, Armani, this is Ramsey and her daughter Luna." Zoo called himself introducing us to this girl.

"Her daughter," I mumbled with a light chuckle. Not only did he not introduce me as his girlfriend like he normally did, but he was downplaying my daughter's role in his life as well.

"Ramsey, this is Love's sister, Armani." Zoo introduced her.

"Oh, I get it now." I said, shaking my head. I could feel myself ready to explode, but I tried to keep it together. Armani looked like she hydrated off negativity, and I wouldn't give her the satisfaction.

"And what the fuck is that supposed to mean? Zoo, I heard around town you were using some bitch and her kids as a knock-off version of my sister and nieces. Now, I see for myself that the rumors are true." She looked at me like I was the most disgusting thing on earth.

"No disrespect to your sister, but I could never be a knock-off version of anyone. Everything about me screams original. Come on, Luna. Let's pick out a toy, and since you *my* daughter, it's my treat." I looked at Zoo for a few seconds, shaking my head before walking off. So many different types of emotions were running through my body, but I couldn't let them show. I was tired of allowing chaos to be a part of my children's life.

"It was nice seeing you, Armani," I heard Zoo say, as I put some distance in between us, walking away.

"Ramsey, baby wait up." Zoo called out, but I kept it moving. I didn't want to be near him right now. I followed Luna from aisle to aisle with a fake smile on my face. I kept my distance from Zoo, but I made sure to send some evil glares his way. This was our routine until we reached the checkout lane. I was ready to go, so I decided not to get the things I had in the basket.

I didn't want him to buy "Ramsey" nor "her kids" anything. I just wanted space away from him.

"Why you being like that?" Zoo asked, rudely slamming my things on the conveyor belt, anyway. Ignoring him, I stood off to the side. I just wanted to go home. Grabbing Luna's hand, I made my way out of the store. I was going to wait by the car for Zoo.

By the look on his face when he pushed the basket out of the store, I knew he was ready to flip out. "Is that what you do now? Why the fuck you keep walking away from me?" Zoo asked, walking into my personal space.

The way Luna squeezed my hand, I could tell she was uncomfortable, causing my anger to rise. I was tired of having my kids on a rollercoaster ride of emotions, because I wanted to date unsure ass niggas.

"You need to back up. You're scaring my daughter." I looked him dead in his eyes. Fire danced around mine. I was so mad right now, and I don't think Zoo understood how pissed off I was.

Looking down at Luna, he realized he had frightened her. Backing away, Zoo ran his hands over his face before popping the lock so he could put the bags away. We were staying at Zoo's house tonight, but I no longer wanted to be around him.

"Take us home." I looked over at him the moment he hopped in the driver's seat.

Clenching his jaw, I could tell he wanted to flip. Looking back at Luna, who watched his every move, Zoo started up the car. The ride to my house was silent, just how I wanted it. I didn't want to argue around Luna. Hell, I didn't want to argue at all. I just wanted my space to get my mind right.

**

"Are you really mad?" Zoo asked, following me around the kitchen. Luna was upstairs playing with her new toys.

"Hell yeah, I'm mad. You claim my kids with everyone else, but as soon as you see your ex's family, me and my kids aren't good enough."

"Ramsey, it wasn't like that."

"Well, I know how it felt. Not only did you disrespect me, you disrespected my child. You also allowed someone else do so as well. It's like, every so often, you want us to compete with the dead." I didn't mean to sound so harsh, but I was just so fed up. "I will never allow anyone to make my daughter feel less than. You often show me you're not ready, and I won't allow anyone to hurt my kids."

I was so angry I was ready to punch Zoo in his face, but I was no dummy. "You speak up with anyone else, any other time, but not once did you come to our defense. That lets me know you feel the same way she does. We can't compete with fucking ghost, Zoo, so we bow out gracefully.

"So, what are you saying?"

"What does it sound like? Ramsey and her kids are done with Zoo."

"So, you saying I can't be a part of my kids' life?"

"They're not your kids; they're Ramsey's kids, remember?" I yelled. "You introduced us like we wasn't shit to you. *This is Ramsey and her daughter Luna*." I mocked.

"Are you fucking joking right now? You're really flipping out over a fucking introduction?"

"Why would I waste my time telling jokes to a man who barely laughs?"

"Fuck, Ramsey I'm sorry. I know I fucked up the moment I said it, but I didn't mean it like that. I love y'all."

"You love us when it's convenient for you. When you need that void filled. We want love that's unconditional. Be real, you feel the same way she does. You feel like we're knock-offs of what you lost as well. You want me, because you can't have who you truly want, which is Love! Same shit applies for the twins as well. They fill the void of Zola and Za'Kiya."

If looks could kill, I would be dead on my kitchen floor right now. I could tell what I was saying hit a nerve with Zoo, but his actions and Armani's words had me in my feelings, so why should I keep sparing feelings?

"I'm leaving, because you're pissing me off right now, and it's taking everything in me not to say or do some crazy shit to your disrespectful ass."

I did nothing to stop Zoo from leaving as he stormed out. I could hear him kicking shit before the door slammed shut knocking my pictures off the wall. Getting up from my seat, I made my way to the front door to lock it. I was trying to tell myself that I was overreacting. My heart wanted me to pretend like Zoo and I didn't have problems. My heart wanted me to be forgiving and understanding, but flashbacks of many sleepless nights wouldn't let me.

Frustrated wasn't the word to describe my mood right now. I tried to get my true feelings together before I woke Zoo up from his dream. Counting to ten in my head, I calmed down a little before shoving Zoo hard as I could a few times.

"Zoo, wake your ass up." I allowed my anger to get the best of me. "Zoo, wake your ass up; you're doing it, again."

"Fuck yes, right here, Love. Fuck, girl, I love you." Zoo moaned out in his sleep, breaking my heart into a million pieces. He was having yet another sex dream about Love.

"Zoo!" I yelled out, shoving him so damn hard I nearly knocked him out of bed. I felt so disrespected. I was ready to go blow for blow with Zoo if I had to.

"Damn, Ramsey, what the fuck?" He yelled. He had the nerve to have an attitude.

"Don't have a fucking attitude with me when you're the one waking me from my damn sleep with your moaning, because you're having another sex dream with Love."

"Ramsey..." he started. The look on his face was apologetic, yet it wasn't enough.

"Save it!" I placed my hand up to silence him. This was another moment where he wanted me to be understanding of his situation, but the sex dreams, I couldn't handle. I know his dreams were something he couldn't control, but that didn't stop me from feeling upset, hurt, and disrespected. I didn't think this relationship between Zoo and I would be this hard. I felt like I was being cheated on as I listened to him moan out in pleasure. These sex dreams with Love happened often.

His apologies no longer made sense to me, I had to let him go for my sanity.

Zoo

It took everything in me not to flip out on Ramsey for all of the disrespectful shit flying out of her mouth. She was crossing a line, and by the look on her face, I could tell she knew it. She just didn't give a fuck.

I knew she was reaching the breaking point of her patience with me. I didn't think an introduction would be the cause that sent her over the edge. I could admit, the last month of our relationship haven't been the best. After seeing her bitch ass baby daddy at my shop, I could admit that I pulled away from her and the twins some. Hearing that nigga threaten to take the twins away made something click in my head, and reality set in. I felt fucked up about the way I was acting, yet the thought of losing the twins scared me.

Ramsey noticed my change, and that caused us to fight a lot. I knew I was fucking up, but some shit was out of my control. Once I got into my moods, it was hard to pull myself out of them. I wanted things to work between Ramsey and me. I didn't look at her and the twins as knock-off version of Love and my daughters. They did fill a void in my life, but not how Ramsey was making shit out to be. I didn't look at her as the "New" Love or Luchi and Luna as the "New" Zola and Za'Kiya.

Ramsey wanted this to be a black and white situation, but it wasn't that simple. She didn't understand that, just because I still loved Love didn't mean I loved her any less.

I could tell by the look in Ramsey's eyes that I was losing her. That was why I decided to leave before shit between us got worse, and we both were saying and doing things we didn't mean. I wanted to say she was overreacting about the way I introduced her, but she had a point.

Seeing Armani standing before me was like looking at Love, causing me to panic. I could admit, it was fucked up. I regretted my choice the moment it happened. I didn't like seeing the hurt look in Rah's eyes. I could tell Armani's words had cut her deep. I knew she was fed up with my fucked-up attitude, and my distant behavior, along with the dreams. I didn't fault her for the way she was feeling. What was new to her was now normal for me.

I explained a little of my story to Ramsey, but what she didn't know was that, the month of May three year ago was the last time my family spent together. I welcomed the dreams I was having, because I dreamed about the moment I spent with them. I knew I was being selfish by wanting Ramsey to deal with me and all my shit. No matter what she thought, I loved her, and I wasn't letting her go. I didn't want to allow her time to cool off. I wanted to make her get over whatever she was feeling, but I knew that wouldn't be fair. I was going to give her time to cool off knowing that would be best.

Chapter Twenty-Four

It had been a few weeks since I decided to end things with Zoo. Let's say I was pretty miserable, and so were the twins.

I guess Zoo thought I was just talking when I told him we were done playing second to his unsure feelings. He would pop up like nothing happened. He would show up unannounced calling the twins' phone to let him in. I didn't want to bring them into our relationship problems, so they didn't know any better. After a while, I had to take their phone, because Zoo was using them to weasel his way back into our life. He even went as far as picking them up from school without my permission or even telling me. I knew he was being spiteful by not answering my calls and bringing them home at ten on a school night, which only caused our problems to become worse.

I thought I was ready to date again, but Dell and Zoo made me realize I wasn't ready at all. I didn't like the drama that came along with being in a relationship with someone. I had to deal with Dell's crazy baby mama drama, only to turn right around to find out Zoo was going through some other shit involving a baby mama and kids as well.

I kind of missed my simple life before the house fire. I missed it being simple and drama-free. I missed the relationship I had with my sister. She was the only one happy about Zoo and I breaking up. I regret allowing my kids to get so attached to him. I was having a hard time dealing with my own heartache, and seeing my kids hurt didn't help any. They didn't understand and I didn't have the words to explain so that they would. I tried to keep their mind off things by keeping them busy, and it worked most of the time. I thought Luchi would be the one giving me a hard time, but Lulu took it harder. She did a lot of crying for Zoo.

Hearing her cry for him made me want to give in, but as her mother, I knew I had to protect her. I felt like keeping our distance was doing the right thing. It was the last day of school, so I was sitting around the house enjoying my off day and my last day of freedom before summer break started when I received a text from Zay. I loved how he still checked on the twins and me to make sure we didn't need anything, although Zoo and I were no longer together.

Text from Zay:

Hey sis what are you into?

Text to Zay:

Just laying around not doing much. Wyd?

Text from Zay:

Shit! I was hitting you up, because tomorrow is the anniversary of Zoo's daughters passing. I really think he could use having you around tomorrow, sis.

My heart ached for Zoo. My kids were my world, I didn't want to think of the thoughts of losing them. I didn't want to imagine half the pain Zoo was feeling . Although I felt for Zoo, I couldn't bring myself to be by his side.

Text to Zay:

I will pray for him, but I think it's best not to be around. I can't keep being a reminder to Zoo of what he truly wants but can't have.

Text from Zay:

Ramsey my brother loves you, and I know this will mean a lot to him to have you by his side. I know you and Zoo are dealing with your own problems, but maybe you can put your differences to the side to be by his side. We'll be at Green Meadows Cemetery tomorrow at two to release balloons for them.

I knew how hard Zoo and his brothers went to bat for each other, so I decided not to text Zay back. I knew he would continue to text until I agreed.

It seemed like Rory knew when I needed her, because her call was coming through right on time.

"Hey, sissy."

"Hey Rory. I'm glad you called." My voice held no excitement like it normally did when she called.

"Oh, my. What's going on now?" Rory asked rolling her eyes.

"Zoo and I broke up, and I'm miserable." I pouted.

"What happened? I was cheering for y'all?" Rory pouted as well.

"I love, Zoo, but it's just becoming too much."

"Fill me in on what's going on."

"I never knew why Zoo felt so connected to us from the jump. He was so drawn to us, but now it's all starting to make sense. When we decided to make things official, Zoo wanted to be open. This was the first time he truly wanted to let me in and when he did, he revealed he had a family."

"What! This nigga been hiding his family this whole time?" Rory screamed cutting me off. I rolled my eyes at her extra ass.

"Yes and no, if that makes sense."

"It doesn't." She looked confused.

"Let me finish crazy ass. He told me he had a family; they passed away in a house fire. His girlfriend, her name was Love, who he had been with for years and their two daughters Zola and Za'Kiya. Also, his girlfriend's mother. He assured me that he was ready to move on. He also told me he was still struggling, but meeting me showed him he was ready to be in a relationship again. I tried to be understanding. Things were going well between us at first. It seemed like everything started to go to shit after the run-in with Lance. That wasn't even the problem. Lance was the least of our worries. Rory, I feel like I'm competing with the dead, and I feel bad because I just want him to move on and just focus on us. I'm his shoulder when he needs to vent. I'm understanding when he wakes up in his moods. I deal with the sex dreams."

"Bitch, what? Sex dreams? Aw, hell naw. I remember when I was dating Kendrick's bitch ass. He had a sex dream about Keri Hilson. I fucked his ass up one time, and that's all it took. Had that nigga sleeping with one eye open most nights. I don't play that shit. I considered that shit cheating. My ass walked around with an attitude for two weeks. Anytime that nigga asked me to do something for him, my reply was to ask that bitch Keri." Rory's tone held so much anger.

"You're too much." I laughed. My sister didn't have it all, but I felt her a hundred percent.

"Everything was building up. Running into his ex's sister is what did it for me. He introduced Luna and me like we meant nothing to him. It wasn't how he introduced me that bothered me so much. It was how he tried to play my daughter. Since day one, he's been all about the twins, and the moment he saw his ex's family, he downplayed our role in his life. The shit was so dry. This is Ramsey and her daughter Luna." I mocked the way Zoo introduced us. "I just don't want my kids to get hurt, because of Zoo's flip-flop behavior.

"I don't enjoy being in a relationship. I've come to realize they're just not for me. I've been doing good keeping my distance from Zoo, although I want to give in and take whatever love he's willing to give me, but I can't be that weak. You know I've been that girl before for Lance. I can't be her for Zoo. I think that's why it was so easy to walk away, because I know where this is heading." I wiped the tears that fell from my eyes. I wanted my relationship with Zoo yet a part of me didn't. I could admit, I was torn and confused.

"It sounds like you're going through a lot, and you're not sure on what you should do."

"Truthfully, I don't, and Zay texted me today asking me to be there for Zoo tomorrow, because it's the anniversary of his family's death. I want to be there for him, but then again, I want to move on."

"I get where you're coming from. I do. Shit sounds messy as hell, but I do believe Zoo loves you. That nigga is too evil to fake his love. His rude ass don't have it in him," Rory laughed. "I know you said you've been understanding of his feelings, but you have to understand losing someone and dealing with grief isn't as simple. He's dealing with three times the grieve. It's not an overnight thing; it's not as simple as you want it to be."

"Rory, I'm not saying he can't grieve their lost. It's the constant disrespect by some of his actions that bother me while he's doing so. He acts like it's a crime that he's trying to move on. If he wasn't ready, why pursue me? Things were fine the way they were between us."

"Did you voice your concerns?"

"No, not really. I didn't think it was necessary. I love Zoo, and I hope one day we could be together, but I realized he needed to figure this out on his own. I can't heal whatever is going on inside him, although I wish I could. I wanted to believe my love could fix all his problems, but emotionally, he's just not there. Instead of me sticking around causing myself pain trying to love an emotionally unavailable man, who can't love me back like I deserve, I accepted that it's not for me and removed myself.

Rory wore a sour look on her face. "I'm sorry, sister. I hate seeing you hurt, because you deserve happiness."

"One day, it will happen for me. I tried. I know everything in life doesn't work out how we want it." I weakly smiled. "I really thought he wanted to be a family. He asked me to have his child." I broke down. For the last few weeks, I been keeping it together pretty well, but right now, I had to let it all out.

"It's going to be okay, sister. I'm here for you."

"I know you are." I smiled at her, trying my best to pull it together. "Hold on, Rory. Let me go wipe my face." I said, placing my tablet on the coffee table.

After drying my tears and blowing my nose, I made my way back into the living room.

"Wait a minute, Rory." I called out as I made my way to my ringing doorbell.

"Who is it?" I called out. I wasn't expecting anyone. I got no answer as I looked out the window. Whoever it was had their back to me. Grabbing the closest object to me, I slowly opened the door. This could have been Dell's crazy baby mama showing up at my house.

"Hello," I called out to get their attention.

"I told you I was here for you." Rory turned around smiling.

"Oh, my!" I yelled, jumping in her arms like a big kid.

We both went crashing down to the ground. I didn't care as I rain kisses all over her face.

"Surprise!" she laughed, uncontrollably.

"Rory, what are you doing here?" I asked, excited. I was still on top of her.

"How about you get your heavy ass off of me then I'll tell you." she laughed, pushing me off of her.

"I'm sorry, but not really." I jumped up from off the ground.

"I've been out here since I called you. I was trying to surprise you. I wasn't expecting you to answer crying. Looks like I blew into town just in time."

"Forget everything I was just talking about. Let's find something to get into." I cheered. I haven't physically been in my sister's presence for almost three years, and I wasn't about to spend our time together moping around over Zoo. All my problems went out the window the moment I saw her face.

"Does Nanna and Jen know you're home?"

"No, I told you when I come home you'll be the first to know. I got in yesterday morning, but I slept my day away. I wanted to be well energized before I made my rounds. Now, come on. Let's pull up on Jen and Maelean Deveraux." Rory grabbed my hand dragging me out the front door.

"Oh, I'll be staying with you for a while until I find a place to stay." She announced.

"You know you're always welcome. I'm so happy you're home." I hugged her tightly. Having my sister home and by my side, I felt like I could take on the world. I had my partner in crime back. I was ready to go out get some drinks and forget about my worries.

**

I told myself I wouldn't be there for Zoo, but I loved him too much not to be by his side. I asked Rory to watch the twins, and she had no problem, because she wanted to spend time with them alone, anyway. They needed to rebuild their relationship all over again. Although I was going out to support Zoo, I wasn't going to bring the twins around, because I was serious about ending things with him. I didn't want to confuse them more than they already were. They didn't understand why Zoo was no longer around.

I didn't have trouble finding where Zoo and his family were meeting up, because I spotted the huge crowd standing around with balloons. Parking, I got out, grabbing the purple and pink balloons I bought. I also bought some flowers and wore the girls' favorite colors.

I felt awkward walking up, because I felt like all eyes were on me. It seemed like everyone noticed I was there besides Zoo. He was bent down in between two tombstones. I saw the way Love's sister looked at me, but I kept it moving. Walking over to Zay and Zoe, I hugged them before giving them a reassuring smile. I hated watching them look so sad.

"Thanks for coming, sis." Zay hugged me again.

"No problem." I slightly whispered. For some reason, I didn't want Zoo to hear my voice.

"On behalf of my brother and the family, I want to thank everyone for coming out to show my nieces, Love, and Ms. Tia some love." Zay announced.

I watched Zoo, and although his back was to me and everyone else, I could tell by the way his shoulders moved up and down he was crying. I hated watching him hurt.

"Zoe, do you mind holding these." I whispered in his ear.

"I got you, boo." He whispered back before taking the balloons and flowers from my hands.

Walking over to Zoo, I placed my hand on his shoulder only for him to roughly shrug my hand off. Bending down, I wrapped my arms around him. I never saw my baby cry, and it truly broke my heart. I didn't know what to say, so I kissed his cheek several times. Turning to face me, Zoo looked deeply into my eyes. His eyes were bloodshot red. Wiping his tears, I kissed his cheek again. Placing his forehead against mine, Zoo pecked my lips.

"I love you, Rah." Zoo took in a deep breath.

I gave him a faint smile before grabbing his hand pulling him from the ground, just as Zay announced the pastor was about to pray before releasing the balloons into the air. Zoo wrapped me tightly in his arms before bowing his head. I didn't know if he thought I would disappear while the pastor prayed or what. It felt weird being this close to him because I haven't seen him in weeks.

After praying, Zoo stood there with his face buried in the crook of my neck, while different family members took turns telling stories about their loved ones they lost. Although Zoo was still crying, I heard him laughing as he listened to Zay tell stories about his youngest daughter Za'Kiya.

I shook my head while Love's sister Armani spent her time of honoring her sister's memory by shading me and trying to make me feel uncomfortable. She told stories about how much Love and Zoo were in love. She decided to end her stories by saying Zoo would never love another the way he loved Love. She even had the nerves to tell everyone to keep him in their prayers, because he was still battling with the loss of his one and only true love. She didn't even speak on his daughters.

This is why I didn't want to come and was now ready to leave. I didn't have time for this mess.

"Please." Zoo whispered once he felt me pull away. I was shocked to hear him say please. I didn't know he even had those types of words in his vocabulary.

I wasn't going to let Armani make this about her. I was here for Zoo, not anyone else, so I was going to ignore the evil stares and shady remarks. Zay asked Zoo did he want to say a few words before releasing the balloons but he declined. Zay should've known he would say no; Zoo kept his feelings about his girls close to his heart.

Zoe had to bring me the balloons, because Zoo didn't want to let me go. Grabbing the balloons and flowers, I gave half to Zoo.

"Sharpies are going around, and once everyone writes their messages on the balloon, I'll count to three, and we'll release them together." Zoe announced, passing out Sharpie markers.

I didn't think I should write a message on the balloons; I didn't know what to say. I didn't want to feel like I was crossing a line. Most of Love's family was already giving me dirty looks feeling like I didn't belong. Zoo poured his heart out on his balloon. I tried to give him privacy, but I couldn't help myself. His message to Love was beautiful. He asked for her forgiveness and prayed that she still loved him. I felt bad for feeling brokenhearted. It was clear that Zoo was still in love with her, and I didn't want to compete with that.

After the releasing of the balloons, I was ready to go. "Wasn't my trip down memory lane with you and Love lovely?" Armani walked up on Zoo and me before I could say my goodbyes.

"It was." Zoo faintly smiled. See, this was the shit I was talking about with him. How could he say he loved me and wanted me to have his kids but stand in my face and agree with his ex's sister about him never loving another.

"I have to get going." I politely said. I would never disrespect his daughters by showing my ass at their resting place.

"Wait, baby." Zoo grabbed my arm stopping me.

"Bye, Zoo, I have to go."

"Wait, Ramsey. I need to see my kids. Please let me see my kids."

"So, you're just going to disrespect my sister by claiming this bitch's kids in front of me?" Armani yelled, causing a scene.

I wasn't about to be labeled as the new girlfriend causing problems, so I walked away. This chick was not about to bring me out of my character. I was going to take her calling me out of my name as her going through something. I was going to give her a pass; I realized today was an emotional day for them.

"Baby, wait!" Zoo called out following me to my car. "Fuck what she's talking about. I need to see my kids. Please just let me see them." Zoo begged.

I stood there looking at him blankly trying to figure out was he just using my kids for the emptiness he was feeling at this moment.

"Look, I came here because I love you, and I wanted to show my support, but I don't think it's best to bring my kids back into the equation.

"Fuck are you here for then? Just to throw it in my face that I can't have you and the twins, either? You don't fucking love me, bitch, so fuck you. I don't need you. Just go." Zoo yelled in my face. I couldn't believe his level of disrespect he was showing me right now.

Armani stood behind Zoo with a satisfied look on her face. Other bystanders stood around watching, looking around at everyone who wore a different emotion on their faces. Most of them smirked, amused at the drama, but I wasn't too surprised about them finding pleasure in my pain.

I wanted to cry, but I held it together, as I made my way to my car. I watched Zoo flip out as I backed out of the cemetery. Zay and Zoe tried to grab him, but Zoo was doing the most. I wanted to go back and give in, but I just couldn't do me and my kids like that. We didn't have to settle for the second choice. Zoo needed to deal with his own demons alone.

Chapter Twenty-Five

Ramsey

With Rory back home, I was excited about celebrating my birthday this year. Last year, I was too depressed about the house fire to celebrate. This year, I was turning twenty-five and ready to party. Zay's birthday was a day before mine, so he invited me to his birthday party. I was skeptical about going, because the last thing he invited me to didn't go over so well.

It had only been a week since the blow-up at the gravesite, and I didn't think I was ready to see Zoo, but I was going, anyway. Rory and I were using any opportunity to have a good time. Nanna was watching the twins along with Ba'Cari. Rory was trying to rebuild Jen and my relationship, so she was attending the birthday party with us as well.

We were getting ready at my house, and so far, Jen wasn't a pain in my ass. She was actually fun to be around. Drinks had been flowing since we started getting ready. Laughing and joking around reminded of when we were younger, only now, we didn't have to sneak into Nanna's alcohol. I was nervous about seeing Zoo, so to keep my nerves together, I was smoking and drinking to keep them at bay. I wasn't fucked up; I had a nice little buzz going.

Arriving at the club where Zay was having his party, I wasn't surprised to see that the place was sold out. Zay was well-known throughout the city. Zoe and his little crew arrived at the same time we did.

"Hey, my baby." Zoe hugged me.

"Hey, Zo."

"Omg, there's two of you chocolate beauties?" Zoe questioned checking Rory out.

"Rory, this is Zoe. Zoe, this is my big sister Rory. She just got home from overseas."

"Yess, I love a bad bitch in uniform." Zoe smiled, grabbing Rory's hand, so she could spin her around in a full circle to check out her curvy body.

"Lies." Jen rudely stated, laughing.

"You're right; who am I kidding. I love a big dick like the next bitch. How's that little boo of yours doing?" Zoe winked at Jen.

"Zoran, don't play with me." Jen threatened.

"Why not? That's what I do with little kids. Auntie Z entertains the babies." Zoe blew Jen a kiss.

"Hey, Rah-Rah!" Amber sing like she was happy to see me.

"Y'all ready to go inside." I ignored her attention-seeking ass.

"Hi, I'm Amber." She said, introducing herself to Rory, which was the wrong move.

"And why should I give a fuck?" Rory asked.

"I guess Ramsey told you about me." Amber laughed.

"Just that you're a thirsty bitch who's only good for sucking dick."

"Oh, wow. I see you're not timid like little Rah-Rah."

"No room for timid when your career is shooting them things. When I shoot, I aim to kill." Rory smirked at Amber. My sister was threatening Amber without coming right out to say it.

"Y'all ready to go inside?" Zoe laughed.

"Let's, before Amber doesn't make it inside. You may never know. One of my bitches could be waiting on the building across the street with a sniper waiting for my cue." Rory smiled at Amber with the most beautiful smile. Like, what she was saying was a pleasant statement.

"Oh, how I've missed you." I laughed, pulling her along, so we could walk inside the club. The look on Amber's face was priceless.

"I can't stand bitches like her. I bet she won't say shit else to me or you." Rory laughed. "Are you nervous?" She asked, whispering in my ear.

"With you by my side? Hell no."

"Quick question, why is it when Rory bites someone's head off, it's cute, but when I do it, I'm a bitch."

"Jen, you already know the answer to that." Rory side-eyed her. The difference between Rory and Jen was that Jen was a straight up hater and negative as hell.

Who was I kidding, I *was* nervous. I was battling with missing Zoo with every passing day. The club was so packed, maybe I could enjoy myself without running into him. I wanted Zay's party to go off without something going wrong, so my plan was to keep my distance and enjoy myself with my sisters.

"Y'all coming up here with the rest of the family?" Zoe yelled in my ear, so I could hear him over the music.

"Yeah, I'm going to get a drink first."

"I'm pretty sure there's drinks already over there." Zoe gave me a knowing look.

"I'm just going to hang out here for a little while." I knew it was rude not to go speak to Zay, but I wasn't ready to face Zoo yet.

"Okay, I guess so." Zoe hugged me before making his way through the crowd over to his brothers. I watched his every move hoping to get a glimpse of Zoo.

"Are we going to hide out at the bar all night or turn up? It's your birthday, too!"

I needed some liquid courage, because I damn sure was about to have a good time. Nervousness washed over me as I felt like I was being watched. I wanted to get up and dance, but I couldn't. I felt stuck. I was nursing my drink at the bar, so Jen and Rory hit the dance floor without me.

I smiled proudly as I watched my sisters' twerk against two strangers. Seeing them have fun, I placed my drink on the bar joining them. I was sandwiched between Rory and Jen dancing. "That's right, big sis. Fuck these niggas. Let your hair down." Jen yelled, cheering me on as I danced up against her.

"Let me get in on this." Zoe danced up to me.

I was glad the hoes he called friends wasn't following behind him, which only meant they were somewhere in Zay and his boys' faces trying to be seen.

Zoe bounced his ass up against me. He was doing more damage on the dance floor than most of the chicks out here, but we danced together for three songs straight.

"Zoe, I asked your ass to come get Ramsey, so I could cuss her ass out. You got side-tracked with shaking your ass the moment you walked over here." Zay said, pulling us both into a tight hug.

"Is there a problem?" Rory asked.

"Damn, Ramsey, you been out here holding out! Is this my birthday gift?" Zay asked in excitement lusting over Rory.

"Not at all. Happy Birthday, Zay; it's nice to finally meet you. I've heard a lot about you." Rory leaned forward so Zay could hear her over the music.

"The pleasure is all mine beautiful." Zay said, pulling Rory close to him. Big mistake.

"You know what, I do have a gift for you. If you don't get your hands off me, I'll have a bullet with your name on it." She smiled. Although her crazy ass was smiling, she was being serious.

"As pretty and as innocent as you look, I know crazy when I see it. I believe you would shoot me." Zay shook his head letting her go. "Come on, I want all my family to chill with me over here." Zay pointed over to the rest of his friends and family.

"Zay!" I whined.

"Come on, Rah. I got your back."

"Okay, first let me get a drink."

"Naw, we have drinks over here." Zay grabbed my hand leading the way.

With every step I took, I felt butterflies in the pit of my stomach. I started to pull away from Zay making him tighten his grip on my hand. I didn't know if I should speak to Zoo or not. The last thing he said to me played over and over in my head. I knew how evil he could be, and I didn't want to play myself in a club full of people.

"Aw, shit. Ro-Ro in the flesh." Zoo's voice caused my heart to skip a beat. He actually sounded happy to see her.

"Don't act like I'm the only one you see."

"Fuck her. She walked right past me like she didn't see me. I'm not about to keep kissing her ass."

"I've been issuing out bullets since I got here. I think I have one left just for you if you keep disrespecting my sister."

"Aye, you can't keep threatening people saying you will shoot them." Zay laughed.

"Why not? I haven't run out of bullets yet, and my trigger finger isn't broken."

Walking away, I found an empty spot on the couch while Rory continued on with her conversation with Zay and Zoo. I rolled my eyes, as I watched Rory laugh with them and Jen talk to Amber.

"Traders!" I rolled my eyes.

"What's up, sis? Happy belated!" Boston sat next to me pulling me in for a hug."

"Thanks, Boss." I smiled.

"Why are you sitting over here looking all lonely without a drink in your hand?"

"Hi, I'm Ramsey's sister Rory." My sister introduced herself before I could answer his question.

"What's good? I'm Boss."

"Nice to meet you, Boss. Do you mind if I sit right here? It's kind of crowded." Rory placed herself in his lap before he could even give her permission. I giggled, because my sister was bold. Unlike me, Rory wasn't afraid to go after what she wanted. Boston looked over at me confused. I giggled, shrugging my shoulders. Rory bopped her head to the music while she texted away on her phone.

"Check your phone." She mouthed to me.

Doing as I was told, I pulled my phone from my clutch.

Text from Rory:

Is dude a cornball?

Text to Rory

Don't you think you should've ask that before you hopped in the man's lap? Lol

"Cornball? I'm a boss baby, hence the name." Boss said, looking over Rory's shoulder. Neither of us noticed he was reading our text message conversation.

"Damn, who told you to read my shit?"

"I didn't need permission like you felt you didn't need permission to sit your ass in my lap. Now, hand me a beer." Boss demanded. Doing as she was told, she leaned forward to get Boston a beer out of the ice bucket that sat on the table.

I looked on smiling. Boss and Rory would be interesting. Over the past year, Zoo's friends and family had become my own. I looked at Boston and the rest of the boys like my brothers.

Jen walked over looking at Rory sitting in Boston's lap with a confused look on her face.

"Damn, bitch, you work fast."

Rory smiled before winking at Jen. She danced in his lap while he leaned back sipping his beer watching the way she moved her body. Everything about Rory was beautiful, inside and out. Her attitude was feisty, but it was hard not to fall in love with her personality. I was feeding off her energy. She had me handling being around Zoo much easier than if I was by myself. She was here for a good time, good music, good laughs, and a lot of drinks. Her being home even put Jen in a good mood, which lately, had been hard to do.

There were girls all over Zay and Zoo. One girl in particular kept catching my eye, because she was all over both Zay and Zoo trying to get both their attention. She was all over Zoo right now doing the most. I tried to brush it off, focusing my attention on anything else but them, but every so often, I couldn't help myself. I had to look their way. He had her bent over, and she was clapping her ass cheeks on his dick while he had the bottle tipped over guzzling down liquor like it was water.

"Don't just sit right here and let some bitch twerk her ass on your man." Rory pulled both Jen and me closer so we could hear her.

"What can I say or do? I broke up with him, remember?"

"So, what. That's the reason why. Because his ass is disrespectful." Jen said, rolling her eyes.

"He's single; he can do what he wants." I said, standing to my feet. My mouth was saying one thing, but my heart was feeling another.

I avoided eye contact as I made my way past everyone. I just needed a moment to myself. I didn't know if I would break down or not, and if I did, I didn't want the hating bitches who watched my every move to witness it. Feeling someone place their hand in mine, I turned around expecting to see Rory, but instead, it was Zoe giving me a reassuring smile.

"Where are you going?" Zoe whispered in my ear.

"I just needed a moment." I forced a smile.

"Let's go sit at the bar. If it will make you feel better, I'll talk shit about these tacky hoes' hair, makeup, and clothes."

"Lets! I'm feeling better already." I laughed. I loved Zoe's messy ass. Grabbing my hand, he led the way. After ordering drinks, he did just what he said he would do. Playing fashion police. Zoe dressed his ass off, so he was on point with club edition of what's hot and what's not.

"It killed me to leave Boss' fine ass, but y'all look like y'all having too much fun over here without me doing all that laughing and shit. Who are y'all over here talking shit about?" Rory asked looking around.

"We were talking about little mama with the two sizes too small heels on. We know that they are Christian Louie's, but baby it's time to let them go. Must be mama's first and only pair." Zoe shook his head, as we watched the chick struggle to stand up straight.

"Baby need to find a seat before she tips over. Baby's legs are as weak as a newborn baby deer."

"I'm not about to deal with you two fools." I laughed "Fuck that noodle leg bitch. Let's dance" Rory yelled, moving her body to the beat.

I was happy to have Zoe and Rory right now. I wanted to be upset about Zoo and all the women in his face, but Zoe and Rory held my attention with their silliness. Rory danced behind Zoe. He was sandwiched in between us. Zoe and I danced face to face.

"Zoe, who is that?" I nodded my head in the direction of Zoo and the chick who danced all up on him. I wasn't quite sure if she was there for Zay or Zoo, because she was hanging all over both of them, more so Zoo.

"That's just, Jada. Zay hired her. She works at the shop now. She's a cool girl. She's nothing to worry about. She's overly friendly with everyone." Zoe danced close to me with his arms wrapped around my neck.

"Aw, okay." I tried not to overthink it, but when someone describes someone else as overly friendly, I think hoe. I didn't like her being all in Zoo's face.

I decided to spend the rest of my night on the dance floor dancing, having a good time with my sisters and Zoe. I wasn't surprised Zoe was on the dance floor with us instead of with his little crew. I wasn't the brightest, but I had a strong feeling Zoe's little crew was only around to get close to a get money nigga that Zoo and Zay ran with.

I thought Zoo and I were both handling being around each other maturely. He was enjoying himself, and so was I. I wasn't trying to stop his shine while he entertained hoes. Jen was trying to coach me into doing the same thing, but I wasn't about to hoe myself out just to piss Zoo off. It wasn't me. I wasn't about to play myself knowing I wasn't looking at these niggas in the club like that.

"So much for maturity," I chuckled to myself as Gucci mane blasted throughout the club.

"Rah, said she through with me,

Don't want shit to do with me,

I don't give a damn, bitch,

You know who I am, bitch." Zoo rapped along with Gucci Mane's song "Fire Data Bitch" staring directly at me.

I shook my head; it was clear Zoo was trying to get a reaction out of me. I wasn't about to embarrass myself by playing into his hands.

Was I pissed right now? Hell yeah, but I wasn't about to give Zoo the satisfaction of showing it. I was going to pretend I was having the best time of my life, unbothered. I know that would piss him off more, although I was hurt by the constant disrespect.

I was throwing back drink after drink, and I couldn't remember the last time I was this carefree, drinking and smoking. I was good and drunk; my feet were hurting, and I was now ready to go home. My bed was calling my name. Rory hadn't been out in so long she wanted to shut down when the club did. I wasn't too fond of staying until closing, because that's when niggas started to act silly, beefing with niggas over silly shit like their shoes being accidently stepped on.

"Y'all grabbing something to eat with us?" Zay asked, as we all exited the club together.

"Naw, I'm already doing too much." I forced a smile.

Zoo stood there staring at me with an intense look on his face. We had gone the whole night without it being a verbal altercation, but by the look on Zoo's face, I could tell he was ready to start. He was drunk, and his eyes were bloodshot red.

"Come on, Rory and Jen. Are y'all ready to go?" I asked, trying to get their attention. Rory was all in Boss' face, and Jen was just in the mix.

"I'm going home with you tonight." Zoo grabbed my arms, so I couldn't walk away.

I giggled, "Boy, you're silly and out of your mind." I said pulling away.

"I done told your ass about walking away from me."

"I don't give a damn." I laughed. I was a silly drunk. I was amused at Zoo's sudden interest in me. He's been getting lap dances and numbers all night, yet he was trying to act like none of this took place.

"Ay!" Zoo's jaw clenched in anger.

"Zay?"

"Ay, Zoo, ease up." Zay stepped in.

"Happy birthday, Brother, I'm heading out." I hugged.

"Ramsey!" Zoo called out.

"Bye, Zouk. Shorty is waiting for you." I had nothing else to say as I walked past Jade. I found it cute how she mean-mugged me like I was getting at her nigga.

Walking over to Rory, she was all hugged up on Boss like they had been together for years. It was clear that he was feeling her, because he was doing a whole lot of smiling at whatever was coming out of that crazy girl's mouth. I looked over at Zoo as Jade leaned in to whisper something in his ear. He and I made eye contact as I smirked shaking my head. This boy was a piece of work.

Snatching away from her, Zoo stormed off, leaving her standing there looking silly. I tried to hold in my laugh, but a drunk wasn't shit. I laughed amused. I was keeping cool most of the night wanting to keep the peace, but if that nigga would've left with her, I would've shown my whole ass.

"Listen," Rory said, grabbing my attention although she wasn't talking to me. It was something in her voice that let me know that, whatever she had to say would be worth hearing.

"I would say that I don't mean to be so forward, but I do. I've been over in South Korea for a while now, and my battery-operated toys stopped doing it for me a long time ago. I'm trying to leave with you and go back to a room. Are you in or are you in?" Rory showed off her beautiful smile, leaving Boss no other option but to leave with her.

"How about your sexy ass lead the way?" Boss smiled. "That's me over there." Boss said, pointing to the Black Audi parked close by.

"Don't wait up, my baby." Rory turned to wink at me, cheesing.

"Where you going?" Jen popped up just in time.

"Hopefully, to get fucked really well." Rory answered with no shame in her game.

"Ain't no hopefully; that shit's a definite. It's hopefully you see them tomorrow, now let's go," Boss slapped her ass roughly causing her it to giggle.

"Well, hopefully, I'll see you in a few days instead of tomorrow. I feel like a nigga fresh out of the joint finally about to get mine." Rory cheered.

"Good night, crazy. Love you!"

"Love y'all. I'll text y'all my location."

"Okay, good night, brother."

"Night, Rah." Boss spoke before grabbing Rory's hand walking off.

"Well, Jen, I guess it's just me and you."

"No, bitch. I guess it's just you." Jen laughed. "I'm leaving with Dude over there; he's giving me a ride home. Good night. Get home safe." Jen walked off before I could speak up.

"Damn, someone could've made sure I made it to my car safe." I pouted, making my way to my car. I didn't want to go home to a big, empty house, so I made my way in the direction of my nanna's house.

Chapter Twenty-Six

Ramsey

I guess you could say I had drunk too much the night of Zay's birthday, because days later, I still had trouble recovering. I had been throwing up like crazy since the night of the party. I didn't make it in nanna's good before I was throwing up everywhere waking them up with my noise. After days of resting with no progress of getting better, I decided to pull myself out of bed to make my way to the drugstore. I needed to buy a pregnancy test to confirm what I'm pretty sure I already knew and what Rory had been saying since she arrived back home from the hotel with Boss, finding me lying across the couch passed out feeling like I was slowly dying.

I was glad Luna was with Jen, and I allowed Luchi to go with Zay to hang out with Cari. I was worried he would see Zoo, and I didn't want to go back to square one with Luchi, and he was finally getting to the point where he didn't ask me about Zoo every day. I knew I couldn't be selfish by keeping Luchi and Ba'Cari apart.

"Are you nervous?" Rory asked, standing in the bathroom with me giving me no privacy. She had been on my back since I told her I was finally going to the store to purchase a pregnancy test. I was done being in denial.

"Yes, I'm nervous, but I wouldn't be too surprised if I am. This was something we planned together before things between us went south."

"How would you feel if it come back you are pregnant?"

"I mean, it is what it is. You know how I feel about my kids, and this one wouldn't be any different. I'm no stranger to being a single mother." I answered, squatting down over the toilet to get on with it.

I was putting on a brave face, yet so many different emotions ran through my head as Rory and I waited for the results in silence. A part of me was nervous and over thinking everything. If I *was* pregnant, I didn't understand why it would happen right now, when we'd been trying for months. A part of me was happy for Zoo, then nervousness quickly washed over me. I knew how quickly niggas could switch up. I didn't know if I was ready to be a single mother of three, but if so, I was prepared to handle my business like I'd been doing.

I was already nervous enough about what I was doing, and the constant ringing of my phone wasn't helping any. Figuring answering it would help pass the time, I picked my phone up to see who was calling. Seeing that it was Jen calling, I quickly answer seeing as how she had Luna.

"Hello." I answered, as I watched Rory pick up the pregnancy test to read the results.

"It's positive." Rory mouthed to me at the same time as Jen begin to cry into the phone. I was stuck on Rory telling me I was pregnant. I was telling myself I was going to be okay, but really, I was scared.

Jen quickly pulled my attention back on the phone call as she cried out to me.

"Ramsey!" she screamed into the phone. "Omg, Ramsey I don't know. I don't know what happened!"

"Jen, calm down, and tell me what's wrong. Is my daughter okay?" I asked in a panic, causing Rory to look at me concerned.

"I'm sorry, Ramsey!" Jen cried.

"Jen, where is my fucking daughter?" I yelled. I was beginning to lose it.

"Someone, um, someone took her from the waterfront park. I only turned my head for a second, and she was gone." Jen yelled hysterically crying. I felt as if someone had knocked the wind out of me at the same time as vomit went flying everywhere.

Was I hearing her correctly? Did this bitch just tell me someone had taken my daughter?